BROOD OF BONES

by

A.E. Marling

Copyright © 2011 A.E. Marling
Cover illustration by Eva Soulu
Graphic design by Raymond Chun
Editors: Dean, Sarah
Special thanks to: Christina, Eric, Jack, Nancy, and Stephanie
First print publication: November, 2011
ISBN: 978-0-9840223-1-1

Seventh Edition

Contents:

*for those living
with sleep disorders*

CAGED
-01-

I never had the knack for staying awake. Consciousness hung over me like a sodden rag, weighing on my eyelids and muffling my ears, yet even my stifled senses did not spare me the indignity of hearing my name screamed across a public place.

"Hiresha!"

The reckless shout could not refer to me, I decided. Another lady of the same name must peruse the bazaar, someone who would consider replying to the immodesty of a raised voice. Why, I was not even in view but safe behind curtains.

Regardless, I trembled in the dimness, my head ringing with remembered shouts. *"Hiresha walks like a sleepy monkey." "Hiresha, you're slower than a drunken sloth."* And, *"How could she ever raise children? Hiresha sleeps more than a newborn."*

My neck burned and flushed under layers of silk and velvet. Gowns that had comforted me in the frigid climate of the Academy now smothered, and I began to pant, sweat running down my back like a millipede with a thousand tickling feet.

I had to disperse the heat building inside me, though deep breaths only drew in more hot air. My lungs smoldered, and my chest refused to move altogether when the worst happened: A woman screamed my name again.

"Hiresha! Don't leave me to die!"

My drowsiness ground against a heat headache, and I could make no sense of the shout. The disjointed words tumbled in my mind, holding no meaning either together or alone.

Don't Hiresha die me leave to.

Leave die to Hiresha don't me.

The carriage in which I was riding slowed to a standstill. A door opened, spilling light over the drifts and folds of my gowns. Jewels covered the landscape of fabric that draped over the seats, and the interior of the carriage glittered like a geode.

My maid bustled within and unhooked my arms from their harnesses of silk. The crisscross of cloth was used to hold me upright while traveling, to prevent my falling forward in my sleep and hurting myself.

I asked, "Why ever has Deepmand stopped the carriage?"

"Couldn't say." Maid Janny tugged on my gloves. "Maybe hereabouts women cry for enchantresses to save them every hour, on the hour. Must amount to a proper nuisance."

"I hardly think the woman meant me. Only Sri the Flawless is expecting my arrival."

"Might be she recognized something about your carriage. Its four white horses. Or the eye-blistering *golden* wheels!" Janny dabbed the sweat on my brow then scuttled out again.

"Maid Janny, inform Deepmand to—Maid Janny!"

The carriage tipped and bobbed as Spellsword Deepmand descended from the driver's perch. His turban glinted with gold thread, and his eyes shone black as onyx above a long beard neatly trimmed into a rectangle. He lifted an embossed gauntlet to assist my step down to the road, yet I only sat and wondered what this was all about and who had screamed. The person in question had taken great liberties with my name.

I peered out across the Bazaar of Fallen Stars. Within merchant tents, open chests twinkled with diamonds. Rugs spread with vials of perfume; a fire breather performed with an orange flash, and a crowd gathered around a cage for the unjust.

"Hiresha!" The woman's cry seemed to originate from the cage. "He'll kill me tonight!"

"She seems rather excessive." I knew something of the severity of crimes punished by time in the cage, and I never went out of my way to meet murderers. "Spellsword Deepmand, I have an appointment with Sri the Flawless at the God's Eye Court. You may take me there now."

"May I take leave to suggest," he said, "that the delay will be worthwhile, Elder Enchantress."

Hearing him use my title in public reassured me. I was not so very old, yet being called "elder" added another comforting layer of concealment.

Both my driver and my personal guard, Spellsword Deepmand possessed a wealth of alertness. I trusted him with my safety and dignity, and if he thought I should associate myself with this outburst then I would.

Taking his hand, I dragged myself from my seat. Sweeps of cloth flowed after me, my gowns spreading from the confines of the carriage in a sparkling cascade.

The crowd gasped, and my spine tightened, while sickness at my own inadequacy wormed its way up my intestines. I was flawed, and they would see it. They would shout it, like they always had.

"*Look! The girl who fell asleep in the privy.*" The taunt boomed in my mind. "*Thought she'd died in there, and when we had the door broken, we all seen her with skirt pulled up. Remember her face? Blinking awake, then gape-eyed like she was choking.*"

Heat billowed from my heart, scalding my chest and rushing to my head. The world blurred and rolled about me. I could not focus on any of the bodies in the crowd, only their staring faces. They were a multi-headed beast, a hydra ready to devour.

"*Her own mother introduced her as an idiot. Said a cobra had spat in her ear. Rotted her brain.*"

I walked with an ornate cane. To be precise, I stumbled forward, and the cane saved me from falling in a heap of silk before the monstrous throng of eyes.

A brick cracked under Deepmand's plated boot, and the isolated noise forced me to realize that the bazaar was hushed. None of the people had spoken. None had jeered. For the first time, I focused on an individual, a woman with a pink cloth wrapped around her belly's enviable roundness. Her short blue blouse would not by itself have covered her pregnancy, and her healthy skin was the hue of amber and lustrous from budding motherhood.

My gowns had tricked her and the rest into not recognizing me. I reminded myself that these people were the virtuous citizens of Morimound, and years had passed since any had seen the girl who had fallen asleep in the street privy.

The same weight of sleep bowed me over now, and I teetered forward, feeling in my plethora of gowns that I waded through a river of silk. I slipped, the cane catching me at the last moment. No one in the predominately male crowd seemed to notice, although my searching eyes caught on another pregnant woman. This one propped a toddler on top of her enlarged belly, leaning far back to compensate for the weight. She had a wilted look, and when she sneezed I feared she would collapse. Her nose ran, eyes a red and blotchy shade of someone who had not slept well for a year.

Meeting expectant women was always bittersweet. Half smiling and half wincing, I approached her, while she held her gaze lowered. I did not imagine this demure person had been the one to call for my help, yet I reached up into the blue and green ribbons of my headdress to remove a jeweled brooch, which I handed to her.

"Sell this," I said, "and buy yourself some help and a few days' rest."

She began to sob, staring down at the cluster of emeralds and gold in her hand, and I shared a moment of surprise: I had meant to give her a topaz brooch and instead had presented a treasure worthy of a princess. Yet I would not think of taking back the gift.

At the sight of my charity, the crowd surged closer. Spellsword Deepmand stopped the tide with single upraised gauntlet. He resembled a gold-and-bronze-plated armadillo, except with a scimitar clamped to his back large enough to decapitate an elephant.

I looked back toward my destination, the cage, only to be accosted by the appearance in the crowd of a third woman flaunting her fertile belly. The coincidence of seeing three pregnant women in a row shocked me like the sharp pain from a biting fly.

After my next steps swayed toward the cage, a voice of an older woman issued from within the bars. "Bless you, Hiresha. Perhaps only one god has cursed me."

Blinking away my fatigue, I saw an elderly matron entrapped within the cage, her fat belly pressed against the slats of brass. She must have been the source of the screams. My lethargic thoughts thrashed about, trying to recall where I had seen her wrinkled face before.

"I am Sri," she said in response to my confusion. "This is who I now am."

"Sri the Flawless?"

As soon as I said it, I regretted it. The Flawless could not be in shackles. I always had respected Sri as the city's arbiter and a woman of sober thinking and propriety, and no possibility existed that she could be locked in this cage, a death sentence fit for rapists and cannibals.

The bars would trap her outside at night, exposing her to Feasters.

Those locked in the cage could not run—nor would bars protect them. An indirect method of execution, the open-air prison dragged out death over hours or days, yet all knew it better to satisfy the Feasters with criminals than leave them to bang on the doors of the innocent at midnight.

This woman already looked half dead, perhaps even three-quarters so. Jaundice discolored her eyes and sleeplessness ringed them, while her white hair contrasted with her sickly yellow skin. The more I peered at her, however, the more I thought I recognized her as Sri the Flawless.

An even more unbelievable possibility presented itself. Entertaining this second idea, I concluded, testified to how sleepiness warped my thinking and how my mindset distorted perception.

Sri the Flawless, the chaste arbiter of the city and four decades my senior, appeared to be not merely fat but pregnant.

IMPROBABLE
-02-

"I am blemished," Sri the Flawless said.

Her hair, renowned for its prestigious length, tangled around her, knotted and greasy. The shortness of her blouse revealed a bulge centered at her waist.

"You turned to gluttony," I said.

The prominent paunch drew the eye, yet her arms had dwindled to yellow sticks, her cheeks sunken as if all the fat in her body had dribbled into her abdomen. I could not help but think that her belly sat higher and firmer than I would expect for a glutton.

"The priests funneled drafts of wormwood down my throat, yet when this refused to shed itself..." She waved to her belly. "...they decided death the most decent course of action."

"You should have resigned," I said, "and secluded yourself before—er—before that grew prominent. How decidedly undignified for a lady of seventy to, ah, pretend to carry child."

Sri, more venerable than any grandmother, surprised me by sobbing like a girl of sixteen. The Flawless had always held society together with her passionless judgment; her shattered persona felt like a betrayal.

"I am unworthy," she said. "Yet, last night taught me how much I want to live."

Her fingers twitched, and she wrapped her arms around herself. She collapsed to sit on her ankles.

"The Feaster, he was kind and inquiring, at first. I hoped he would spare me because of my condition." She held herself closer, digging her arms into her abdomen. "Now I'm afraid he'll come back tonight."

I steadied myself with both hands on my cane while endeavoring to make sense of the scene. My thoughts slithered from my grasp, and I slumped toward sleep.

Sri the Once Flawless said, "I want to taste the wines I've never tried, to explore the lands I've never seen, and to love. I know it's not too late to love, and I want a good man to help raise the child in me."

She caressed her unreasonably round belly.

"You can save me, Hiresha. Your Spellsword can cut through these shackles."

Her hand wobbled as she reached through the bars, beckoning to Deepmand. The scimitar belted to his back glinted with gilded scrollwork patterned in a tempest of lightning.

The crowd murmured. Deepmand turned to regard me, waiting to hear what I would say. The eyes of the citizens bore into me, demanding an answer.

"I will thank you to refer to me as 'Elder Enchantress Hiresha,' young lady." I had not meant to say that last part to the white-haired woman—the words had slipped out like loose pages in an old tome—and shame silenced me for three long seconds. "They—the priests who sentenced you to this cage may have misinterpreted the wills of their gods. I will inform them of the impossibility of your pregnancy."

White locks of hair fanned out as she shook her hair. "I am what I am. For months I couldn't keep more than crumbs down. My hair has thickened, I piss more than a dog, and even my poor old breasts have perked up."

Her lack of propriety forced me to gasp. "A reasonable explanation exists for all those symptoms."

"For all?" She eased her belly against the bars.

My inability to think of an explanation in no way removed the possibility one existed. Even if pregnancy seemed the most visible answer, the idea could not be countenanced. I had never heard of a woman who bore a child at such advanced age. If a white-crowned woman could conceive, then the event would be as rare as a red diamond. She would never survive the birth.

"Even if you were pregnant," I said, "you presumed too much in recalling me all the way from the Mindvault Academy. I am not one to conceal others' improprieties. Or mine. Not to suggest I have any." I could not believe I just said that.

"I admit I committed a selfish act," Sri said, "and the gods revealed it. Yet, I pled for your return only for the sake of the other women of Morimound."

"Yes. As the Flawless, you served as the paragon of virtue and restraint for them."

A thought waddled to the fore of my mind: I had assumed Sri had meant harming its women indirectly by scarring Morimound's reputation, yet she might have been thinking of another effect. She had said something about a transgression. I wished my thoughts would follow the speed of conversation.

More tears ran down her face's wrinkles. "You may be right. Perhaps they are all pregnant because of me."

I started. "What did you say?"

"Have you not seen? All the women of Morimound are with child."

My thoughts froze in my head and refused to move. I had to speak without thinking.

"I most certainly have seen nothing of the kind. I have seen a trend, yet . . .no, it's beyond possibility. Utterly impossible. The women of Morimound have upstanding morals, their threads of fate the brightest in the world. Did you say 'all the women pregnant?'"

"And all for just as long."

My heart pounded blood into my head, scattering my thoughts even farther. I could not focus on anything. It all seemed a nonsensical, childhood dream. Yet, I knew I did not dream because if I were sleeping, I would not feel so exhausted.

"You, Sri the Once Flawless, can only be suffering from dementia."

"Ask any woman here, any man. They will tell you I speak truth."

The crowd mumbled assent.

"Hysteria," I said, "cannot prove true a delusion."

"Then go to the God's Eye Court," Sri the Once Flawless said. "You must believe the priests."

"I will go, as sanity is obviously in need of a champion."

In order to turn, I walked forward and sideways, following the course of a semicircle to ensure that my gowns swept behind me. The Once-Flawless' words left me befuddled, and I would have fallen over on the way to the carriage if Maid Janny had not leaned over my gowns to steady my shoulder.

Children chased each other over the square, laughing and pretending to snarl as they chanted a rhyme:

"The Lord of the Feast comes,
How many heads has he?
One, two, three,
One, two, three.

When sun sets, he hungers,
Will you escape, my boy?
Wait and see,
Wait and see."

The children halted their games at the sight of my gowns. Some clutched at one another and exclaimed in astonishment; the rest ran after me to touch the satin and silk trains. Usually, the sight of children would have provided a pleasant respite, yet my encounter with Sri had upset me beyond diversion.

Once I stepped into the carriage, I revolved in place, one foot moving at a time, to wind my trains inside. Maid Janny wrestled in the last of my folds. "You may open the curtains," I said.

The Once Flawless had spoken the most intolerable claims. A few minutes' observation of the city would provide all the evidence necessary to prove her wrong. With a clack of hooves, the carriage rolled up the street, and I gazed out a window.

Morimound rose from the savanna on a man-made hill of golden-brown brickwork. A pair of step pyramids crowned the city, one ziggurat for each god. The highest third of the White Ziggurat gleamed with the sun behind it, the fiery orb appearing to balance on the structure's highest terrace.

Wood smoke from kilns enticed my nose, teasing me with memories of childhood that tiredness kept just outside my mind's eye. Above the rooftops, canvas blades revolved on windmills, which drove pistons to sluice water into the city's wells and flush refuse through an unsurpassed sewer system. I felt joy at the sight of Morimound, the greatest city in the world, alongside my fear that someone would recognize me, point, and laugh.

On the street, men backed into merchant tents to let the carriage pass. Three children ran after us, their pregnant mother struggling to keep up. I clicked my tongue in annoyance, although one more woman with child hardly attested to anything. I would need a larger sampling to form a judgment.

My eyelids began to droop. Deepmand's shouting from the front of the carriage faded to a mumble as if liquid filled my ears.

"The elder enchantress returns! Make way for the...."

My blurry eyes distorted the world, and I felt I was underwater and gazing up through the rippling surface. Brick houses three stories and taller seemed to sway and bend over the street. My head lolling with fatigue, I floated away from reality.

Once I had seen a girl who fell into a city well; her head had struck on the way down. She had sunk with arms open, hair fanning around her, peaceful because of the concussion. Now I wondered if she had been struggling in her mind, but had only been able to twitch her fingers as she drowned. I felt as helpless.

Flashes of wakefulness came like gasps of breath; I watched in numb terror as the next woman entered my view, leaning back in her gait to counterbalance the weight of the child inside her. The following woman was similarly blessed, her belly bobbing at each turn of crank as she drew water from a well.

I dipped back into my own private well, the transition between world and dream. This time, I did not fight the sinking sensation.

I must not have really seen seven pregnant women in a row, one old enough to be a great grandmother; my own bias had mistaken their plumpness for motherhood. To dry myself of sweat and to gain perspective, I would sleep.

In the blackness of my mind, marble steps appeared before my feet. I descended them, feeling heavier and heavier as I trudged closer to dreaming. Upon reaching the hundredth step, the stair vanished, and I leaped.

My weariness dissolved, the muddle of my thoughts clearing. I became weightless.

A.E. MARLING

LUCID
-03-

I brushed one slippered foot on a circular dais comprised of one thousand glittering diamonds. The black slab of an operations table lay before me, the stone indented to accommodate the average human figure. A wall of the same basalt rock ringed the laboratory, and tiered ebony platforms followed the room's curve. In each step of dark wood, a shelf glowed with a luminance of tools and baubles.

The wall possessed no ornamentation, and neither doors nor windows marred its surface. Above the shelves, my favorite jewels drifted through the air, lighting the round room with their multicolored hues. Sapphires in flight shone like the blue of hot flames, while clusters of rubies and amethysts orbited like flocks of songbirds.

I Attracted a towel embroidered with gold to my hand, and it flew from a shelf through the air to my outstretched fingers. An enchantress's primary power was to draw objects toward her, and Attracting came so naturally to me by now that I did not consider it a spell so much as a polite invitation for an item to jump into my palm.

All the shelved baubles stored memories of complex magic scripts, and the golden cloth I held was no exception. At my touch, the cloth shone, and hundreds of targeted Attractions pooled the sweat in my gowns into droplets, which were Burdened until they rolled down my stockings and away.

I swiveled in the air, streams of bright fabric trailing my arms, until I faced a full-length mirror. The levitating looking glass did not reflect my image but my memories; it would reveal visions of my past, whether or not I had been sufficiently clear-headed to acknowledge them at the time.

Sri the Once Flawless appeared in the mirror, and understanding flashed into me. A tumor in her liver had swelled within her abdomen, mimicking the shape of pregnancy. Its corruption had spread to her brain and there increased the production of her feminine oils, which stimulated her hair follicles and mammary glands. Dementia then explained the rest of her raving.

Having restored reality, I beckoned to the mirror. Images of the other six women blinked by within its crystal-covered silver, their imminent motherhood revealed not only in their bellies but also in the fullness and vibrancy of their black hair. Two even flaunted pregnancy masks: The darker pigmentation speckling their cheeks and brows would have arisen in the second trimester.

I could not believe it. The probability of seeing six pregnant women one after another was a thousand times less likely than one in forty-eight hundred. I calculated the vast numbers by visualizing beads in pyramid piles and then counting the colorful mountains all in a glance.

Desperate to break the trend, I batted a few floating rubies away from my head and commanded my mirror to show a memory from earlier in the day. I had parted a window curtain as the carriage had rolled through a gatehouse in the city's Flood Wall. Seventeen feet tall and seven and three-quarters thick, the wall would protect Morimound from summer torrents as well as from greedy invaders. I knew its specifications because I had designed them and planned its construction in an idle hour at the Academy, and my gold had paid for its stone.

We had entered the fringe of the city, Stilt Town, where shanties and shacks stood on wooden platforms, five feet above the ground. The elevation would prove unnecessary now, due to the Flood Wall, and thus newer buildings squatted closer to the mud. Wooden structures rotted in this climate; an odor of mold tingled the back of my throat when I recalled the scene.

Men had stared at our passing, as had one woman, who had paused in stringing fish out to dry. I jerked my eyes away from the reflection of her round belly.

"Your point is made, goddess," I said. "No need to direct more pregnancies into my path." The Fate Weaver must be punishing me, for returning to Morimound before ridding myself of the sleeping disease.

My somnolence was part of the goddess's divine plan. It had to be. Her gift—her curse—gave me tremendous advantage in the study of enchantment because the magic could only be accessed during sleep. Only when I had fulfilled my role in the Academy would the Fate Weaver allow me to find a cure and return to a life of wakefulness in my city home.

I had even hosted the funerals of my parents outside the Flood Wall, amid ripened rice fields, in order not to offend the goddess. I never should have heeded Sri's letter. Passing through the gates had been a sacrilege.

Each pregnancy I saw was a penance, a reminder of my own insufficiency. I had always imagined myself with a family, yet everything came in its proper time. Before children should come marriage, and before marriage should come a bride's capacity to stay awake at her wedding.

Ache spread from my chest to my abdomen, and my throat contracted by thirty-five percent as a desire to cry tingled behind my eyes. I disallowed myself tears in my dream.

Forcing my mind away from thoughts of childlessness, I willed my mirror to depict what I had seen in the Bazaar of Fallen Stars. Sri's yellow skin warned me that I would need to obtain help for her immediately: If the Feaster did not kill her tonight then her wormwood-destroyed liver would drown her in her own toxins tomorrow.

The people in the crowd now appeared before me in perfect clarity. The faces of the men were strained, the skin below their eyes swollen from poor sleep; I detected more alcohol in their collective breaths than I would expect. They eyed each other with distrust, one scowl even suggesting murderous wishes. When they looked upon my gowns and me, they displayed a mix of hope, avarice, and uncertainty.

Not particularly pleased, I shifted my concentration to the women. The first I observed sold green and orange melons, and her belly was comparable in shape to the sizeable fruits. Another female lifted sheets of blue and pink cloth, draping them for display over her prominent midsection.

Feeling increasingly breathless, I focused my mirror on the faces of the women. Even when they smiled to entice customers, their facial musculature displayed undertones of apprehension common to potential mothers. Less usual were the daze and paranoia detected in their wide, skittering eyes.

One woman's visage opened in fear when a man cornered her between two merchant stalls to demand who had fathered her child. I should have liked to remind him to be civil, yet the carriage would have moved well past by now.

In the cold serenity of my laboratory, I could control my panic. The explanation for all the pregnant women needed not be divine in origin. Morimound's priests perhaps had ordained that only women bearing children should venture outside today, for some inscrutable reason.

This would also account for why so few women traversed the streets, a mere one for every eight men. The rest would be residing in their homes. My focus swept over the buildings, up ladders leading to doors that stood an average of ten feet above street level. Per custom, people had painted messages beside the ladders, conversations between residents, passersby, and guests.

"At their table I ate the finest melon-seed curry in my life," read one line.

Below it was scrawled, "You are always welcome, Saral Manjeet."

"I hope to enjoy it again tonight. May your bricks never crack and your gems ever shine."

On another home's wall, I read, "The Fate Weaver has blessed Uma with beauty. May she bear many sons."

Lower down appeared, "Basu Trillspa and Uma are wed on this day. Let them Ever Thrive."

Those salutations I expected. Closer to street level, the more-recent messages caught my attention.

"Yami either swallowed a nest of crocodile eggs, or she should get married."

"The home of Parth, a bad thread who has wronged my sister."

"She is no Flawless."

"Preeta couldn't keep her skirt on."

"They are all rotten threads."

"Damodar will die for what he did to Kanti."

"Never Flawless."

"Fate Weaver spins ugly web, not even Flawless spared."

The view of my mirror zoomed from one wall to another, from painted insults to anger chiseled into brick. I had never seen such hatred here, and all were written within the last two months.

The accusations drove me to re-inspect the pregnant women I had seen. I bobbed toward one mirror, and swaths of velvet and silk flowed around me, weightless and drifting. Only half the women wore twined marriage necklaces; the rest were unmarried. I checked them all again and again, multiple times a second, their reflections spinning past.

This could not be right. I must be missing something, some citywide jest of which I was not aware. Or Diamond Way had an uncharacteristic amount of ill will between competing merchants, who had written their arguments on walls. And as for the unmarried, pregnant women, I must have observed a sample unrepresentative of the city.

A peculiarity even more difficult to explain was that all the women had appeared to be in the same trimester: the final one. I had always prided myself on my ability not to speculate prematurely, yet this last detail splintered my composure into shards of boggling color.

"All the women of Morimound are with child." The memory of Sri's words echoed in my dream laboratory; jewels trembled in the air. "And all for just as long."

She had to have lied. Rather, the Fate Weaver must be guiding me toward a future of insanity. The mirror now showed myself, mouthing my promise not to return to Morimound, while the images of the recently seen women squeezed around me, entwining me in tangled arms and between rotund bellies.

It was too much. I had to stop thinking. I had to flee my laboratory.

To exit my dream, I Burdened myself, my magic increasing my weight until I smashed through the diamond dais below me; sparkling jewels scattered and faded into blackness.

I awoke in a blissful stupor, in the shadow of the White Ziggurat. As we traversed to the west side of the step pyramid, its gypsum plaster shone red in the late-afternoon sun. The carriage rolled past lotus gardens and beneath arches formed of the draping roots of banyan trees; we stopped alongside the elliptical court of God's Eye.

Deepmand the Spellsword opened the carriage door and announced me. "Elder Enchantress Hiresha, recipient of twenty and seven honorary gowns, and the Mindvault Academy's Provost of Applied Enchantment."

Of course, I did not wear all twenty-seven gowns. That would be ridiculous. I only wore six; the rest were interwoven over my back and trailed behind in a procession of resplendent color.

The occupants of the court gawked at me, and I returned their stares, open-mouthed. Women stood in a line around the circumference of the court, yet, no, I could not call them women. All younger than fourteen, these girls had not yet accustomed themselves to their maturing bodies, and their gangly limbs teetered as they tried to support the weight of their pregnancies.

Two girls backed away from the rippling spread of my gowns as I staggered forward. I searched their faces and those of male acolytes in the center of the court for signs of suppressed humor. This had to be a jest. The priests had known I would return today and had prepared an elaborate and reprehensible hoax at my expense.

Their faces seemed surprised and otherwise indecipherable. I would know no more until I slept.

I asked, "What is the meaning of this conspiracy?"

A cluster of acolytes bowed their heads and parted around Abwar, the Priest of the Ever Always. I recognized him by his robes; he wore the representation of the sun adorning cloth the shade of green peridot, and a long sleeve flowed behind his arm as he gestured to the girls.

"Praise the Ever Thriving, Always Dying! These pregnant women are all virgins."

GODSENT
-04-

"We have you to thank, Elder Enchantress," Priest Abwar said, "for this miracle."

I slumped on my cane for support, and my head rolled up then down as the world seemed to tilt under my feet, to the point that I might fall over backward into the sky. Nothing here made sense. Everything was wrong.

Spellsword Deepmand said, "Lustrous Priest of the Ever Always, I assure you the elder enchantress was not responsible. She has not left the Academy for over three years."

"Observe the bowed head of the elder enchantress." Priest Abwar strutted among the acolytes, his green sleeves flapping as his hands beat the air in time to his words. "Her humility is commendable before the deeds of the divine, of which she served a part. Five times by flood and once by raider's blade, the holy city of Morimound has been cleansed by death. The Ever Thriving, Always Dying reaps and sows. He takes life and births it anew."

The eyes of the girls bulged at the priest, and not simply from alarm. The internal pressure caused by their pregnancies doubtless contributed to their ocular protrusion.

"Morimound has reaped six floods of death. There will be no Seventh Flood, thanks to the Flood Wall constructed by this lustrous enchantress, this jewel of our city. Now the

Ever Thriving, Always Dying has repaid our suffering. He has sown in these wombs a harvest of life."

Priest Abwar slapped his hands onto two distended bellies, and the girls cringed, one backing a half step away from him.

"Now that the Flood Wall protects us from another catastrophe, the souls of the drowned are safe to return to life once more. This renewal heralds a diamond age for Morimound, a time of growth and wealth."

He lifted his arms toward the Garden Ziggurat, its terraces lush with fruit trees and ferns. The sun dipped below one of its lower sections.

"Tell the city, my acolytes. The steps of the Garden Ziggurat will run with the blood of twenty oxen. No, fifty oxen! I will perform the sacrifices myself for this divine gift."

Among all these pregnant girls, the mention of blood reminded me of childbirth. Women so young tended to die in delivery, along with their babies. The thought wracked my insides with nausea, and stomach acid burned its way up to my tongue before I could swallow it down.

The words of the priest confused me, and I hesitated to believe them. I had lost faith in the Ever Always. Sacrifices of the lives of animals as well as my own years of life had yielded me nothing.

If Priest Abwar spoke truth, then this miracle would rival the ones I had learned as a child: The Ever Always had rained fish on the city to feed the hungry. A bestowed melon had grown with each cut of a knife. An army of attackers had transformed into monkeys.

"Look around you, Enchantress," Priest Abwar said as he beamed with ruddy cheeks and swinging jowls. "We are witnessing the wonder of the city's Seventh Age."

Every woman in Morimound was pregnant, except for me. The thought stunned me, and Abwar of the Ever Always was grinning about it.

"This is a matter most grave," I said. "Pregnant women face seven deathly dangers. The yellow-eyed death. The shaking death. The bleeding death...."

Spellsword Deepmand cleared his throat, an unwelcome distraction. I strove to remember all seven deaths.

"...The white-bloat death. The childbed death. And the fainting death."

I feared I had forgotten one. Deepmand sighed, and I noticed the raised brows and horrified faces of the pregnant girls.

Abwar of the Ever Always shrugged. "He reaps and He sows."

The priest's uncaring attitude toward the lives of these girls disturbed me.

A man's voice whispered from behind my shoulder, "Elder Enchantress Hiresha, I prophesied your coming."

The voice surprised me, and I swiveled my head, one eye seeing past the profusion of silk spreading from my neck in frills, scarves, and collars. Morimound's second priest, Salkant of the Fate Weaver, had slunk behind me in a manner most discourteous. If one had the habit of sneaking up on people then bells tied to one's feet would be a matter of simple courtesy.

"I didn't expect you so soon," Priest Salkant said. "I only sent out a messenger last month. The Fate Weaver must have guided you here with all eight of Her hands."

Salkant of the Fate Weaver wore black robes patterned with blotches of venomous yellow. Cobwebs stuck to him, and he had lost a few finger joints on both hands, no doubt due to carelessness in regards to spider bites.

"Priest," I said, purposefully leaving out the honorific of "Lustrous" because he had snuck up on me, "I must have passed your messenger on my journey."

I refrained from mentioning that the Once Flawless' message had brought me here, as an association with her at this moment seemed of dubious repute.

He glanced at the green Priest of the Ever Always and said, "I fear Abwar has mistaken the signs. The webs do not confirm this to be a divine act, nor one of benevolence. If anything, the strands point to the opposite."

"How could this be anything but an act of divinity?"

"This the webs do not tell, and I worry. Morimound's women…that is, all those my acolytes spoke to…they haven't quickened."

"Not felt a kick?" I was dumbfounded. "They are in their third trimester, are they not?"

"Most unusual, I know."

"Unusual? It is an implausibility too rude to be considered."

"Fate decides what is possible," he said, "not you or I."

"You old spider," Priest Abwar interrupted, "what're you whispering to the enchantress? And you won't be wheedling away all the credit, because I don't have to read webs to foretell that she will one day be known as the city's paragon."

Salkant of the Fate Weaver nodded. "Lustrous Enchantress Hiresha, at the center of every web I see the patterns of the outcast, the sage, the secret benefactor, and the spinster. These all refer to you."

"I find some of those implications abrasive, Priest." I again refrained from calling him "Lustrous Priest" due to his effrontery. My mind reeled at what he had said about the lack of quickening, unable to fully grasp the ramifications.

"From the center, the strands grow tangled and senseless. You must right them or break them. You will bring about Morimound's salvation, or its destruction."

Abwar of the Ever Always asked, "What's this about destruction?"

"I am no spider at the center of a web," I said, although in the next instant I wondered if I had said something foolish. The temperature had begun to escalate within the insulation of my gowns, the heat boiling away my thoughts.

"A spider? Certainly not." Abwar of the Ever Always stroked his jowls as he regarded me. "A flood of fabric, maybe. Yes, I like that. 'A flood of fabric with a froth of jewels.' I want a scribe to write that down."

Salkant of the Fate Weaver leaned so close that I had to suffer his stale breath. "You must guide the city through its time of strife, as its arbiter."

"Through its time of plenty," Priest Abwar said, smacking his own bulbous green belly. "You will be the first among jewels, the Flawless of Morimound."

I tried to work out if they had suggested I become the city's highest judge. I believed they had, yet I could not conceive of it. If I spent all my time officiating the city then I could never return to the Academy and cure my somnolence. My head had grown light with heat, and I widened my stance to form a firmer tripod with my cane to stop swaying.

I knew also that the Flawless could never marry.

"I cannot accede to this." The thought of staying in this city with so many happy mothers agonized me. "I must return to my position and studies at the Academy."

"The future of the city depends on you, the webs leave no question to that."

"Stay and witness Morimound's diamond age."

"You do not need me. Free Sri the Once Flawless from her cage and return her to this court as arbiter. You can hardly fault her for an act of divinity." Then again, I recalled that she had said something about her shame.

"I had forgotten about her," Abwar of the Ever Always said. "No, I don't think we can pronounce her the Flawless a second time. Her proportions no longer seem suited."

He made a rounded motion with his hand over his gut.

"I saw no sign of her reinstatement in the webs," Priest Salkant said from behind my shoulder. He picked cobwebs out of his hair with two partially amputated fingers. "Historically, the priests have chosen, well, young women. Because purity of decision requires...."

He stole a glance at me.

"...purity of vessel."

"Of course she's pure," Priest Abwar said. "Look at her, she's untouchable."

I asked, "Just what are you insinuating?"

"It is true," Priest Salkant said, "the Fate Weaver has placed the elder enchantress at the center of the Loom of Life. As the Flawless, her thread will be long and all-encompassing."

"I cannot be the Flawless. My travels to other nations have worsened me, and, well, I am not Flawless." My fatigue blemished me in every way.

Abwar of the Ever Always said, "With the condition of the rest of Morimound's women, we can't be too particular. With the laying on of hands, she becomes the Flawless."

"No! I insist not!" My imperfections would displease the gods and bring the city to ruin. I had only become an enchantress for the chance of curing my somnolence, and I refused to trap myself within yet another tedious role.

Priest Abwar reached out and slid his hand up my sleeve to fondle my arm. Salkant of the Fate Weaver traced a finger's two-remaining knuckles down my neck.

Heat washed and crashed inside me, and I felt as if I had dived into a bubbling, sulfurous springs. I was drenched; nauseating steam spread through my chest.

"Look at her sweat," Priest Abwar said. "She burns with the power of the gods!"

Salkant of the Fate Weaver nodded. "And trembles with the weight of destiny."

Priest Abwar withdrew his hand first and turned his gaze to the goggling, pregnant virgins. "Acolytes, return these bundles of blessings to their homes. Sunset nears."

The priests left, and the girls began to plod away from the court. Once I resumed control of my breathing, I said,

"Spellsword Deepmand, you should have stopped the priests from inducing me. I mean, inducting me."

"My apologies, Elder Enchantress." He laid a gauntlet over the gilded plates covering his chest. "The priests speak for the gods, and I thought your protestations appropriately humble."

Maid Janny lifted her face from its formerly demure position. "You should've known something was deeply wrong, with her acting humble."

After a firm sniff, I underwent the process of turning around to return to my carriage. Pregnant girls stood still to watch me pass, and I recalled the priest's egregious claim that they had not quickened.

"You will have felt your child kick, of course." I gestured to their gravid figures.

They looked among each other, nervous, saying nothing.

"Or a fluttering, a tapping, something reminiscent of a growling of the stomach?"

A few girls appeared uncertain. One said, "I don't think so, Madam Enchantress."

"Nonsense. All women in your advanced state quicken, all those with child."

"Then you must be right," one said.

"Doubtless so." Yet, I did not feel reassured. Quickening was a crucial event, when the Fate Weaver tied a soul's thread to a child. Its absence was unthinkable.

Agitated, I approached a group of mature, pregnant women who had waited under a banyan tree during the proceedings. They were embracing the virgin girls, perhaps their daughters, and accompanying them away into the gardens.

"You," I said to one, "have you quickened?"

"Me? No."

"What about you?"

"No, Lustrous Enchantress."

"And you? You must have quickened."

"I don't think so, Flawless."

"Do not call me that." I stormed through them in a flurry of gowns to the next cluster of women. "Which of you have quickened?"

They looked away and held their silence. The air seemed to have left the sky, for I could not breathe and I gagged on my tongue. The ground appeared a long way below me, and I fell toward it.

I landed on my cane, catching myself. Deepmand steadied my shoulder.

"Elder Enchantress?"

I fled to the next pregnant pack, finding the same lack of response.

Reaching out, I touched two of their bellies. "Do you not understand? You would have felt your babies move, you had to have felt them."

They shied away from my desperate tone, and I tugged at a glove, at last pulling it off. My bare hand gripped their engorged waistlines, one after another. Once I finally thought I felt something then realized it was the shaking of my hand.

One girl asked, "Why is it so important? That we quicken."

"Because...because...."

Rather than answering, I reached to touch two more women, feeling nothing but a tautness of skin, and I tried yet another but found only stillness. My hand remained on that abdomen, as I felt myself too weak to lift it.

"It means the Priest of the Ever Always is wrong. About all of you. There is no life here."

UNCERTAIN
-05-

Night Three, Third Trimester

I should not have said it, not in front of the pregnant women. The guilt struck me on the walk back to my carriage, and I began wringing my glove. Maid Janny coaxed the cloth from my fingers to pull it back over my hand.

Their children had to be deformed. I could think of no better explanation, and I grew dizzy imagining so many babies paralyzed in their wombs, perhaps entirely lacking legs and arms. The thought horrified me, washing me with deluges of heat and shockwaves of cold, and by turns I felt I would dissolve or shatter. I swayed and sweated, propping one hand against the coiling root of a banyan tree for support.

This could not be. I had to be wrong, yet any reassuring thought flew from my reach. I had to enter my dream laboratory to clear my mind.

Staggering into my carriage, I closed my eyes to see the hundred marble steps descending to sleep. I ran down them, even as the stair trembled with my anxiety and melted from the heat. The final step lifted me into the black, round room without doors.

Feverish warmth subsided into a chill. My dream maintained a cooler temperature to facilitate thinking, and a filigree of frost rimmed my memory mirror. Disordered thoughts flashed nonsense images and flickers of color over the glass. I gripped my head and forced the nonsense away.

Something was amiss in the bellies of the women in Morimound. If they carried babies, then those babies could never live.

I had heard once of a pregnancy that held no life, only thousands of pearls of skin, bubbles of flesh that multiplied until the mother burst. The midwife's story had sounded incredible and, if it was true, would account for an eighth path to death for mothers, in addition to the retching death, which I had forgotten in the court.

The midwife had thought that "froth womb" swelled a mother's belly faster than a true child, and I did not believe that was the case here, given the women I had seen thus far. The length and quality of their hair and nails gave me an estimate of how long they had carried, as those areas were affected by the feminine oils released in pregnancy. The fact brought small solace because if the women did not suffer from froth womb then they faced something that I had even less capacity to explain.

I could mull over the potential causes, such as an epidemic of tumors, yet I sensed the sun had set in the real world, and Sri the Once Flawless would be helpless in her cage. The priests had poisoned her with wormwood then had left her to the mercy of Feasters, condemned for a pregnancy over which I doubted very much she had any control. I could save her; I would save her, lawfully as the Flawless.

Awaking, I directed Deepmand to travel downhill toward the execution cage. Maid Janny entered the carriage and then closed the door behind her.

"You can drive tired horses to death if you like," she said, "but you won't have me outside at night. My tastiness would be the death of me."

"The relative tenderness of your tissues is beside the point," I said. "Feasters do not consume the physical."

"Nothing worse than a picky eater."

Janny sat across from me, scrunched against the sideboards. The carriage had been built to hold six people, permitting her just enough room to squeeze inside among my gowns. My enchanted earrings shone blue light over her grey dress and bonnet, which she filled with an amorphous body. Freckles scattered over her face like air-bubble inclusions in an emerald.

Her smile lines remained even as she lowered her chin and frowned. "I know, I know. They slurp souls or some such. Found a girl in a gutter once. Thought she was sleeping drunk and had gone and ruined her dress. Slapped her, and she was cold as used bathwater."

"Maid Janny, every word you speak further elucidates your ignorance. Feasters do not imbibe souls. Their magic drains power from fear."

"Don't care what all they eat, if it comes from me. Breastfeeding was bad enough."

"It is an honor of motherhood."

She fretted in her seat, knuckling her chin. "We shouldn't be out and about at night. We shouldn't, we shouldn't."

"You should have more confidence in Spellsword Deepmand," I said. "He is trained to defeat Feasters, and I suspect Morimound to have the second least incidence of them of all the major cities."

"Easy for you to be brave. A Feaster would go hungry rather than listen to you lecture about its dining etiquette."

Maid Janny infuriated me. True, I had to forgive her much for her labors scrounging underneath my gowns to remove used chamber pots. She made her low opinion of my views obvious, while I took every opportunity to point out her deficiencies. Beyond the bickering, we shared nothing in common. In short, we were inseparable friends.

She peered out at the deserted and dark streets as they whisked past. "The men in robes said something about gods, but how do they know the women didn't all have a good tumble in the loft?"

"Exactly what are you implying about the strong-fibered women of Morimound?"

"That they had some belly on belly. They sweet-dreamed. Aired the mattress. Paid the lord."

"Maid Janny!"

"Oiled the sword. Danced the sheets. Husked the corn."

"Did you neglect to hear the Lustrous Priest pronounce those women virgins?"

"Poor girls. They missed the best part of having a baby."

"You refer to no more than a means to an end," I said. "Maid Janny, it is well that you are unattractive, or you would be entirely insufferable."

"It is well you're rich. Or so would you."

To deceive Janny into thinking I cared nothing for her words, I engaged in sleep.

As jewels meandered overhead in my laboratory, I estimated fifteen more minutes would elapse before Spellsword Deepmand procured the key from the jailor then returned to the execution cage to free Sri the Once Flawless.

Janny's uncouth tongue reminded me of the admonishment of the Fate Weaver's priest: The pregnancies might not be divine in origin.

A physical explanation seemed less than imaginable. I trusted Morimound women to know whether or not they were virgins, and few of their faces showed an excess of guilt when the priest proclaimed the girls as chaste. The pregnancies of elders such as Sri the Once Flawless rendered a theory of normal conception even more dubious. If geriatric fertility was widespread then I could rule out all means less than supernatural.

I pondered in mid air at the center of the circular room, my gowns drifting around me. To prevent them from enveloping me entirely in a satin cocoon, I batted them back from my face as if parting curtains. I also dimmed the jewel lights, with a thought, for an environment more conducive to meditation.

For the first time, I regretted learning no more than a general education in the less proper magics. I knew of none whose primary or even tertiary effects could cause anything resembling a pregnancy. The intricacy of spellcraft involved would require proximity of the practitioner to the woman, in all probability necessitating physical touch to achieve the most efficient and precise delivery of the magic.

The lack of quickening made this situation altogether more ominous. A spell that had seeded them must have gone awry, unless causing misfortune had been the magic-user's intent. I wondered who would do something as unspeakable as cast stillborns into wombs.

If a woman did not bear a healthy child then she bore anguish. The thought of my people suffering sent prickles running over my skin, as if spiders crawled over my hands and up my sleeves. I could not allow anything to tarnish Morimound, which was the beacon of decency and civilization in a world full of catcallers, lepers, loan sharks, jewel dupers, murderers, and bureaucrats.

An amethyst flashed from its place on the shelf, signaling that we had arrived at the cage and Deepmand was speaking my name for me to wake. I Burdened myself, smashing through the dais and back to the real world.

"Elder Enchantress Hiresha," Deepmand said, his voice reverberating in the carriage, "we are not the first here tonight."

MURDEROUS
-06-

As I muddled myself into focus, I grew aware of lights outside the carriage and a ruckus, which shocked me with a fear that I had somehow slept to the dawn. I began to flush at the embarrassment of leaving Sri the Once Flawless out all night.

The lights shifted before me, and, after blinking, I perceived lamps with flames leaking from their brass nozzles, carried by men around the cage. Stars shone in the sky, and it was still night. At least I thought it was, yet the premise conflicted with the presence of civilians outside.

I overheard men speaking in the crowd. "When the Feaster shows, throw these nets on him."

"Will they hold him?"

"They hold cheetahs, don't they?"

"Right, then we'll see how he likes eating swords."

"I will abolish the Feaster."

These last words came from a man armored with shield and scimitar. I identified him as a Bright Palm by his radiance, his glow most marked in the veins of his hands. His presence explained the boldness of the other men, as his magic rendered him immune to Feasters' fear attacks. This failed to make me pleased to see him.

The Bright Palms had no respect for the divine. Neither did they approve of the weighty fees I charged for my enchanting and regeneration services. Their magic could heal faster but not better, and it leeched the Bright Palms' emotions, rendering them passionless constructs of flesh.

An idea struck me: As the Flawless, I could order the Bright Palm to leave the city. I hesitated to exercise that power, however, because his open vest and loose, sheet pants suggested he was a Morimound native.

Sri the Once Flawless spoke from her cage. "Did you imagine a Feaster would come with the street alight? Even cockroaches are smarter."

A citizen asked, "You expect us to catch him in the dark?"

The Bright Palm stood silent and expressionless. The other men looked at him, and one said, "Suppose we can't help but catch him, with a Brighty to help."

Another man lifted his lamp toward the cage. "What say we kill her instead? Was her disgrace what caused my Salha to grow in a motherly way."

I realized I should leave the carriage and order Deepmand to free Sri. My desire to sleep outweighed my sense, and the voices outside grew distant.

"Heard today that it wasn't nothing to do with the Flawless. The Ever Always is having his way with us again."

"All I know is none will wed my daughter now. We should kill the Flawless, to be on the safe side."

I dragged myself from the carriage. Deepmand steadied me when I stumbled.

"I was, I am the new arbiter of this city," I said with slurred words. "Sri the Once Flawless is innocent and will be released."

"You can't do that," a man said, "she's the bait."

"By edict of the priests, I am..." I could not bring myself to say "the Flawless." "... I have the authority to order you to disperse."

"But I just tapped this barrel. Men, fortify yourself with my best red wine, and you'll catch a Feaster yet." A one-armed man paused from passing out clay cups to bow to me. "With the lady's permission, of course."

"I concur with the Once Flawless," I said. "This is not a proper way to catch a Feaster, and everyone must return to their homes as promptly as possible."

The Bright Palm spoke in a monotone. "We know the Feaster's lair. We will seek him there at dawn."

I attempted not to cringe. "You know where he lives?"

"At the Mitul house on Rainsweep Street," the one-armed man said. "Most of the neighbors have suspected for years, but mistress Mitul is a gem. Hated to drag her son onto the street and beat him to death."

Spellsword Deepmand asked, "The Feaster is living at his mother's house?"

"Yes," the man with only one arm said. "Wine?"

Maid Janny smacked her lips behind me, but neither she nor I accepted the cup. Deepmand's armor plinked as he tapped his gauntleted fingers against it.

He asked, "Then why did you not attack yesterday, during daylight?"

"Takes time for men to build their courage. And wine."

"Why did you need more than one man?" Deepmand waved to the Bright Palm.

The one-armed man noticed a cut on his thumb, which he thrust into his mouth. Once he had sucked away the blood, he said, "Will give them something new to talk about. Too much 'who bedded whose daughter,' if you understand me."

Worrying that fatigue would slump me onto my side on the street, I forced my eyes as wide open as possible. "Then this gathering may continue, as long as it avoids disturbing the surrounding occupants. Deepmand will take Sri the Once Flawless into my care, however."

None of the men with weapons attempted to impede the Spellsword, likely due to careful consideration for his excess of two hundred pounds of arms and armor. Gautam Deepmand would not have the capacity to move if not for his Spellsword ability to activate Lightening enchantments, which I had crafted into his gold-etched bronze.

I sensed him Lighten one leg and one arm at a time as he marched forward. His armor fitted together without chink, the plates on his legs additionally reinforced to support the weight of his torso. The scimitar on his back was too large to be wielded by a normal man, and I took pride in the enchantment in the silver-tinted diamond on its hilt.

Through force of will, I reached my carriage before falling asleep. I could not expect myself to stay awake at night when all civilized people slept.

My respite was brief. The amethyst in my dream laboratory pulsed, and I faced it with dread, knowing I was wanted awake.

Upon returning to the world, first I noticed a stink. Then I saw Sri the Once Flawless in the carriage with me, wearing her tattered skirt and blouse.

Deepmand said, "Your pardon, Elder Enchantress, but when I asked where I should deliver mistress Sri, she could make no reply."

The wrinkled, jaundiced, and swollen woman said, "I can't go back to my house at the top of the hill, as it's for the Flawless. Did those do-nothings declare you the Flawless?"

"They believe they did, yet I am not the Flawless. I cannot be."

"I didn't believe I could either." Sri laid a hand on the outmost of my six layers of sleeves, her veins bulging under her shriveled skin. I worried her touch would soil my gown. "I suppose I was right, in the end, but I think you are stronger. With an elder enchantress in the court, the city has a chance to escape its fate."

"And what fate would that be?" I asked, worrying about the women and their motionless wombs.

Her head drooped. Sri's bent back brought her chin close to reaching her belly. "I admit I've had nightmares of a flood. Only it wasn't a flood of water. It was worse, somehow. Strange as it sounds, in the dreams I always thought my baby and I had caused it."

"It is natural to have anxious dreams, while carrying a child." I squinted down at her abdomen.

"These were not normal dreams. I felt I could see the future, without reading a web."

"Vivid dreams are also typical in your state," I said. "Do you have any family at whose home you could stay?"

"I have nine grandnieces and twelve grandnephews, and I would never do them the injustice of asking for hospitality. Their reputations may never recover."

"Neither can you stay at an inn. It would be below your dignity. My manor is empty." I had commissioned the mansion five years ago but had never entered it. "You may stay with me."

"I could never ask you for such a favor."

"You did not ask. I invited." My eyes dropped to the wrinkled mound of her pregnancy. "There is one detail...have you quickened, Lady Sri?"

"I should have by now, shouldn't I?" She dabbed the corners of her eyes with the sleeves of her blouse. "Do you think the wormwood has hurt my baby?"

"That, I will determine tomorrow." I would regenerate her liver then as well, in private. Enchantment magic was not suitable for public eyes. "Spellsword Deepmand."

"Elder Enchantress?"

"We will stay here tonight, so you can ensure that none of our people come to harm from Feasters."

"As you wish, Elder Enchantress."

In three seconds, I had fallen asleep. Reviewing my prior conversation with Sri, I noted her self-deprecating comments, which, combined with facial slumps around the corners of her mouth, indicated intense shame. I would have to ascertain the cause, as it seemed less than warranted if she numbered among the faultless-yet-pregnant virgins. My own reputation might diminish by housing Sri, I realized, yet I had already agreed to host her. Until proof of wrongdoing surfaced, I intended to give preference to the aged lady.

I also contemplated the Feaster situation in regards to the condition of the city's female populace. Although responsible for cowardly hunting the weak, the Feasters could not be at fault for the peculiar pregnancies. Their magic was no more than illusion, fleeting things of shadow that evaporated under daylight.

A Feaster had almost killed Sri, yet he could have played no role in her unnatural condition. He might, however, have seen or heard someone who had, such as another magic user, one powerful enough to keep Feasters at bay as he crept from house to house at night, touching each woman as she slept.

I would confront this Feaster tonight, and he had best behave himself.

DECEIVED
-07-

"Inform Deepmand to depart for Rainsweep Street."

Maid Janny hiccupped in surprise. "But that's where the fear nibbler is!"

"Do not dawdle. I must arrive before the dawn."

"If Feasters it is, I'll have another cup."

While Sri the Once Flawless dozed across from me, Janny returned to the carriage, wrestling with my gowns for room. Her cup remained vertical, never spilling a drop as we raced over the streets.

Janny gulped her wine in a fashion less than civilized. "Wonder if the city has any lady Feasters with the big bump."

"Excuse me?"

"There are lady Feasters. I've seen Bright Palms nail them onto temple doors," she said. "Think any here have the breeding belly? The jug full of trouble? The nine-month bellyache?"

"Why would they not?"

"Heard they couldn't. If peppers give me the burns, eating all that fear must blacken their insides. You know, shrivel their wombs, no children. Now that I think of it, might not be half bad."

"Do not be absurd. They have all the requisite reproductive organs."

"Just how much do you know about their re-productive organs?"

"I have received an education at an academy of higher learning, the benefits of which you could not begin to appreciate."

"I'll drink to that." She upended her wine glass.

Janny's impertinence gave me an excuse to contemplate her dismissal. My finger would point out from the carriage, and she would leave, too surprised for a retort.

With my next breath, I remembered her helping me on my first days in the Academy. She had guided me up walls along gravity-defying paths, huffing as she did from the weight of the child she had carried inside her, too. Maid Janny had been young then and I younger still, a girl lost and frightened in an upside-down world.

No, I would sooner do without one of my hands than part with Maid Janny, although I would never admit it to her.

I turned my eyes away from the vulgar woman. My study of Feasters had begun after one of those mornings when my drowsiness swamped my perceptions, shut out all potential for satisfaction, and forced me to consider the benefits of killing myself. This avenue of thought had focused my attention on Feasters, whose magic was rumored to cure all deformity and afflictions. As a Feaster, I might escape my endless fatigue.

My ruminations of becoming a Feaster had spiraled into obsession, which I had escaped only by reassuring myself that no theory existed as to how a magic of fear and nightmares could cure so much as a hangnail. True, a disproportionate number of lepers became Feasters, yet illusions might cover their disease rather than cure it. I reminded myself of that now because I would soon face temptation.

My gaze rested on the sleeping Sri. She faded in and out of view as my eyelids fluttered closed, yet I saw her clearly in my laboratory, through the hovering mirror.

Her white hair reached her ankles, or it would if its tangles were brushed straight. The hair had thickened near her scalp because of her pregnancy, yet otherwise the condition did not become her. Stretch marks crisscrossed with wrinkles over her abdomen, while her nails had cracked and dulled, and her skin had discolored to the pale yellow shade of a toadstool.

I could purge her blood of wormwood and restore her liver. Even so, I judged she would not survive the last months of pregnancy, let alone the birthing. My magic could save her but not all the city's elderly matrons. Each family would lose its grandmothers.

I remembered with fondness my grandmother Sandu, the only female relative who had not beat me for forgetfulness and oversleeping.

Although a frown line etched the brow of Sri the Once Flawless, she slept with a smile. She believed she could bear her child, raise it, and find happiness. I could not help but wonder if I would feel the same way if I had resided in Morimound six months ago and had become pregnant like all the rest. I had sufficient strength to bear a child. I was not too old to raise it. My somnolence might not be inherited. The possibilities cramped my stomach.

Worst of all, I suspected increasingly that the children would be stillborn. I imagined what I would feel after carrying a baby inside me for nine months, pouring a thousand hopes and affectionate thoughts into her, braving constant fears of miscarriage then the trial of childbirth, only to hold my daughter for the first time and find her shriveled and lifeless.

The pain of that possibility was too great, and I had to wake to dampen my thoughts.

The carriage stopped, and Deepmand helped me step down to the street.

Maid Janny said, "You expect me to go out there? The Feaster might pounce me."

"You may stay with Sri the Once Flawless," I said, turning to read the writing on the wall of the home before me.

"Alali Mitul," the wall read, "the Ever Thriving bless you. Your caring is most deserving, your generosity true."

Under that couplet, flecks of paint and discolored bricks indicated passages had been scrubbed away. A persistent someone had carved a message, "This roof hides a...." The final word had been removed by chipping bricks from the wall.

Stars in the east sky faded. The street behind us gleamed from nearing day and the incoming lamps of the crowd, led by the Bright Palm and his raised scimitar.

I lifted a gloved hand to the house door. "Deepmand, we cannot wait. I must speak to the Feaster, before the Bright Palm interferes. Bring him to me."

Maid Janny spoke behind us. "You expect me to stay in the carriage by myself? Sri hardly counts, she's old."

The door shuddered when Deepmand thumped it with his plated hand. "Open this door, by command of the Flawless."

"I am not the Flawless," I said.

"Open the door, in the name of Elder Enchantress Hiresha."

The spellsword's vociferations and knockings failed to bring about a response, although I believed I saw a light move behind the shutters. The east sky had turned pink. Deepmand smashed the door to splinters with an armored shoulder.

Women screamed inside, and I heard Deepmand's muffled apology. Outside, men waved scimitars and yelled, "Get the shadow swallower!"

"Bring 'im out so he can see the dawn!"

Despite their words, the men abstained from following Deepmand into the house. The Bright Palm's neck flashed with the magic flowing up his arteries as he eyed the second story windows.

I followed his gaze to see shutters swing out and a man jump to the street. The black-bearded man landed on his feet, but the sight of my gowns seemed to startle him. I wondered if this was the Feaster. When two citizens charged him, he snapped his gaze away from me and threw a sack; it opened in a burst of hornets.

Buzzing insects landed on the citizens' faces, and the men dropped their weapons and howled, slapping at their cheeks. The man I presumed to be the Feaster gulped in air, and his belly expanded, his paunch slumping over his belt buckle. More disturbing than the sudden growth was a darkness that swirled beneath his stretched skin like spilled sewage.

"Deepmand, your presence is requested." I failed to keep a frantic note out of my voice. A hornet's large, segmented body crawled on my arm, and I felt it bite through my glove. Telling myself it was an illusion only partially lessened the sting.

Two men with nets approached the Feaster, who reached into his own mouth and pulled out a sword, an obsidian blade sliding between his lips like an overlong dark tongue. In a sweep of shadow, the black sword chopped off a citizen's hand. The man stumbled back, clutching the stump of his arm.

The Bright Palm shoved his way through the crowd, and when he passed me, the hornet on my glove vanished. The Feaster spotted him, and the fear-eater's face twisted with horror. He turned to try to run, his sides swaying and jiggling with his sudden fatness.

Scimitar raised, the Bright Palm closed the distance between them, his veins shining through his skin in a blur of white.

"Stop him!" I reached toward the Bright Palm with fingers hooked, knowing he would catch the Feaster in seconds and decapitate him.

In a spray of bricks, Deepmand leapt through the second-story window; rather than falling, he sailed overhead. He had activated to the fullest his armor's enchantments of Lightening, and for a moment, a man wearing two hundred and twenty pounds of arms weighed nothing.

He arched through the air, overtaking Bright Palm and Feaster. His flight stopped when he Burdened himself, plunging straight down. I admired his technique; he smashed between pursuer and pursued, pulverizing the bricks he landed on. His armor absorbed the impact and channeled its force up his legs to his torso. Deepmand batted away the Bright Palm's scimitar with his gauntlet, yet when he swung his arm to do the same to the Feaster's blade, the obsidian edge sliced through Deepmand's enchanted bronze.

A disembodied arm clattered to the ground.

Obsidian could never cut metal. I knew it was impossible, an illusion. Apparently, Deepmand knew it, too, because he reached for the Feaster with his seemingly missing hand and bludgeoned him to the street with a fist temporarily unseen but nonetheless weighted with gold knuckles.

Deepmand's arm reappeared, and before the Feaster could wriggle away, the spellsword planted a metal foot on him and compressed. The Feaster writhed, gawking up at a sky that brightened with dawn. I moved toward them through the mass of citizens. When my gowns rippled around their feet like flowing water, the bystanders sucked in their breaths and shuffled back.

"Masterfully done, Spellsword Deepmand." I inclined my nose to the Feaster. "Now, degenerate, I suggest you answer my questions."

WRETCHED
-08-

Day Four, Third Trimester

"I never hurt anyone. Never killed them." The Feaster wiped at an inky substance dribbling from his lips. "I'm just cursed. Please don't—"

"That is quite sufficient sniveling," I said. "First, did you witness anything untoward during the night, between five to seven months ago?"

"No, nothing." He clamped his pudgy hands over Deepmand's boot, failing to budge it.

"You have sufficient time, degenerate, to consider your answers, yet none to try my patience. Did anything seem out of place on your nightly escapades?"

"Wait, yes, there was demons made of flames."

"There *were* demons." I corrected him.

"They chased me down the streets, the demons did, always after me with their knives, and me just hungry and drenched in the rain and always so hungry."

Deepmand asked, "Flame demons, in the rain?"

"No, no, no, it wasn't raining then. Only later."

I did not know if he spoke truth, yet I would in my dream. "As a Feaster, you have an olfactory perception of fear. Correct?"

"No, I swear by the Fate Weaver I never did!"

Deepmand leaned farther over him. "The elder enchantress asked if you can smell fear."

"No, no! Well, a little."

"Then," I asked, "has any home contained occupants who seemed particularly fearful in the past months? Or, when the pregnancies became obvious, did any household lack fear?"

"Do not listen to it." The Bright Palm edged toward the Feaster with his scimitar lifted. "Their kind will say anything to avoid justice. I insist on the right to avenge the meek."

The fat man wailed. "Lord of the Feast, save me!"

Deepmand glanced to me for approval then caught the Bright Palm's descending scimitar, yanking it from his grasp. By activating an Attraction between the dorsal sides of his gauntlets, he snapped the blade in two.

The Bright Palm's face never changed as he watched his sword broken, and with a voice that might have commented on the relative humidity he said, "You are aiding a thing of lies and despair. Desist, or the Order of the Innocent will condemn this city."

"Does this look like aiding to you?" I waved to the pinioned Feaster. Fortunately, I had anticipated this point of contention and planned in the dream what I would say. "I have enchanted seven swords for Bright Palms, which together will have slain dozens of Feasters. I am not their ally."

"What you have done in the past is irrelevant. Morimound is shielding this Feaster and harming the meek."

I did not like how he attributed my actions to the city, although I admitted that he might have some grounds for doing so. The Bright Palms had already condemned me multiple times, for the prices of those enchanted swords, and their toneless disapproval no longer bothered me. More flustering was the thought of my city receiving condemnation, the first step on the path to a declaration of righteous war.

Unsure of myself, I glanced to the spellsword, yet he only bowed his turbaned head. I heard a woman's voice behind me.

"He can't help himself. Arsumi is a good boy at heart, and never wanted to cause hurt."

A woman I understood to be the Feaster's mother wrung her hands among the wreckage of the house's door. Four children peeped their heads out from behind her.

The Feaster pawed at Deepmand's boot, gasping for air with which to speak. "Let me go! Or my sisters and brothers will kill you."

"That I doubt." I glanced back at the children in the doorway.

"No, my other family."

A coldness seeped through me. Although I did not consider myself susceptible to physical attacks, a Feaster's magic could circumvent my defensive enchantments and frighten me to no minor degree. I remembered the pain of the sting and wondered what Deepmand had felt when his arm had been lopped off at the elbow.

The citizens had backed away from me, or perhaps from the Feaster, and they thrashed their scimitars in the air, indicating that they hoped for the entertainment of the Feaster's death.

I began to think I should have Deepmand kill him, although I had planned otherwise in the dream. Granted, I had not fully anticipated the ramifications of my actions, and I wished I could rest to analyze my situation.

Dawn's light crept over the street, and the Feaster gasped as his skin bubbled and fumed. His mounds of flesh collapsed, shrinking him to the size of a boy with far too many ribs showing. His beard withered until only awkward fuzz remained on his chin. The day had turned him from a menacing man to a sickly adolescent.

Afraid to go back on choices made while asleep, I turned to the Bright Palm. "Feasters, I can stand. Impertinence, I will not. The, er, the gods have chosen me to serve this city, and I judge that delaying this boy's—I mean this degenerate's—execution is the best course of action."

Men in the crowd groaned. "Why not do him? He's right there and pinned."

"Feaster, I will grant your temporary freedom, if you promise to search for unexpected fear levels. You also must speak with any brethren you have in this city, few as I trust they are, and then return to me with a full report."

The Bright Palm lunged for the Feaster. Before his fingers could close on the scrawny boy's throat, Deepmand shoved him aside.

"Yes, yes, I promise I will," the Feaster said. "I will, I will!"

"I want you to swear in the name of the Lord of the Feast." Anecdotal evidence had suggested this was an effective way of ensuring a Feaster's cooperation.

He paled, one eyelid fluttering in a series of tics. "I mah-mustn't do that."

"And why ever not?"

"No, no, I can't. He's close." His gaze darted to the streets around him. "He's always close. Aiiaaahhhh!"

The Feaster convulsed and vomited a fan of black liquid over the street bricks; it boiled to nothing in seconds under the sun. The boy stopped twitching, his moans quieting to whimpers.

I tried a few more times to convince the Feaster to commit to the oath, yet I grew convinced he preferred to die than presume himself on the Lord of the Feast, a fact I found disconcerting.

"Then, degenerate, I will advise you to leave your family's house, as you are disgracing them."

I realized I should not have said that, because I might not be able to find him later in another dwelling. The shadow walls of sleep closed around me; I made a shooing motion to the Feaster then turned to the crowd.

"Accosting this Feaster, or this household, is forbidden by order of the God's Eye Court."

Deepmand returned to my side, and the Feaster scampered back in the dimness of the house. The Bright Palm gazed after him with a placid face.

Not trusting the Bright Palm to obey local law, I accosted two acolytes as they walked the streets on an early-morning task. "Assign city guards to protect this house during the day," I said.

Permitting Maid Janny to assist me into the carriage, I observed that her hand trembled. She said, "However did you manage? You never flinched or fainted, and I was obliged to do both for you."

"I was in no danger, from illusions," I said. "Reading the texts prepared me for that much, although not for how disgusting and pitiable Feasters are."

Sri the Once Flawless had scrunched herself into a corner of the carriage, and she was shaking her head. "He seemed sweet, at first. I thought he would free me from the cage."

"Your intelligence must be impaired, from toxins accumulating in your blood. I will see to your convalescence at my estate." The words left my mouth with more confidence than I felt, as I planned to view the interior of her womb at the same time. If I found a stillbirth then I would be obligated to attend to it with my magic: Not an easy task nor a pleasant one. "Deepmand will now convey us there."

Once asleep, I saw that the Feaster had lied about demons chasing him through the streets. He had told the truth concerning an absence of anything strange five to seven months ago, at least to the extent he had pondered it.

The Feaster had scanned the streets around him after mention of the Lord of the Feast, and I too examined the alleys and avenues through the mirror, finding nothing. The boy had screamed and gone into spasms but not in fear of strangulation from the Bright Palm. In that case he would have glanced in the glowing man's direction. His eyes had instead unfocused; the terror had been from a memory, I judged.

The only evidence of the legendary three-headed Feaster in Morimound was no evidence at all: a caricature, crudely drawn in charcoal on the wall between two homes, glimpsed by me yesterday. Contorted and bloated, the figure resembled a leaping bullfrog with the heads of a screaming man, a snake, and a crocodile.

This act of vandalism upset and unsettled me, and I washed it from the mirror with a sweep of my hand.

Uncertain whether or not I had gained anything this night, except an enemy in the Bright Palm, I focused on the unsavory prospect of pulling Sri into my dream laboratory, where I could cure her. The process was always unpleasant, and completing it in Morimound would not be ideal. To be precise, it would be illegal.

APPALLING
-09-

I rubbed my eyes. "Maid Janny will escort Lady Sri into one of the guest rooms, and I will follow."

A gaggle of servants negotiated Sri the Once Flawless out of the carriage and carried her away on a gravel path, one holding her knees, one her back, and two more her shoulders. She mumbled, her head rolling and eyes unfocused.

"See that she is bathed," I called out after them.

Spellsword Deepmand shook his head, his beard sliding over his armor. "I fear the Lady Sri has little time left."

"Fortunately, the Fate Weaver placed me in her path."

"An amulet will heal her?"

The safest and fastest way for me to regenerate Sri would be to draw her into my dream for a custom enchantment. Deepmand knew this, and he had lifted one black, bushy brow, no doubt concerned that I meant to break the Propriety Pledge, which I did. A professional statute forbade enchanting outside the Academy's walls, to protect the dignity of our magic.

Before I could think how to reassure him, a clop of hooves approached, ending with the sound of someone dismounting, and a male voice spoke nearby. "A spellsword, I see, so they must've given the correct address."

Deepmand swiveled one leg at a time to turn as a man in a foppish red coat trimmed with lace stepped into view, his face powdered to an absurd degree.

"Elder Enchantress Hiresha, Provost of Applied Enchantment, I am Tethiel, interim ambassador from Jordania."

For a foreigner, he pronounced my name well. Beginning with a high sound, he avoided stressing the harsh middle syllable and ended with a resonant "ah."

"You have my attention, Ambassador. Jordania exports some of the finest topaz in the lands."

"Jordania values them so highly, Enchantress Hiresha, that it sells all it can. I believe you requested my assistance, and I am at your service."

I realized I had remembered wrong: Jordania mined fewer topazes than garnet jewels, and the ambassador had made light of my mistake. He must wonder how someone with such poor mental faculties had risen so high, and I could not even recall where I had met this man before, although I felt I must have.

"When did we first meet, Ambassador?"

"Why, just now. But I have it on good authority—or perhaps not so good yet much trusted—that your powers of observation match those of the Opal Mind, the empress enchantress."

Well used to sycophants attempting to ingratiate themselves to my wealth, I hesitated only a moment before saying, "If we never before met, then I could not have asked you for assistance, and I see no need for this conversation to proceed. I bid you good day."

Even after his defeat, the fop held my gaze and had the audacity to tell me his place of residence. To that impropriety, he bowed only from the neck, as if between equals, and I added Jordania to the long list of nations I would never visit.

Deepmand lifted a hand, to help me down from the carriage. "Elder Enchantress, may I present your estate and manor, Sunchase Hall."

Gravel crunched under my slippers. Scores of servants bowed along the path to the doors, touching the hems of my gowns as I passed.

I had seen the manor before in my dream, where I had designed its construction, but never witnessed it under true daylight; the morning sun streamed off the crystal windows like molten gold. I grinned even as I sucked my breath through my teeth. I had hoped to arrive here under more joyful conditions, such as wakefulness. I batted my gloved hand over my yawn.

"Lustrous Elder Enchantress, we have waited five years for this day." A servant with a white beard and a black turban lowered himself to greet me when I entered my manor's stairwell entrance hall. "I am Pallam Obenji, and I will ensure all you desire is yours while staying at Sunchase Hall."

"What I desire is irrelevant, Mister Obenji," I said. "What I need is privacy to tend to the Lady Sri."

"I recognized the great lady instantly, even with her recent...alteration." He ushered me down a corridor hanging with monochrome green tapestries. "You are a veritable paragon for bringing her in, and she is an honor to your home."

We stopped in front of a guest room. I saw Maid Janny tucking Sri into a lavish bed while other servants filed out the door.

"Your ring." I pointed to one of two diamond rings on the smallest finger of Mister Obenji's right hand. "I require that."

"This?" He gave the ring a half turn. "It is a family heirloom."

"My gold will buy you more heirlooms."

After a deep breath, he twisted the ring off his finger and handed it to me with a bow. I nodded to him, thankful that I now had the resource to heal Sri.

"Deepmand, allow no one inside, under any pretense."

The spellsword peered down at me, kneading his lips between his teeth. He had to know what I intended, and I wondered if he would try to stop me. As a representative of the Mindvault Academy, he would be as concerned as any about my breaking the Propriety Pledge and revealing the secret of enchantresses: Accessing our magic required our going to sleep. Entirely too much lewdness surrounded the name "enchantress" without the world knowing we slept with the swords we imbued with power.

He and I both had grown up in Morimound, although Deepmand had a decade before I. Sri had arbitrated during both our childhoods, and I at least had always seen her as something priceless and pure. Witnessing her in this state had to pain him, too.

Without nodding or giving any other sign of consent, he said, "I understand, Elder Enchantress, and you will not be disturbed."

When the door closed behind me in the guest room, I began to doubt that Deepmand was correct about my not being disturbed. Bringing another into my dream laboratory required physical contact, an inordinate and repulsive amount of physical contact.

"I trust, Maid Janny," I said, "you will be good enough not to remember today."

"'Forgetfulness is your greatest asset,' that's what my mum always said." She winked and began untying my gown laces.

Maid Janny was a regretful necessity. I might as well be wearing chains and padlocks, for all my capacity to undress myself. I spent most of the wait half-asleep, and I had little memory of anything that occurred before I slipped under the covers with Sri and slid the diamond ring onto her right pointer finger.

The Once Flawless had not spoken, and I was thankful for her comatose state. Wrinkled and discolored though she was, she thankfully was not the most unpleasant person I had been forced to sleep alongside. Few dared to tell dukes and kings they stank, and nobility seemed to be bred for their hairy moles, along with the occasional weeping ulcer.

Sri smelled of scented soap. I tucked my chin over her shoulder, reaching around her watermelon waist and easing myself closer for maximum skin contact. We both wore nothing, only our undergarments. I closed my eyes and found myself on the stair, my hands empty for the moment.

I walked downward, alone, darkness undiluted on either side of the marble steps. Upon reaching the last step, I grabbed at the air, and Sri appeared in my arms as I lifted into my laboratory.

The elderly woman disappeared from my grasp just as quickly and materialized on the indented stone of the black operations table. Even though I no longer wore my gowns in the real world, they swirled about me here in their full copper-and-silver-threaded majesty.

"Hiresha?" Sri blinked awake, her eyes following the yellow topazes flitting past her nose. "By the gods, where are we?"

"Your consciousness is not required." I reached toward a shelf and Attracted a silver pillow. The magic bauble sped through ten feet, to my fingertips, and I brushed it over Sri's cheeks.

She closed her eyes again with a sigh. The spell would hold her in a deeper sleep and prevent her from remembering anything.

My first order of business was to search her hair. In one second, I had found thirty-four lice; one had even crawled onto my arm. A spell of Attraction crushed the nuisances against a quartz crystal I held between two fingers.

A sapphire honey jar leaped from a shelf to float above the operation table, followed closely by a series of vials holding powdered gemstone. Together they contained spells that would clear her blood of bodily contaminates as well as any residual wormwood. Flecks of light leaked down from the glowing trinkets to sift over her while I prepared to repair her liver.

I Attracted a cluster of blue diamonds from a shelf and positioned them in a sparkling pile atop the right side of her belly. The diamonds spread outward, circumscribing her abdomen in a revolving circle. The skin they passed over became invisible. Yellow globules of fat nestled against a reddish plaiting of abdominal muscles, all of which faded from sight below the descending diamonds.

The liver appeared, a bulging, slimy thing the color of sulfur. I pinched my nose although I could not in truth smell it through the transparent flesh. The organ bore no tumors, and was crowded by a bright pink womb, which I would investigate shortly. I lifted my hand, and a scepter with a purple jewel spun, end over end, into my grasp.

The scepter embodied my most coveted enchantment: regeneration. The spell involved hundreds of Attractions and Repulsions over infinitesimal distances, targeting bits of matter I did not fully understand in units of flesh I could not see, the process multiplied a vast number of times per inch of intended re-growth.

Once I had set a few parameters in the spell, I lifted Sri's hand with the diamond ring. It was the only real gemstone here, the one thing capable of maintaining the enchantments once I woke. I touched it to the scepter then to a rack of vials, and the diamond began to glow pink.

Realizing I had been less than gracious in procuring this necessary jewelry, I sighed. At least I would be able to return it to Mister Obenji once it had returned Sri to health.

Her safety now assured, I gathered my courage to view the state of her child. I was less than hopeful and felt a buzzing twinge in my stomach. Focusing my mind, I willed the blue diamonds to reveal another section of her abdomen.

The smooth muscles of her womb entered my view, followed by a layer of spongy crimson. I held my breath, preparing myself for my first glimpse of a godsent child.

I blinked, realizing I had pushed the jewels too far. The spell had removed from the visible spectrum not only the anterior of the womb but also the child's skin, revealing a tiny bone hand, its finger joints glistening with cartilage. Often, babies in the womb would clench their fists, yet these fingers lay flat, its wrist resembling a collection of white pebbles. I pulled back and noticed that the skin between the fingers was a translucent yellow, a surprisingly similar shade to cartilage.

To obtain a better visual of the child's skin, I withdrew the spell a tenth of an inch and saw the gelatinous membrane of the birth sac. Again, I had gone too far. Even as that thought flitted through my consciousness, I observed something that caused my mind to scream, adrenaline gushing into my arteries like sparks exploding from my heart.

Through the filmy covering of the birth sac, I could still see the whiteness of the skeletal hand. No skin covered those fingers.

Moving my diamonds forward bared the sight of the hand surrounded by more bones, cartilage connecting finger bones to what appeared to be leg bones and ribs. Neither believing nor understanding what I saw, I flung aside the blue diamonds. Sri's spotted skin reappeared, hiding whatever lurked inside her.

Panting, I found myself chewing on gloved knuckles. My head seemed to pulse with flashes of white, the white of the interlocked bones I had discovered. The mishmash of ribs and femurs dug into my mind, and I gripped my temples.

I asked myself what I had seen. Not a stillbirth, I thought, but something fleshless, a pandemonium of bones.

All at once, I grew aware of a pressure, the sensation of a stranger's hand on my shoulder. Alarmed, I pirouetted, gowns sweeping aside gemstones. No one was behind me, yet I still felt the presence.

I could be feeling the hand of a god, the Ever Always. The divinity, or something else, had wormed its way into my dream laboratory, into my most protected of places. I felt vulnerable, horrified for my safety as well as by what I had found in Sri's womb.

If a god peered into my dream, he could kill me with a thought.

"I—I did not mean to interfere." I kneeled awkwardly in mid-air. "Forgive me. I will...I promise to...."

I could not think of what to promise, only of the gaze that felt like molten wax dripping on my skin. I had to escape, had to get free. In a blink, I smashed down through the diamond dais and left the dream.

MISSPOKEN
-10-

I staggered from the doors of Sri's room, Maid Janny lacing the last of my gowns onto my back. Mister Obenji, the elderly servant with the black turban, bowed then tried to look past my tide of fabric.

"Lustrous Enchantress, I hope there is chance for the good lady's recovery."

"She will progress," I said distractedly.

My wobbly legs took me to a parlor with green upholstery. I could not sit in my gowns, so I leaned sideways onto a couch, my face pressed against the cushions as I focused on breathing through chest spasms.

I no longer felt watched by an unseen force. All I felt, rather, was sickness on an empty stomach. Squeezing one eye closed then another, I tried to rationalize the thing that was not a child lodged in Sri's womb. I had been too frightened to view more than its closest part. Nor did I feel any desire to rush back and investigate.

Shivering despite my six layers of gowns, I now understood why Sri had not felt a quickening. The not-child had fused bones and could not move. My head trembled from side-to-side at the thought. The strangeness, the nonsense of what I had seen tore at me, and I could not believe that every woman in Morimound carried what I could only assume was a curse of the Always Dying.

"Sri has to be an exception," I muttered. "A fluke. A horrid, horrid—"

"Did you speak, Elder Enchantress?"

"No, Deepmand."

After several minutes sprawled on the couch, I convinced myself that I had witnessed a very rare birth defect. The other women most decidedly carried healthy babies in their wombs. The presence I had felt in my dream might not have been a god. A magic user could have interposed his will. In theory.

I turned my attention to all those in the city who might suffer from childbirth, although I had no reason to suspect they would bear anything but normal children. True, the mothers I had spoken to last night had denied quickening, yet they could have been in error. Others might have felt life within them.

I had to focus. I could not lose control. I had to stay calm and stay silent about what I had seen. If any breath of it reached the people then they might panic. A terrified citizenry could attract Feasters and cause even more problems.

My thoughts were spinning away from me. Increasingly, I dreaded the idea of more not-children—of unchildren— within Morimound mothers, inside my people, ensconced in their daughters.

Only twelve years had passed since an old friend, Harend Chandur, had told me of the birth of his daughter. During my residence in the Academy, I had exchanged several letters with him, one of his first detailing pride in his newborn son, another of his daughter five years later. The news had pained me more than I would ever admit.

I decided to visit Harend Chandur today, to reassure myself that his daughter had quickened and could not be pregnant with anything untoward. Maybe she was not even pregnant. She would be only twelve.

As I heaved myself up from the couch, Spellsword Deepmand cleared his throat. "Would you wish to view Sunchase Hall, Elder Enchantress?"

"I am in no mood for frivolities."

"You look glassy," Maid Janny said. "You'll feel better with a meal in you."

"I will take my breakfast at the estate of Harend Chandur."

"My apologies, Elder Enchantress," Deepmand said. "It is past noon, and I was unaware you had received their invitation."

"I will receive one, once I arrive."

Janny obtained directions to the Chandur estate, and we departed from my manor grounds. When the carriage passed through the gates leading down from the High Wall, I rapped my cane on the roof.

"Maid Janny, your diminutive mind has misremembered the directions. Harend Chandur lives in the Island District."

"And he couldn't have moved, in the who-knows-how-many years since you've last been here?"

"He would not have, downhill of the High Wall. His family is one of the most established in Morimound."

"Then I'll ask the gate guard over there, as his figure looks rather well established." She winked at me. "Wouldn't you say?"

Averting my eyes, I resolved to sit and doze while Janny's incompetence sent me to the wrong address. I was relieved to find that the unnerving presence from my dream was now gone, although I avoided looking into my mirrors.

We arrived at a house with three stories but in all other ways deficient of a manor. Janny shuffled to the door and back.

"Faliti Chandur said they'd be delighted and honored and whatnot for you to dine with them this evening."

My mind labored over the concept of Faliti being the wife of Harend Chandur, who both temporarily lived here, outside the Island District. I assumed their manor was undergoing repairs.

Faliti I remembered all too well from my youth. Leering over me with her aggressive and mannish chin, she had said, "Resha, you don't deserve to be a mother. You'd smother your children by falling asleep on them." She had stolen Harend, the only man who had tolerated my falling asleep between dances and, once, in mid-conversation.

"Maid Janny, did you neglect to tell Faliti Chandur that it is not now evening?"

"Must've slipped my mind."

"You may take my hand as I exit the carriage."

"Mind that I don't take both hands. The honor would be too great for my weak heart."

The door of the house opened when I approached, and Faliti glared down at me. The sight of her broad shoulders and square chin sparked fear, even after all these years, and I missed a step.

Faliti closed her open mouth, and I realized that she had not glared so much as gaped in shock. The sight of my gowns morphed her face through several different expressions, and although I could not distinguish them now, I planned to savor them later.

"I am not prepared to receive you, Resha—uh." Faliti balked as if surprised she had called me by my childhood name and knowing she had blundered.

"Faliti Chandur, you may address me as 'Elder Enchantress.' I have come on behalf of the priests and the divine gods to see to the safety of your daughter."

At the mention of her daughter, Faliti dropped a hand to her own pregnant belly, and despite myself, a flush of resentment crept up my cheeks. I swept past her, and she skirted away when one of my gowns rippled past her legs.

"By the Ever Always! Are your dresses quite safe? One just grabbed my ankle."

Lightening enchantments in my gowns caused them to undulate more than expected, lending them an appearance of animation. I saw no reason to put Faliti's mind at rest and maintained my silence.

"And you, er," she said to Deepmand, "your boots are cracking my floorboards, ant-ridden such as they are."

"My apologies, Madam. I will Lighten my step."

I walked through the rooms of the first floor, noting items of refinement, such as a tapestry of peacock feathers, amid otherwise bare furnishings. "Is Harend Chandur present?"

Faliti tidied some sewing stuffs. "He's meeting his merchant friends at the White Ziggurat, so he can lose more money."

"Then you may now introduce his daughter to me."

"I'm sure I would, but she's recovering and bedridden, and I wouldn't be a fit mother if I taxed her strength with visitors."

Argument required more mental dexterity than I usually commanded when awake, so I had little recourse than to repeat myself. "You have my permission to take me to her bedside."

"Alyla is not seeing anyone. She's in no state to."

"She will see me. My presence is most salubrious." I walked past Faliti as she ground her teeth.

Finding no bedrooms on the first floor, I looked up a ladder leading to the second story. It had a gentle incline, similar to a stair, but stepping on the rungs would prove difficult with my oscillating sense of balance and inability to see my feet.

Hoping I was not fated to fall once again in front of Faliti, I gathered as many of my skirts as I could and explored the first rung with my slipper. Stepping up, I tried to find the second rung, yet velvet and silk slithered around my foot. I had to step on my skirts, although this made me sway and tilt, my shoulder brushing the wall; letting go of my gowns to catch myself only aggravated my plight, with satin blocking any possibility of a subsequent step.

I tipped backward and knew I would fall in a most dreadful and undignified way. Faliti had committed an act of negligence in employing this ladder, her disregard tantamount to assault with intent to injure.

A.E. MARLING

Gauntleted hands gripped my shoulders, and Deepmand carried me to the second floor in a leap that cleared the whole ladder. Relief made me gasp, and my knees knocked under my skirts as I strode down the hall, dragging my gowns out of the way so that the spellsword could stop levitating and rest his feet on the ground.

I avoided Deepmand's gaze, ashamed that I had needed his assistance for this most simple of tasks. I wished, for a moment, that I could activate enchantments when awake as a spellsword could. Of course, such a practice would be neither possible, for an enchantress, nor dignified.

A voice quavered down the hall. "Mother, do we have guests?"

I stepped into a bedroom and saw a girl sitting up between pillows, her swollen abdomen rising from beneath sheets. Her slender limbs caused her to resemble a pale spider with only four legs; her skin was waxy and sickly as white jade. The square chin she had inherited from Faliti sat at odds with her smaller frame and timid eyes, which were reddened and bulging.

If fate had permitted then I could have married Harend, and Alyla might have been my daughter. The inside of my chest felt rubbed raw. I asked, "I wish to know, have you quickened?"

After roughly a dozen blinks at my gowns, she still failed to find voice to answer.

"Have you quickened, child? Oh, and I am Enchantress Hiresha."

She swallowed and said, "I'm afraid I don't move too fast anymore."

"I mean have you felt your baby move?"

"Oh." Her lashes flickered over large, beautiful brown eyes. "I'm not sure."

With little insulation in the form of physical bulk, she should have felt each kick as a stab. She should have been sure. My fears dragged my gaze away from hers.

I doubted that so slight a girl could give birth safely, certainly not with a labor shorter than twenty-four hours; I imagined her ordeal, a lifetime of agony compressed into a day of blood and strain, and then I saw her final contraction producing not a pink, healthy child but a thing of bones, a god's cruel trick, an unchild.

It could not be. I promised myself it *would* not be, and I felt a current of excitement and a deep sense of meaning that made me know I was exactly where I was meant to be, nestled in the pattern designed by the Fate Weaver. The goddess had guided me here to save this girl from grief.

Regretfully, said goddess had yet to provide any clue as to how I could help her and the other thousands. If I but knew how a letter might reach the Fate Weaver's cavern palace at the center of the world, then I would have written a stern complaint.

CRAVING
-11-

Faliti stomped into the room. "She shouldn't be like this. If she'd been stronger, she wouldn't be this way."

I eyed Faliti's own motherly belly. "All the women in Morimound are pregnant."

"My daughter has no right to be. Alyla could've dodged it, if she had the will to do anything in her life except spread her legs for some alley boy."

Alyla hid her face behind her hands and sobbed. I felt I should comfort her, although I did not quite know how. My gloved hand glittered as I laid it on her knee, and I wondered if a gentle squeeze would be a suitable demonstration of affection. When I tried it, the fleshless knee jabbed my fingers.

I said, "Priest Abwar has proclaimed these pregnancies as godsent."

"God or alley boy, she couldn't have said 'no' to one less than the other. I tried to build something out of her, but the Fate Weaver spins some thick and others thin."

I, of all people, knew that.

"Are you still having nausea, my child?" I spoke the motherly address without thinking, and the words tasted bitter on my tongue. She was no child of mine.

Alyla glanced at her true mother then looked down.

"No, she isn't," Faliti said. "She has trouble seeing."

"Blurred vision is common from increased—"

"You've been at it again, you disgusting girl." Faliti pointed at the wall behind the bed, where the bricks had cracked and chipped. She brushed clay flakes from Alyla's shift and sheet. "And here are the crumbs. What are you, some mud-eating pig?"

She slapped Alyla then pinched her cheeks to pry open her jaw.

"Spit it out, girl. Out with the brick you've eaten, or I'll throttle it out."

I noticed a chunk of clay between two of Alyla's teeth, and her tongue was yellow. "This is also common." Disturbingly so, given the uncommon thing I feared was inside her.

"Eat no more of our house or it'll crumble, as poorly built as it is. You have shamed us in front of my important guest. Do you see her, Alyla? See the gemstones strewn about her? I knew her when she was poor and stupid, and now I bet she earns more in a year than your father will in his whole life."

When Alyla tried to meet my gaze, her eyes lost themselves among the mazes of copper and silver thread embroidered in my gowns.

Faliti said, "Say something to the enchantress. Prove you may be dumb, but you can at least speak."

Alyla's spindly fingers gripped her belly as if she felt the need to cling to something. "You honor the roof of... of our home, and we in-invite you to live here as our guest."

Faliti cuffed the back of her head, ruffling her dark hair over her eyes. "Why would you say that? The enchantress owns the largest mansion in Morimound and would never want to stay in this fly-pen."

At the sight of her hitting the girl, my hand rose to my mouth, and I held back a sob. I wondered how Faliti could strike something so precious, could abuse a gift given by the Ever Always: a child of her own blood.

Deepmand shifted beside me in a clink of metal, and he tugged at his beard.

I left the bedroom before I had a fit. Descending the ladder almost killed me even after Maid Janny had climbed up to hold my shoulder.

Once safe on the ground floor, I said, "I will dine here."

"Surely not, Enchantress," Faliti Chandur said, walking down the ladder. "We're reduced to drinking tea and eating field peas, nothing I could serve you."

"Maid Janny will retrieve my meal. And tea is the only suitable drink for women of childbearing years."

Janny muttered, "And who'd want those years?"

She returned from the carriage with a basket and my ottoman, and she helped manage my skirts while I approached the padded stool. Faliti could use a normal chair, which she did, setting in front of herself a bowl of eggs and rice.

Faliti asked me, "Why did that enchantress choose you, anyway? Those years and years ago. Out of all of us working the rice paddy, she picked you."

"She saw me sleeping in the rain."

"That's not a reason."

"I have significant aptitude for enchantment."

"I don't believe it. She could've taken any of us to your land of fancy dresses."

Janny cut my broccoli florets into quarters, and she shucked greater beans, which had been steamed. She placed a napkin and silver fork into my hands.

"That can't be what you eat," Faliti said. "That's food fit for the muddies working fields."

"After a certain point," I said, "quality of sustenance is independent of cost."

"You're mocking me. You came to this house to gloat and mock my ill fate."

My hands began to tremble, so I hid them under the table. "Faliti Chandur, you are fortunate beyond measure."

She barked a laugh. "You call unpainted bricks and only one servant fortunate? And look at you, the woman with the city in her hand, and you never had to stoop for it. You never were forced to carry a man's child or weep over a miscarriage!"

The bowl of egg and rice smashed against the wall, and I stared from its dribbling yellow chunks back to Faliti. She sat still and composed as if she had not just thrown her meal.

She asked, "Did the priests really make you the Flawless?"

"I am not flawless."

"Well, I know your plan, Resha. You will try to take Harend from me, but I won't let you. He's mine and still will be no matter how many gems you flash in front of him."

I glanced at her marriage necklace, a twined chain of gold bearing a diamond. "Faliti Chandur, you will refer to me as 'Elder Enchantress Hiresha,' or not at all."

I struggled up from the ottoman then left the house.

As Deepmand drove me uphill, I pondered the potential truth of Faliti's claims. My dream held more than my laboratory, and one of its other rooms contained a portrait of Harend; I had thought to one day wed him even though he was married to Faliti.

I saw no point in marrying anyone until I could stay awake between kisses.

The carriage stopped at the God's Eye Court, and acolytes and petitioners gathered as close around me as they dared. "Lady Flawless, I have a dispute over aquifer shares."

"And I represent a man wrongly trampled on the very streets of this city."

"The bridal price hasn't been paid for my daughter."

"Quiet!" I raised my hands, my sleeves fanning out in a spectrum of fabrics ranging from red to green to purple. "I am only interested in babies, mothers, and—most to the point—babies inside mothers. Acolytes, you will make reports of women's general health, size, weight, and how many per thousand have miscarried and quickened."

The day simmered, and I strained to remember what I had planned next to say.

"Make special note of any not pregnant. Furthermore, you will bring women ordered by their age and place of residence for my examination tomorrow in this court."

As the acolytes formed themselves into work teams, a one-armed man approached me and kneeled to touch one of my myriad hems. I lifted a hand both in acknowledgement and to cover a yawn. My mouth snapped back shut when he spoke.

"Elder Enchantress and the Flawless of Morimound, someone is murdering our women, and I can tell you where to find him."

A.E. MARLING

LETHAL
-12-

"Tell me of this murderer, and do so without calling me 'Flawless.'"

The one-armed man winced as he rose to his feet. I believed I recognized him as the wine merchant from the previous night.

"I spend most days in the bazaar, long enough to see things, you understand. I'm Anlash Niklia, vintner of Anlash's fine wines, including the legendary Liquid Diamond."

"I did not ask your occupation. Did the pregnancies incite the murders?"

"The pregnancies? No, not at all." He ran his only hand through his long, wavy and oiled hair. "Well, in a way. With so many women being as they are, and many wishing to be—hmmm—less so, they find certain merchants who sell certain herbs. Do you understand my meaning?"

"I am not one to understand meanings." I bit my tongue, realizing what I had just said.

"I'm sure I meant no disrespect to your virtuous personage. But some of less repute buy, well, poisons meant for the child they carry."

The sun burned above me, and sweat seeped from my headdress and ran down my brow.

He said, "Only, the herbs aren't just poisoning their wombs, they're killing the mothers."

I clenched my cane, trying to exhale as much of the heat inside me as I could. Nothing angered me more than mothers coming to harm, and I thought of Sri and her liver rotten from wormwood. Yet, I could not dismiss such herbs as a potential means of freeing any women who carried an unchild, although I maintained hope that some women had normal babies. Some must have quickened.

"Name the herbalist responsible, immediately," I said.

"Noblin, southwest bazaar."

"He will be apprehended without delay."

"I also wanted you to know, Elder Enchantress, having my fine wines served in your manor would give me the greatest of pleasure."

"I have no interest in intoxicants."

"But you were so interested in my information. I hoped that interest could spread to my wares, as it were."

"I think I understand. Very well. For your assistance, you will have my patronage." As I left the court, acolytes hopped away from my gowns. "Deepmand, the carriage."

While sleeping, I considered how I might help Alyla and all the rest most at risk in childbirth. I could pull one girl into my dream and perhaps find a way to dismantle the unchild, if unchild I found, yet such an effort would be futile on the citywide scale. Since I would require an hour with each woman, the labor would take years and would obliterate the Propriety Pledge, revealing the enchantresses' disgrace.

Herbs such as wormwood might make such a labor more feasible, if the will of the Ever Always could be surmounted

A.E. MARLING

by poisons. I doubted that, and thus I had to hope the women had been seeded by a mortal's magic.

We arrived at the bazaar seventeen minutes later. The crowds parted to stare at me and at my back, and I remembered I wore a golden hump, which I sometimes forgot about because it weighed less than air. In the Mindvault Academy, a curved spine signified the seniority of an elder enchantress, yet I realized the implication was lost here. My golden hump bewildered onlookers, although I would not do without its enchantment, for my safety.

Someone to my right whistled. "Wonder what the enchantress hides under all those clothes."

Deepmand stepped to face the speaker but apparently failed to spot him in the crowd. To counter the indignity, I lifted my chin to new heights.

"Such lasciviousness," I said to Maid Janny. "Men confuse 'enchantress' with 'wanton charmer.'"

"How unfair. Doubt you've charmed a single person in your life."

"Quite right, Maid Janny. Oh dear, are those Bright Palms?"

"Hark the signs! Hark the signs!"

Two Bright Palms shouted at the passersby from a podium constructed of rice barrels. "The Lord of the Feast hides among us, but by three signs you will know him...."

I strode past merchants hawking their wares and competing with the Bright Palms in volume to see who could cause the most headaches in a day.

"Alligator oil, for all your tooth pains!"

"Wildebeest roast, killed by my son's own spear!"

The Bright Palms continued their ranting. "...The Lord of the Feast has no teeth to speak mercy...."

"Get your cheetah cub here," a red-faced merchant shouted. "Nearly tame!"

"...no ears to hear your pleas...."

A woman merchant bowed to touch the hem of my nearest gown. I could not bear to look at her, wondering if she carried an unchild within her.

"...and a black triangle on his brow, where soul left body."

I glanced at the Bright Palms as they began their chant anew. Before seeing the Feaster's horror at his mention, I had hypothesized the Lord of the Feast to be a myth invented by the Bright Palms to garnish attention and support.

We traversed to a stall with hanging herbs and a pungent smell. A foreigner stooped over a ledger, his white whiskers tufting out below his wire spectacles. When his nose tipped up toward me, lenses enlarged his eyes into watery black pits.

"Herbalist Noblin," I said, "you are selling poisons to the women of Morimound."

"What? Who're...who...oh my, but I'm not poisoning anyone."

"Wormwood is a poison."

"A poison is a substance and a dose. I swear on the honor of the Founder that I never gave a poison dose, and I have the notation to prove it."

He shoved the ledger toward me, tipping piles of herbs and a mortar off the side of the table.

"You will see," the herbalist said, running his fingers over lines of squiggles on which I could not focus with my mind thick and my gowns smothering, "that I wrote down the herb and dose, and here the recipient's sign. These are times when I refused to give a second dose."

"This list appears to be pages long," I said. "If so many asked for a second dose, the first must not have been especially efficacious."

"I admit I could've received poor batches of black cohosh and slippery elm bark. The rue and mugwort have had fewer requests for second doses."

"Maybe the first dose is killing them," I said. "Spellsword Deepmand, take herbalist Noblin to the nearest guard. The city will hold him, until I judge what the Fate Weaver has spun for him."

A gauntlet clamped onto the herbalist's hand, and he groaned as Deepmand dragged him across the square. I followed, having otherwise no idea how to find my carriage. After we had deposited the herbalist, a school of acolytes blocked Deepmand's path.

"Lustrous and Elder Enchantress Hiresha."

The man's voice came from behind my right ear.

INCOMPLETE

-13-

Priest Salkant of the Fate Weaver stepped into view. His words would have startled a few drops of urine out of me, if not for my impeccable bladder control.

"Priest," I said, again inclined to leave out the "Lustrous" honorific.

"I have seen an event in the webs, which you must know about, but no one else. With your permission, I will whisper it in your ear."

"I am not in the habit of receiving whispers from men, yet in this case, I will acquiesce."

His robes bore the yellow on black coloration of an orb-weaver spider, and as he leaned toward my neck, I had a jolt of fear that he would bite me. Instead, he covered both sides of his mouth with his fingers and half-fingers and garbled something in my ear.

"Excuse me?" I said.

He whispered again, and amid the clamor of the bazaar and with my thoughts moving at the speed of mold, it sounded something like, "Severs mud in cry fiefdom."

As I believed I could determine what he had actually said in my dream, I merely nodded.

He leaned back, his chin upturned in a frown. "You understand why news of this gravity could not spread."

"Indeed not."

"There is no confusion in the weave. A certainty, I'm afraid."

"I wish I knew what to say."

He said, "We can do no more to prepare ourselves than live these last years to their fullest."

"I will contemplate this."

Priest Salkant tapped his fingers together, gaps forming between the amputated ones. "Sometimes I believe all these soon-to-be mothers as an omen of it, though if that be so, it's a pitiless one indeed."

Not understanding the reference, I let my attention solidify on his hands. "I could regenerate those fingers."

I regretted my words even before Priest Salkant gave me a puzzled look. Utilizing my magic on him in Morimound would be another transgression of the Propriety Pledge.

He waggled his truncated fingers. "I hardly notice them anymore, and I understand that healing a finger would cost me an arm and a leg."

"My fees are high to discourage pestering, yet I would not charge a priest of Morimound." I sighed inwardly, realizing I was encouraging him.

"You are indeed the Flawless, but I'm sure you have more important concerns than a few fingers."

"Of your two assessments, the latter is undoubtedly true. May your life's thread be long, Lustrous Priest."

In leaving, he laughed, although I did not see why. I wanted to determine what he had whispered with minimal delay. Inside the carriage, I bid Maid Janny hand me the herbalist's ledger and the pouch of wormwood, a dried plant with the appearance of a fern with short fronds, which I emptied out on the street, observing as I did the rain of dried plant matter. A page of the ledger turned under my fingers every second, my eyes glossing over the notes.

I broiled in my own sweat, yet I forced myself to begin descending toward sleep.

On the twelfth step, I heard a boy shouting. "Mister Spellsword! Mister Spellsword! Tell the enchantress that Lady Sri has fallen, and Mister Obenji fears the worst."

THREATENED
-14-

I pushed the carriage door open. "My boy, did Lady Sri break any bones? Has she gone into labor?"

His eyes popped at the sight of me. "Uh, she landed on her side, and now her hip is swelling like a corpse in summer. Oh, I shouldn't have said that. Fast feet and slow thinking, that's what they say 'bout me."

Irritation flashed through me at the thought of Sri the Once Flawless leaping from her sickbed only to break a bone. She seemed to have the audacity of a youth without the mistake-absorbent body.

"Elder Enchantress," Deepmand said from the carriage perch, "I will make full speed for your estate."

"No," I said.

"Elder Enchantress?"

I touched my fingers to my forehead, which burned. Sri had likely shattered her hipbone and would die of internal bleeding within days. My magic could save her, yet the spellcraft would require hours, while a Bright Palm could heal her in seconds.

More to the point, I did not think I was ready to confront another unchild, or feel again what might be a god breathing into my dream.

"My boy, run back to the manor with an acolyte of the Ever Always, and have him splint her leg and give her milk of the poppy. Then proceed to the nearest sanctum and beg a Bright Palm to heal her. Make certain you tell them she is destitute."

"Des-ti-tute. Right."

I waved him away then slumped back into my silk harnesses. Panting, I thumped my cane against the ceiling.

"Move to the shade."

Once I slipped into sleep, I summoned my mirror to show my conversation with Salkant of the Fate Weaver. After I blotted out all the other sounds of the bazaar, his whisper echoed in the laboratory.

"The Seventh Flood will come in my lifetime."

All the floating jewels held still, and with a wave of my hand, the mirror turned black. Fears mixed inside me with pangs of helplessness; I curled up, drifting in the air in an approximation of the fetal position. My gowns spread out for twenty feet in a pool of blue, purple, and black fabrics, intermingled with red satin, dashes of white scarf, and islands of green taffeta.

The mirror sounded the whisper again, so I could be sure.

"The Seventh Flood will come in my lifetime."

Sri the Once Flawless had dreamed of a Seventh Flood that would destroy the city in a wave not comprised of water. Likewise, the Third Flood had not involved overflowing rivers but invading foreigners, and I could not help but wonder if the Seventh Flood related to the mass pregnancies.

I wanted to believe that the Fate Weaver had brought me back to Morimound to help the women, yet her priest had predicted doom.

Priest Salkant must have misinterpreted the webs, I reasoned. The Flood Wall I had built would prevent torrents of muddy water from drowning Morimound's people and sweeping away the majority of their homes.

Still, I felt I had plummeted through a thousand feet of icy air without clothes.

To distract myself, I summoned the herbalist's ledger, and it fluttered open inside the mirror. I read each page at a glance, seeing that Noblin had first sold less dangerous herbs but had run out. Most women had tried to obtain a second dose, and when he refused them, they returned again, signing under different names. It was evident from their style of pen strokes. Through deception, the women received second, third, fourth, and, in one case, fifth doses, in the hopes of expelling their pregnancies.

Either the herbalist had trouble identifying people through his spectacles, or he had allowed the women to escalate the dosage without thought for their health. I suspected the former, in the light of the horror on his face when I had accused him of murdering the women.

The godsent children seemed to have a resiliency to poison. Normal babies had the habit of wasting away in the womb from intoxicants that gave no more than passing trouble to their mothers. These women had swallowed dose after bitter dose of wormwood. I feared for the health of Alyla because her angry mother had purchased four doses. Although Faliti Chandur had not signed under her correct name even once, I recognized her handwriting.

The reflection in the mirror changed to show Alyla, the whites of her eyes yellow from damage to her liver caused by toxins. I had missed it at the time, yet I judged her mother had poisoned her with the herbs to try to rid her of the baby.

In a second mirror, I studied my memory of Sri the Once Flawless and her rough and cracked fingernails, signs of depleting bone strength, common enough in the pregnant yet dangerous in elders. The grandmothers of Morimound would continue to break bones; their hearts would stop, and their veins would burst from the stresses of pregnancy.

Sri was seventy-three years old, while Alyla had only lived twelve. For both, the dangers would intensify over the next two months, during which they would likely give birth too soon, and if they survived to gaze on what they had borne, they would in all probability be suffocated by grief.

I had to do something, for the thousands of women in serious risk. Either I had to watch the old and very young succumb to deadly childbirth, or I had to succeed where Noblin the herbalist had failed in terminating the pregnancies. The thought induced me to retch.

Although my magic could serve to expel a pregnancy, I loathed the idea. In addition, I could not go to sleep with thousands of women, no indeed. Wormwood also seemed to have failed in the worst way thus far, apparently insufficient to overcome the spell or divine will responsible. I hoped to find out which power was at work; knowing the cause of the pregnancies might present a safer course of action.

In the short term, I had to save Alyla. Her breath had reeked of wormwood, and if Faliti gave her another dose then she would likely perish before even beginning the trial of labor. Her mother might not listen to my warnings, yet I trusted that her father would. Harend Chandur would be spending his day at the White Ziggurat, or so Faliti Chandur had complained, and there I would make an appearance.

While peering at Alyla through the mirror, I realized her angular and spindly features shared little with the bone structure of Harend Chandur, giving me ninety-five-percent confidence she was not his true daughter.

Outrage stopped me from breathing, and I might have passed out, if I were not already dreaming. I would never have betrayed Harend, had I been able to marry him.

I awoke sticky with sweat, and I bid Deepmand drive me to the White Ziggurat. We arrived in minutes, as he had shaded the carriage nearby in an Island District mango orchard.

I left the carriage and craned my neck upward to gaze at the White Ziggurat, its gypsum plaster glaring brighter than snow on a mountaintop. Acolytes in white robes and merchants in finery walked together on the steps, talking on the ziggurat's terraces.

After arriving at the base of the stairs, I stopped. I could manage a few steps in these gowns, if I was careful, yet I feared the heat would incapacitate me before I reached the first terrace; a faint would result in injury. By no means could I endure the one thousand, one hundred and eleven steps leading to the ziggurat's summit. Neither could I employ one of the sedan carriages, due to the volume of my gowns. Removing my adornments was not an option: Only their lavishness bewildered others into taking me seriously.

I walked into the path of two acolytes, my silks blocking their way. "A silver coin for whoever finds Harend Chandur and mentions my desire—my wish to speak with him. I will await him in the shade of that tree."

"We'll return faster than flies, Lustrous Lady." The acolytes sprinted up the steps, making a game of it.

"Walk," I shouted after them, "or I will not be the one to piece together your broken skulls."

The banyan tree I had chosen overshadowed the road and, being in plain sight, would not cast suspicion on the respectability of the meeting.

My stomach kneaded itself while I thought of encountering Harend again at last. My father had polished diamonds for his father, who had been a master gemcutter, and I had thought his family unimaginably wealthy, in my youth. The other girls had teased me, saying he only liked me because we did ill-fated things together at night. We most certainly had not. Sleep had imprisoned me from sunset to sunup, and in evening and morning, too, when my mother had tired of kicking me and let me lie.

My head began to nod, even though I stared at the blinding ziggurat to try to stay awake.

"Elder Enchantress, may I make a request regarding my family?"

"What? Ah, you may, Spellsword Deepmand."

"Thank you, Elder Enchantress. Given your new position as the Flawless, I think it possible your residence in Morimound may be of significant duration."

"I will thank you not to associate me with that title, and my departure will come as soon as I judge the city safe."

"May the Fate Weaver grant swift success to that endeavor, Elder Enchantress." Two ziggurats of gold embellished his breastplate, designed after the structures towering above us. "My request was whether my family might reside in your manor, for as long as I have the privilege of protecting you."

I bowed my head, allowing the folds of my headdress to cover my grimace at the idea of the children of another woman running through my halls. Like Alyla, one of his children was illegitimate, sired when Deepmand guarded an enchantress away from the Academy and his wife. The foreigner woman had claimed her baby premature, yet the boy's healthy birth weight spoke against it.

The alternate parentage might not have been as obvious to Deepmand, and I had never mentioned it because he seemed to treasure the child and his wife. Sometimes I even thought she cared for him, although she had a strange way of showing it.

"My wish has always been to return here for my retirement," Deepmand said, "and I will begin the arrangements to move my family to Morimound. In the happy event of your sudden success and departure, I would still be able to join them in two years."

I said, "Your family will be provided with a respectable residence in the city proper."

"Your generosity humbles me, Elder Enchantress."

Tilting my chin to peer at the gilded globe of his turbaned head, I rubbed my upper lip against my teeth. "Deepmand, there is something of which you should be informed."

"Yes, Elder Enchantress?"

"I may need to—that is to say it is possible—I may be required to treat another woman." If I drew Alyla into my dream then I could determine immediately if she too carried an unchild and what might be done to help her. In my estimation, the Propriety Pledge was meant to stop young enchantresses from foolishness, not to thwart the Provost of Applied Enchantment from doing essential work.

"A woman other than Lady Sri?" Deepmand's lips folded inward, disappearing in his beard. "My concern lies in matters of...propriety."

"My concern, Spellsword Deepmand, lies in the wombs of our people." I waited until two men in robes passed out of earshot before continuing. "Not everything may have progressed properly."

He frowned. Maid Janny looked up with concern, asking, "Buns not cooking right in the ovens??"

"Shush!" I lifted a hand to her, my eyes still on the spellsword. "It may be necessary."

"If it is necessary," he said slowly, "then I will assist you in discretion. Elder Enchantress, I believe the gentleman walking toward us may be none other than Harend Chandur."

I searched for the symmetrical face and well-proportioned physique I remembered from my youth, and I kept looking even when someone stood before me, blocking my view.

"Resha, is that you?"

DISAPPOINTING
-15-

The familiar voice came from a man past his prime, his back slumped, his double chin shabbily shaven. His eyes were dull, and they could not meet my stare.

I knew this was Harend Chandur, yet the sight jarred with the portrait of him I had painted years ago in my dream. A tightness spread down my throat into my chest, as I thought how unfair it was that in addition to my having to spend my life far from the city I loved, everything in that city had the inconsideration to change in my absence.

"It is I," I said.

"I wasn't sure I'd see you. You avoided me on your last visits, didn't you? Ah, anyway, they say you've come to lead the city to prosperity, and everyone is buying goods. Even Nilmar Tightfist gave me a loan today."

I had often thought of what I might say to Harend when next we met, yet much of it no longer seemed suitable, especially not with Deepmand and Maid Janny beside me. My resentment toward Faliti brought one fact to my lips.

"Are you aware your wife has forged your handwriting, twice, to ask me for money?"

He sighed. "It's my own fault, I refuse to ask for handouts, and the gods haven't blessed any of my ventures."

"The fault cannot be yours, unless you knew of the forged letters." I had thought Faliti had written them to discourage me from writing Harend, yet I could discriminate her imitative scrawl from his with ease.

"I didn't, but I don't blame her. We're sending our son through the empire's martial university, and the tuition is turning us to paupers. Couldn't do less for him, though, because he's the hope for the family."

"I have not had the privilege of meeting your son, yet I did see your daughter today. There is something I wished to tell you about her."

Harend fingered the threads of a frayed section of his vest. "Yes? She's a good girl, though, I admit, not everything I expected."

"What are you implying?" I wondered if he suspected her mother's unfaithfulness.

"I guess I'm comparing Alyla to her brother, which is less than fair. We were counting on a good bride price for her, and she's ruined that by, well, you've seen her."

"Her current state does not negatively reflect on her fate's thread. That thread may be short, however, if Faliti continues to poison her."

"Poison? You mean her complaining?"

"With wormwood, to purge the pregnancy. You must intervene."

"It's not really poisoning then, is it? Alyla won't have much of a life, if she has a child now."

"She will not have any life," I said, "if she dies."

"Faliti wouldn't harm her. Alyla's been sick, but isn't that expected? Who'd know what's best for her, if not her mother?"

"I would. You must stop Faliti from giving her another dose of wormwood."

He threw up his hands. "Fine. I'll mention it to Faliti, if you think I should, Resha."

Distaste pervaded my mouth as if I had eaten bread that I only now realized was spotted green. Something more than Harend's appearance conflicted with my expectations.

I said, "You cannot call me that anymore, Mister Chandur."

"I suppose not. The Flawless of Morimound, then?"

"Nor that."

"You sign your letters 'Elder Enchantress Hiresha,' but your friends couldn't call you that."

"Everyone calls me that." Hearing him say my title made me feel as lifeless and dusty as book stacks in the Academy library.

He glanced to Janny, who had her head down, and to Deepmand, who scrutinized anyone who walked close. When Harend Chandur's gaze fell on my cane, I became self-conscious.

"This may sound odd," he said, "but I once thought we'd have more between us. I can see now the Fate Weaver had greater plans for you."

"I am uncertain what you mean. There could be no greater aspiration than to raise a family in this city."

"But look at you." His eyes followed the train of gowns, which wound around the trunk of the banyan. "You're a city patron. You built the Flood Wall."

His words faded, slipping farther and farther away as I labored to keep my head upright and my eyes open. "You will wish to return home, Mister Chandur, for your daughter's sake."

"You're right, and, um, Elder Enchantress Hiresha, it was amazing to meet you again."

Before I realized what he was doing, he clasped my hand. My fingers wriggled, and I tried to scan the street, to see if anyone witnessed the improper gesture.

He plodded off, and I let go of myself, slumping on my cane. My eyes blinked shut; the world darkened, and everything in me felt as if it weighed twice what it should.

Janny guided me back to the carriage, and I plunged into sleep. A shock awaited me, in reviewing my meeting with Harend Chandur. I had waited years to speak with him, only to find a man indecisive and scarcely capable of mustering the resolve to save a girl's life, even if she was not his true daughter. At the mention of her, his face had shifted from embarrassment to sorrow.

His thread of fate was a flimsy one. I did not know what I had ever seen in him.

A tearing feeling crossed through me as if a tether connecting me to the world had severed, and I could not help but think that I floated in the laboratory because nothing filled my body: I was a hollow woman.

Not feeling ready to face the real world yet, I decided to correct an imperfection in my dream.

I threw myself upward, toward the dome roof, and airborne jewels swirled in the wake of my gowns. Although this circular room had no doors, a skylight at the top of the curved ceiling opened to the night sky, and my jump carried me through it. Stars above glittered green, pink, and purple;

they were jewels I had thrown to the sky in moments of frustration.

Among them loomed the moon, full, dim, and red; some would call it a blood moon, yet I preferred to think of its lighter edge as the hue of amber and its darker face as the shade of spessartine gems. I had Created the moon in replica of a lunar eclipse I had once witnessed at sunrise, which had required the heroic effort of waking predawn.

I Burdened myself, landing on the laboratory dome then Lightening my body and leaping off again. The roof fell away behind me, along with an island of rock on which the laboratory drifted in the sky, leaving nothing below but a drop of three thousand, two hundred and fifty-one feet to the ground.

I glided in my gowns.

The rush of the chill air caressed me as I spread my arms to encourage my sleeves to billow outward. Silver streaks of rivers raced closer, below on the savanna. Leaning to the left, I circled through the air down toward a dark hill on the flatland, its rough surface growing distinct as the homes of my replica of Morimound became more visible.

The White Ziggurat I had Created glistened blue from the light of my earrings as I swept over the step pyramid, down to the street of Diamond Way. The buildings and empty merchant stalls in the bazaar reformed to represent the changes I had seen.

My slippers landed on the street. I Lightened myself to nothing and sprang off the bricks, sailing into the air. Whisking over Rainsweep Street, I decided to leave the door to the Mitul house forever broken, in memory of the confrontation with the Feaster. Although no children peered out from this doorway, glowing jewels inside leaked light of blue and red out onto the dark street. I did not permit myself the indulgence of replicating other people, and the city was empty, except for my jewels and myself.

I vaulted back toward the ziggurats, past the High Wall and into the upper section of the city, the Island District. My estate encompassed a grove of strangler fig trees, their trunks weaving around host trees to crawl their way to the sunlight. The roof of my house steepled in pyramids, one on each of its wings, and I touched the eastern marble pyramid with my hand and pushed off to coast to the front doors.

Quartz windows rippled with the light from my earrings, and I ghosted inside and up a curving stairway, into a dining hall set with porcelain that had never been used, by chairs in which none had ever sat, below chandeliers that had never been lit.

An ache built within me as I passed from dark room to silent hall. Dim moonlight fell on a painting, a portrait of a young man as seen through all the blurry hope of an adolescent girl; Harend Chandur gazed down at me from the shadows of his picture frame. Shaking my head, I waved a hand, and the paints faded and transformed into the wood of a jewel display case. A rainbow of corundum stones whisked past my shoulders to arrange themselves in place of the man I had never had the right to call mine.

I felt I had to scream, or I would die. I asked myself where the harm would be in wailing here in my dream, where none would ever hear me, except myself.

Outside, my laboratory had descended closer to the city. The mound of rock obscured a patch of stars. I calculated my trajectory then hurled myself toward the floating island in one swooping arc; the ground and city plummeted away from me, and my insides felt squeezed down into my thighs. Dropping as planned through the laboratory skylight, I kicked off the wall to the diamond dais and returned to the waking world.

Aches in my legs and back caused me to groan, as they often did; I wore an enchanted opal, which flexed opposing muscle groups throughout my body, causing me to exercise in my sleep.

"We have arrived at your manor, Elder Enchantress." Deepmand appeared relieved that I had woken before full darkness.

Outside my carriage, the open front doors of my manor glowed with candlelight, windows blazing in the colors of sunset. The sight pierced me like a shard of diamond in the eye: My home looked so welcoming, so full of warmth, that for a moment I assumed someone else's family must live there.

EMPTY
-16-

Night Four, Third Trimester

The manor servants insisted on giving me a tour. I knew I should not compare the home they had labored over for years to the one I had Created in my dream, yet the similarities disoriented me while the discrepancies upset me.

"We now approach the guest rooms," Mister Obenji said, tapping his glinting fingers together. He wore at least ten rings, all of excellent design. "Here you will find Lady Sri convalescing."

"No Bright Palms have deigned to heal her yet, have they?"

"One has promised to come tomorrow, at noon."

I was determined to be present at that time to ensure the Bright Palm did not refuse to heal her because of some technicality.

My earrings lit the sickroom with a bluish-white glow. Sri the Once Flawless lay in bed, belly up; her yellow skin had whitened to a pallor, and her pupils had constricted from the milk of the poppy. Her gaze strayed to Mister Obenji, whom she blinked at with both eyes in a peculiar manner. He touched her hand and asked if she needed broth, another pillow, or more milk. She shook her head, brushing a lock of sweat-plastered white hair off her brow.

Mister Obenji left the room to confer with Deepmand. I gestured Maid Janny to lift the coverings, and I observed that Sri's hip was well splinted. A mass of bloating purple skin still protruded from her side, rivaling her pregnancy in size.

Sri touched her lips with thick-jointed fingers. "Hiresha, what do you think of Mister Obenji? Is he not dashing?"

"He seems competent."

"Yes, but is he potent?" Sri cackled.

"While under the poppy's influence, you should endeavor to speak as little as you can. To maintain your dignity."

"I've had enough dignity for four lifetimes," she said. "I winked at him. Do you think he noticed?"

"You did not wink."

"I did so. Five times."

"Those were most decidedly blinks."

"It takes practice," Janny said and displayed a most inappropriate lowering of the eyelid. "I'll help you learn."

"You will do nothing of the kind, Maid Janny. Lady Sri, once you are healed, I must insist you walk with a cane. In fact, I will require all mothers over sixty to do so." I grew conscious of my own cane, which would place me in the same class as grandmothers. "Make that two canes, one for each hand, to prevent falls."

"I didn't fall," Sri said.

"Of course you did."

"Only after my leg broke. It cracked while I was walking, then I fell."

"Your pregnancy clearly has diverted too much blood from your brain. You fell first." I had never heard of someone breaking her leg while walking. I wondered if it was possible that the unchild had so leached Sri's bones of mineral to strengthen its own twisted skeleton that she could no longer withstand her own weight.

Leaving the sickroom, I heard Deepmand speaking to Mister Obenji. "...she does appreciate the work you've done. Only, she prefers everything just as envisioned, and understand the stress she's under."

"I see." Mister Obenji pivoted to face me. "Ah, Lustrous Elder Enchantress, you will doubtless wish to retire now in the east wing."

"I would rather not." In the east wing waited the rooms of my never-family.

"Was there another room you wished to see first?"

"No."

"I would recommend the gardens, were it not night."

As if under a spell of compulsion, I followed Mister Obenji's turban into the east wing. My bluish light pushed the darkness back, revealing a door set with a misty green stone, the room of Chrysoprase, my daughter, who would be my greatest happiness in life. I wondered if an opportunity would ever come for me to bring her into existence, or if she would remain worse than dead: an unborn.

I had already picked names for my progeny, as well as planned them the happy childhoods and lives that I had never had. Now, walking past their empty rooms, I felt my hopes for them being ripped away.

Using my cane to drag myself forward, I shuddered as I passed a door with a magenta gem, the room that would have to belong to my firstborn son, Beryl. Next, a stone the hue of fire glinted from the wooden portal to Carnelian's room; her beauty would have brought her fame. Last came a stone of grey ripples, where Agate would have grown up, his depth of intelligence lofting him to rule.

With each year spent attempting to cure my somnolence, I dwindled closer to barrenness. Insufficient time might remain for courtship and raising a family. Time was kidnapping my children, one by one.

My legs lost their ability to move, while a coldness spread outward from my abdomen, numbing everything. I felt the urge to flee to my dream and carve gems in isolation for days.

Past the four jeweled rooms, the door to my chambers yawned open. The master bed inside was terrible in its broadness. Mister Obenji touched the silk sheets and spoke, yet I could not hear him, my mind grating and screeching from the opportunities of my life closing.

In a corner of the room hung a contraption of rope and beams, as if ready to assist my suicide. I was familiar with this harness; it supported me in silk shackles while I slept partially reclined, sitting on an ottoman. I could not lie down in any bed in my gowns, and dressing and undressing would take hours from my already short days.

My eyes swung from the expanse of bed and its hoard of pillows to the hanging rack of the harness, and my mind yelled at me to flee. When I tried to retreat, my gowns trapped me. I whirled halfway around then capsized. Maid Janny lunged to support me, and she too teetered in the blinding disorder of my dresses, until Deepmand seized and righted us both.

"I cannot stay here," I said. "Deepmand, the carriage. I need the carriage."

"Elder Enchantress?"

"I must leave at once, to, to check on Alyla. Yes, she was sick, and she invited me to stay at the Chandur residence as their guest. I will accept. To do otherwise would be unadulterated baseness."

I gained the safety of the carriage before losing control. Tears flooded my face. Maid Janny appeared to wish to hug me, yet fortunately my gowns prevented her from coming close; she contented herself with holding my arm and patting my cheeks dry every few seconds.

Finding myself in my laboratory, I realized I must have fallen asleep. Suddenly clear of mind, I saw that I could not stay at the Chandur address, as it would allow for too many unbecoming implications.

Awake once more, I rapped the carriage roof. "What induced you to disturb the night with these trotting horses? Most negligent of you."

"My apologies, Elder Enchantress. I would be happy to return you to your manor."

When I told him yes, Maid Janny gave me a look.

"I change my mind no more often than necessary, Maid Janny."

"Far more often than folks change their underclothes, and that's a shame for all involved."

Amidst city-wide uncertainty, I found the constancy of Janny's insults most refreshing. I could not bear the thought of anything unnatural happening to her.

Affecting a disgusted turn of my head away from the maid, I said, "Your ideas alone must be sufficient to cause indigestion, Maid Janny. When we arrive at the manor, I will take my repose in the smallest of guest rooms."

I felt I needed sixteen hours of sleep to recover, yet tomorrow morning I would receive reports on the mass pregnancies in the God's Eye Court. Then I would learn whether or not I was pitted against a god.

DIVINED

-17-

Day Five, Third Trimester

Five hundred bulging, bobbing abdomens poked their belly buttons out at me as I stood at the center of the court and of the city. The expecting women surrounded me, their fleshy protrusions blocking any attempt to escape.

Tall women stooped over their bellies, while short women leaned back. Women of bountiful bodies carried their pregnancy proudly and naturally. Those women who had done less than their duty at the dining table stood awkwardly, their bellies swelling as if they had swallowed a teapot. Some boasted stretch marks, and all had amber skin with the luster of motherhood.

The acolytes had arranged the mothers by age, and I felt a strong twinge of concern for the youngest, those wobble-legged girls between twelve and fifteen, who wiped their noses every minute and who looked lost behind their bellies.

The sight of the grandmothers made me feel wretched. They tottered about with the canes I had required of them, and many acolytes assisted by holding them by the shoulder. Their bellies hung below their bent walk, pregnancies weighing them down as if stones filled their wombs.

After surveying the five hundred women, I sat on my ottoman. Then I leaned forward on my cane and descended into sleep. In my laboratory, I analyzed the girth of the bellies relative to the women's age, height, and weight, determining the vast majority to be close to their third trimester. The consistency frightened me because I would expect it of the Ever Always, the god's will manifested without pause or exception.

I awoke to see that the acolytes had replaced the first women with a second sample of five hundred, taken from throughout the city. After observation, I returned to my laboratory, noting whispered conversations I overheard as I drifted to sleep.

"Hope this doesn't take much longer. These days I pass more water than a bridge."

"Having many nightmares?"

"Yes, but I had them with Falipa, too."

"I keep reminding Father it was the Ever Always seeded me. He still hits me."

"He has no right to that, and I'll tell him so. Had to be a god what done this. Even my rhinoceros of a brother couldn't have gotten between all these legs."

"Do you think something might be wrong?"

"Why would it? This babe is part of the divine plan."

"Yes, but I thought the enchantress frowned at me."

"She might've scowled, a bit."

"Must be on account of her being the Flawless. Gems can't keep her as warm in bed as a man."

"See how her head bows as she thinks? She looks so wise."

"She's speaking to the gods, she is."

The scene in the mirror changed, black lengths of hair draping of many different lengths. The feminine oils produced in pregnancy richened hair quality. Because I knew that hair grew an average of a half-inch a month, I could estimate the women's date of conception by analyzing their locks. I determined that most were between day eighty of their second trimester and day six of their third. I could not be certain whether they had all conceived in the same hour, in the same instant, or over the span of a few weeks.

Although I would expect no more than a quarter of Morimound's women to be fertile in any given week, even mothers in their prime, a full seventy-one percent of them appeared to have been seeded in a short span of time.

In the following two months, the incidence of pregnancies rose to ninety-seven percent. I believed that every woman before me was pregnant now, although those of lesser width had been carrying their child for only a few months or less.

The variation gave me some solace; I did not see why a god would delay his will. Anomalies suggested more of men and their magic, elements with which I could contest, and these inconsistencies might grant clues to the origin of the spellcraft and the thinking of its user.

I awoke to say, "Present those mothers who have miscarried in the last year."

The acolytes checked their clay tablets, called out names, and ushered about ninety women onto the court's marble. Their bellies extended to a lesser degree than average and not past their breasts.

"These women must have miscarried five months or more ago, to be obviously pregnant again now," I said. "Did any others lose their children in the last three months?"

"Not that we found, Lustrous and Elder Enchantress. Some women in that time, regretfully, passed into the goddess's eight arms."

His mention of the deceased singed me like a spark landing on my arm.

I judged that those who had miscarried had done so in the same period when the rest had become pregnant, and they quickly got with child again. Whatever had caused this fertile epidemic had seen fit to terminate natural pregnancies and replace them with the supernatural. Or perhaps it was not intentional but a mere corollary of the power that had affected all the women simultaneously. Both possibilities seemed ominous.

Physical beatings seemed to have had no effect on the pregnancies. I studied several women with inflamed cuts caused perhaps by belt buckles and others marked with blue, yellow, and purple bruises.

I imagined myself having grown in a family way as a girl, being whipped bloody by my father and punched by my brothers in attempts to shake loose my shame and save my bride price. One woman had a belly entirely discolored, the skin puffy with black blood and green pus, as if she had slammed herself against a wall to kill the bony child inside her, who refused to die.

Maybe the unchildren could not die. Maybe they were the progeny of a god.

Sweat turned my gloves sodden. I felt too hot to keep air in my lungs and had to pant to avoid passing out.

"Are there…have you found any women in this city who are not pregnant?"

"None of the girls eleven or younger are, Lustrous and Elder Enchantress."

"The Fate Weaver has spared them, at least," I said.

The acolyte consulted his tablet. "One out of four women in Stilt Town are without child, and most of the muddies who live beyond that are as slim as rice reeds."

"Kindly dispense with the similes, young man."

"Er, I'm sorry, Lustrous and Elder Enchantress. We believe not all the women in the city have, I mean, some have not...."

"This is no blushing matter," I said. "Out with it."

"Yes, well, I've heard a few are not pregnant, but we didn't find any when collecting this thousand."

An acolyte beside him said, "There's always Yellow-Back's daughter."

"The 'Yellow-Back?'" I feared I had heard him wrong.

"Oh, I meant Priest Salkant of the Fate Weaver. Everyone knows his daughter has kept her purity."

"You should refrain from speaking of your betters, except with their proper titles."

"Yes, Lustrous and Elder Enchantress."

Blood pounded in my head with excitement at the thought that Priest Salkant's daughter had escaped the fate of so many. This meant something, and I hoped to discern what with a visit to his estate, today.

"Acolytes, group the women by proximity of residence."

Amid the hubbub of reorganization, my gaze wandered up the overgrown terraces of the Garden Ziggurat. Priest Abwar had kept his promise to redden its steps with blood.

The sacrificed oxen roasted in bonfires at the base of the ziggurat, and acolytes of the Ever Always served the meat to the assembled women, who ate with fingers slick with fat. The mothers stood before me now, this time arranged by residence.

As soon as my slippers lifted above the diamond dais in my dream laboratory, I saw a pattern. Women belonging to wealthier families displayed less of a swell from crotch to ribs; those who lived higher up the hill of Morimound had become pregnant later than the rest, by an average of a month.

The mass pregnancies appeared to act like a flood, reaching those lower in the city first and then rising upward. I remembered Priest Salkant's warning of the Seventh Flood, as well as how Sri described a nightmare in which the flood came as something more dangerous than water.

As frightening as childbirth was, I preferred its danger to that of a real flood, and the pattern did not fit in other ways. Many of the poorest, those who lived among the mud of Stilt Town, had not become pregnant, although a true flood would have drowned them first.

Blinking my eyes in the sunlight, I said in a resigned tone, "Last, I must know if any of the women have quickened."

"Some believe...a few would like to think they've felt their child move." The acolyte clutched his tablet as if clinging to the side of a cliff.

A sigh shuddered out of me, and I rested my forehead on my gloved palm. The majority of women had entered their seventh month of pregnancy, and they all should have been blessed regularly by kicks. Those who hesitantly said they felt their child move might have confused the sensation with gas traveling through the intestines, and I was beginning to accept that their wombs all bristled with bones.

I needed to help them, somehow. First, however, I had promised to attend Sri the Once Flawless.

The carriage had rolled its golden wheels to the edge of the court, where the women flocked to peer at the white horses, some petting their braided manes. Deepmand beckoned the women to clear a path for me.

With a clomp of hooves, the carriage passed between parks of hanging vines and plots of jasmine, toward my estate, where I hoped to find a Bright Palm healing Sri. I realized that if he did not, I would have to fight for her one life with my magic, at a time I most needed to focus on saving the lives of many.

CONNIVING
-18-

I felt immoral appreciating the spectacle of my estate. Although I kept my gaze down, I could not help but hear the bees and glimpse the reds of my hibiscus gardens. Nor could I avoid the agony of the marble splendor of the stair in the entrance hall, or daylight streaming onto gilded hand railings from windows with diamond-shaped panes.

"Mister Obenji," I asked, "has the Bright Palm arrived?"

"A boy has been sent to escort him here, Elder Enchantress Hiresha."

"Excellent. Now, if the Bright Palm asks, you must attest that Lady Sri is fifty-eight years old."

"Why, the Lady Sri is even younger than I thought."

"Do not persuade me of your senility, Mister Obenji. She is seventy-three. However, the Bright Palm cannot know it, or he will not heal her."

"He would let such a lady die? Have they no mercy?"

"Bright Palms lack all feeling and act in accordance with a set of tenets. They heal neither the elderly, nor the rich."

"I admit, Elder Enchantress Hiresha, I feel a measure of apprehension."

"I have planned what to say. You need only support me."

"And I will do so gladly," he said. "Ah, I believe I see the Bright Palm on the path."

I squinted out the window into the gardens, yet even after rubbing my eyes, I failed to distinguish the Bright Palm from the gardeners.

Mister Obenji adjusted his turban and strode out the doors. "Greetings, Lustrous Bright Palm, and welcome to Sunchase Hall."

A man wearing sackcloth halted his march before the steps leading up to the doors. His fingertips glowed. "I must go no farther," he said. "Anyone living in such a prison of decadence could have no use of my blessing. I would not doom their soul to more years of luxury."

His slack gaze fell on me, and he spoke in his monotone.

"Hope remains for even your stifled soul, Hiresha of Morimound. Liberate yourself of wealth. The Order of the Innocent will accept its burden for you. Then you may receive my blessing."

"It is not I who needs healing, Bright Palm. My destitute guest is dying."

Mister Obenji said, "You must help her. She would not even have the coin for a funeral."

"This woman, she is a relative?"

"No," I said, "and her family would not accept her. She is cast out and without support."

The Bright Palm took the stair's first step then paused. "She has your support, and you are condemned."

"She may stay under this roof," Mister Obenji said, "but she is fed only rice and beans."

"I promise to throw her out onto the streets," I said, "at the first available opportunity."

The Bight Palm walked through the doors. "Take me to this worthy soul."

I felt uncomfortable beside the Bright Palm, aware of his uncanny strength. Even with eyes turned away, I could point out his direction; the power flowing in his veins created a sensation of pressure in my skull.

As we arrived in the sickroom, Sri the Once Flawless cried out. "Mister Obenji! What a pleasure to see you again."

"We have come with help, Lady Sri." He knelt beside the bed, and she gave his nose a playful squeeze.

The Bright Palm touched the silk sheets. "I disapprove of this as a place of healing."

"I will have flax blankets sent for, straight away," Mister Obenji said.

The Bright Palm's face stayed neutral as he looked down at Sri. "How many winters has she lived?"

Mister Obenji said, "She's youthful at fifty-eight."

"She appears older," the Bright Palm said.

"The sun has aged her skin prematurely," I said. "She deliberated her days away on the God's Eye Court."

"I believe she has lived more than sixty years," the Bright Palm said. "Her time has been spent."

Sri wailed, yet the Bright Palm seemed not to hear her as he turned to leave. He would have departed by the time I thought of something to say.

Mister Obenji defied his own aged body and leapt in front of the Bright Palm. "You must heal her. She carries a child who will never live a single year of life unless you intervene."

I believed the Bright Palm considered, although his face gave little sign of it. He said, "Expose the wound."

Sri held the covers over herself. "Not in front of Mister Obenji!"

"Worry not, Lady Sri," he said, kneeling beside her and taking her hand, "I will gaze only into your beautiful eyes."

Maid Janny lifted the covers, and the Bright Palm laid his hand on Sri's swollen hip. White light pulsed down the veins of his arm, spreading from fingertips until his hand held such power that I could see it even with my eyes closed. The light leaked into Sri, her bluish skin turning pink, and the bruises shrank.

"Sri," I asked, "why did you rise and break your hip anyway, instead of sensibly staying in bed?"

"Heehee." She touched one of the curled ends of Mister Obenji's white mustache. "Maybe I saw someone worth falling for."

Thrusting my chin outward in disgust, I glanced back to her most prominent feature and thought of the unchild growing inside her like a bone tumor. "Bright Palm, I will donate twenty gold pieces to your order, if you direct your magic into her womb."

"We are not mercenary, unlike you," he said. "Still, I will see if the nascent one needs healing."

The light flowed deeper inside her, tracing paths to her heart and down again, pooling in her womb's nutritive sac. It percolated farther, the pattern of veins blurring white in her abdomen; I planned to analyze the sight in my laboratory.

"There is no injury," the Bright Palm said. "I have completed the blessing."

Their magic worked in an imprecise manner, strengthening the body to mend its own wounds. Apparently, Sri's constitution did not know where to begin with the unchild.

I pursued the Bright Palm on his way out of my manor, to guarantee he did not abscond with any small treasures, "for my own good." As he approached the front doors, Spellsword Deepmand said, "You have done a good deed, Bright Palm."

"I serve the innocent," he said.

The doors opened onto the view of a man riding a horse up the gravel path. I recognized him by his satin coat as the fop ambassador.

"Enchantress Hiresha," he said, "I hope you have not corrupted this simple Bright Palm with your gold. We wealthy are such a poor lot."

"Those of my order may handle gold safely," the Bright Palm said. "We are immune to avarice."

"And for that," the fop said, "you paid no more than your humanity."

The Bright Palm regarded him with a statue's gaze. The fop withstood it, his hands resting in an overly relaxed manner on his saddle horn, although his horse stiffened as if preparing to bolt.

The Bright Palm said, "The richness of your clothes speaks to the poverty of your soul."

"A respectable soul of good quality costs entirely too much to maintain," the fop said, "and I find your clothes pretentiously poor."

My brows lifted in astonishment. I always had wished to say something similar but had never done so, and I wondered how the Bright Palm would react. Of course, he lacked the ability to take offense at the slight.

As if he had not heard the insults, the Bright Palm marched down the hibiscus path and away from the manor.

"Ambassador," I said, "you waste your breath arguing with a Bright Palm. Their minds are intractable."

"To sway opinion should never be the motive of argument. I argue only for pleasure."

"A most impractical philosophy. Ambassador, since you were not invited to Sunchase Hall, you may now leave."

"I came after witnessing the parade you gathered at the God's Eye. You do know that nothing good will come of those full bellies."

Narrowing my eyes, I wondered if he could know of the unchildren. His tone had been calm, not at all conspiratorial, as if he merely had a low opinion of infants in general. "I find your flippancy offensive," I said. "Deepmand, inform Mister Obenji to never allow this person on my property again."

"With pleasure, Elder Enchantress."

"In that case, Enchantress Hiresha," the fop said, "I will await you at the High and Dry Inn. You have the power to see everything, while I know everything but see nothing. Together, we have much to discuss."

Again, the rapscallion presumed to invite me to his quarters. Wishing I could demonstrate my offense with a sharp heel turn, I dragged my gowns around and into the manor.

Once the doors shut behind us, Janny said, "He's a handsome gent, isn't he?"

"He powders his face," I said, "a sign of lasciviousness and deceit."

"I have noticed," she said, "that women here paint their faces."

"Painting is entirely different. Quite respectable."

"Of course." She grinned in a most childish fashion. "Also noticed he sweated under all his fancy yarns. You should meet him and discuss how stifling clothes can be, ask if he might suggest a way to find relief."

"Maid Janny!"

"I could ask him for you, if you'd like."

"Your effrontery is only surpassed by your impropriety. Now, if you will assist me, I must contemplate."

We had reached my guest room, and Janny helped secure my arms to the harness to facilitate my sleeping. Although embarrassment had accelerated my heart rate, I required only a hundred seconds before I lifted into my laboratory.

I reviewed the portion of the fop's conversation when he had mentioned the women's "full bellies." No guilt or shame disturbed his face then, too little emotion at all to suggest he knew more than he should about their wombs' unwelcome guests.

For the remainder of my sleep, I prepared myself mentally to meet Salkant of the Fate Weaver and his non-pregnant daughter.

ISOLATED
-19-

The priest had shed his yellow and black robes to work bare-chested in his vineyards. Over his sweat-glistening potbelly dangled a wonder, a paragon diamond. The size of a strawberry, this emperor of jewels threw specks of prismatic light over the moist dirt and green grape leaves. The priest pruned the vines, shears clutched in his partially amputated fingers.

"I know you bargained with a Feaster, *Flawless*," he said accusingly. "A scorpion-tailed spider revealed it in her web."

"It did?" I could think of nothing better to say.

"I studied the silk prophecies, in which your pattern lies always at the center. But because you will prevent the Seventh Flood, or provoke it? I realized I could not be certain."

The priest's words stung me and increased the temperature within my gowns from broil to roast. Under my breath, I said, "I am not the Flawless."

I stood on the path at the edge of the vineyard, unable to approach Priest Salkant, as the vines tied to wicker supports grew too close together to allow my gowns clearance. And I would not be seen walking on dirt.

"I judged the Feaster innocent," I said.

"They never are."

"Innocent of involvement in the mass pregnancies. I solicited his reconnaissance in exchange for a postponement of his sentence. The transaction was both reasonable and upright."

"Will people see it that way?" Priest Salkant had narrow shoulders and a thin head, forcing one to speculate on the relative size of the brain. Below his line of sight, a spider with translucent orange legs and a bulbous yellow abdomen crawled up his flowing canvas pants.

"They should concern themselves with the imperiled state of their wives and daughters, rather than a few societal parasites," I said. "Not to imply that *it* is a parasite, but you have a certain eight-legged individual close to your knee."

To my horror, he lifted the spider by its abdomen between two finger stumps. He placed it on a vine post, speaking all the while. "You stopped a Bright Palm from slaying a Feaster. You may as well have taken a bone from a wolf and expected not to be bitten. Morimound cannot afford condemnation by the Order of the Innocent." His shears snipped away grape leaves. "If the reputation of Morimound suffers, our trade will diminish. If our mercantile clout diminishes, we become vulnerable to invasion."

"The state of our unmarried women poses a greater threat to our reputation."

Priest Salkant had moved far enough down the row of grapes that I was uncertain he would hear me. I walked uphill, to the other side of the vineyard, annoyed that he would consider his plants of greater import than myself. More so, the truth of his words agitated me.

I waited for him to tread into the range of polite discourse. "Lustrous Priest, the mothers must be well nourished, for a chance at delivering their...their babies. I request shipments of sardines totaling forty-three tons. In addition, a mandate to eat egg and spinach daily to replenish their blood."

Although I expected him to call an acolyte to arrange the task, he only nodded and continued his clipping. I realized he expected to remember the requests, something I would never trust to my waking memory.

"Then, Lustrous Priest, all that remains for me to do is examine your daughter."

"There is no need. The Fate Weaver has assured me of her safety."

"As an anomaly, she may give insight into the condition of the other women."

"The benefits of seclusion for young ladies is no secret, and I am proud that Kishala has not lived an unguarded day in her life."

"Nonetheless, I must insist."

The priest rammed his shears into a belt loop then led me into his manor. The clutter of his furnishings and gaudiness of his chandeliers demonstrated a lack of taste.

We approached two women wearing scimitars who played a game of stones. The one with the spinning stick let it fall as they hefted themselves to attention in front of a brass door. Their bellies jutted outward.

"Men know to guard their gold," Priest Salkant said, "but daughters are far more perishable. Observe the slot at the base of the door that permits the passage of necessities into the chamber and undesirables out. Kishala, it's me."

He rapped a signet ring against the brass portal, and a bony hand reached out from under the door, giving me a shock. The priest squatted down and cupped the hand in both of his.

"I make a point to hold her like this every day. I am not an uncaring father, after all."

Maid Janny cleared her throat behind me with a strangled noise, which would have been rude had it been louder.

"Spellsword," Priest Salkant said, "if you would situate yourself out of sight, I will open the door."

"By your order, Lustrous Priest." Deepmand's voice sounded a tad stiff as he clanked around a corner.

"You will note, Flawless Hiresha, that I carry the only key."

I shook my head at the honorific as Priest Salkant unlocked the door, and I noted the portal's thickness. The flickering light inside attested to a room free from windows. A wealth of candles burned with the scent of jasmine.

The priest strutted into the chamber. "Kishala, I brought you a gift. A visitor, Elder Enchantress Hiresha. One day, you will have the same grandeur."

I met the stare of a girl with an unfortunate resemblance to her father, her body with so little breadth that it appeared compacted. Her face was narrow enough to give the impression that her eyes were mounted on the sides of her head, although her gaze assessed my gowns with calculation. She wore only a silk shift.

The girl asked, "Am I to be an enchantress, Father?"

"Perhaps, my hatchling. Perhaps."

My gaze had wandered past her to an overflowing bookshelf then to hanging planters of ferns and small flowering plants growing toward the candles. Tables were strewn with maps, glass bowls on tripods full of bright fishes.

Jealousy tasted in my mouth as overripe lemon, not for the girl's imprisonment but for the forethought given her by her father. My own parents had never considered me more than a nuisance. The priest believed the lavish confinement best for her, a point I would not argue, not then.

My skin itched and twitched as I thought of her imprisonment. I worried she would be ill prepared for entering the world, no matter how well read. Her leanness also concerned me.

I asked, "Are you underfed?"

"We have talked about this," Priest Salkant said. "You must eat more, Kish."

The girl shrugged, the motion subtle with her truncated shoulders.

I asked, "Do you never leave the safety of these walls?"

"Father takes me to the roof garden twice a year. He even lets me decide what to plant, and I have written essays on horticulture, if you'd like to see."

"That will not be necessary," I said.

"So much more will grow outside, it's amazing." She reached to a planter, touching pale white flowers with her fingertips. "We haven't gone out this year. Father says it's not safe."

"Something is negatively affecting the women of Morimound," I said, "yet your father's consideration has protected you. Lustrous Priest, I believe that will be all."

The girl asked, "Can't you stay and tell me about enchanting?"

"The Propriety Pledge prohibits my doing so."

"What if father apprenticed me to you?"

"Many depend on me now, young lady."

"Then, goodbye, I suppose. You have made this a memorable month."

Although the size of the room had allowed most of my gowns to enter after me, I found myself unable to turn. Maid Janny heaved at the avalanche of silks, the gowns slipping from her grasp to spread outward in new directions. When I left the chamber, my raiment compressed in the doorway then swelled outward in the hall.

The priest locked the door behind him. "You will not wish to leave without tasting the estate vintage."

Maid Janny mumbled behind me. "I need a drink, after seeing that poor girl."

"Most kind of you," I said to the priest, "yet I must return to the God's Eye Court."

"A golden-web spider dictated that you would stay. I always have a bottle on ice, along with a comparison. And I thank you for not mentioning you are the Flawless. Kishala studied law, before I realized the Fate Weaver had chosen you for the position."

"I am sure she deserves it more."

"Perhaps this weave is better, though. The position would have required her exposure."

In a parlor, he uncorked a bottle and trickled into a glass a fluid with the coloration of dilute urine, which he subsequently forced into my hand.

"Here you are, the second best wine in Morimound."

"I am afraid, Lustrous Priest, I must decline. Alcohol makes me drowsy." In point of fact, it stupefied me.

"Just a sip, then."

Scowling down at the pale fluid, I lifted the glass. It tasted exactly like what it was: rotten grapes.

"Now, experience this vintage. I enhance its flavor by exposing the grapes themselves to the maximum possible sunlight."

He thrust me a glass with considerably more wine. I wanted to refuse, yet I deemed he would have taken it as a slight. The wine stung my mouth in much the same manner.

A smile stretched over the priest's face, admittedly no great distance. "Is it not bliss? I drink nothing else."

I took a proffered handkerchief from Maid Janny and scrubbed my lips. "A staggering accomplishment."

While Priest Salkant turned to pour more wine into another glass, I passed mine to Janny. She tipped it upside down, drinking the fluid in two gulps then returning the glass to me, now empty.

"By the Fate Weaver," he said, upon turning around again, "you must have enjoyed it!"

"Indubitably, although I must excuse myself. I am expected at the court."

"May your thread shine."

Spellsword Deepmand accompanied me to the carriage. Once I reached my flying laboratory, I considered how the daughter reinforced my theory of tactile spellcraft. The walls surrounding Kishala had thwarted the pregnancy-evoking touch. For the sake of sanity I decided to assume I dealt with magic users, with mortals I could hope to understand and surmount.

Now I had to locate the perpetrators. The Feaster had claimed not to have seen anything during the night. Therefore, I would have to speak to the acolytes about other possible groups who had the opportunity to touch every woman in the city.

A brief analysis disturbed me with the thought that the acolytes themselves, through their duties, would have had access to the greatest number of women.

CONSENTING
-20-

As my gowns fluttered outward from my carriage, I pointed to the nearest acolytes, picking one representative of each god. "You and you. Attend me at the center of the court."

Once we had gathered apart from the bystanders, I spoke in a low voice.

"These pregnancies were not caused by a god but by magic."

"No, the Ever Always filled the wombs with—"

"This magic came from one person, or one group of people, who touched each and every woman. You two must discern who could have laid their hands on so many, six months ago."

One acolyte pointed to the other. "Those of the Fate Weaver touch women, they take a lock of hair before reading their destinies."

"But we don't read every woman's web, no more than a few thousand a year," the other said. "I'm more suspicious of Abwar of the Ever Always. His hands seem to get most everywhere."

The Ever Always' acolyte crossed his arms, grey sleeves sliding over each other. "No one man could've touched all Morimound's women. Not even a group of men, without someone noticing. We are witnessing a god's work."

"Then it is a work of cruelty," I said, striding off the court.

I sat in my carriage and tried to think, yet, naturally, I could not until I dipped into sleep. The acolyte's words frightened me with their reason: Nobody could have touched all the women, not without notice. Either I had to find who had witnessed them or admit that I confronted the will of a god, against which I would be powerless to protect my people. Women would die or give birth to something other than children, and Morimound would become infamous.

There had to be more to learn about the unchildren. I willed my mirror to reflect the image of the Bright Palm's magic as it branched white into Sri's womb. The light traced along distinct paths from a pulsing center and divided into the shape of a white sphere; this surprised me, as it seemed to indicate that the unchild had blood flow. A heart beat in rapid flashes. I realized I should have expected this because nutrients would have to reach the bones for them to grow, yet the concept of the unchild as a living entity and not some totem of death did not in any manner grant comfort.

A glimpse of it while I was regenerating Sri's liver had frightened me away before I could better understand it. A closer observation of the unchildren's internal workings might lead me to their makers. Each second of ignorance blistered me, and the thought that bones might be elongating by the hour in Alyla goaded me into such an overwrought state that I Repulsed my mirror against the wall, shattering it. Shards collided with the floating jewels. Fearing the glass would scratch the malachite gems and moonstones, I willed the glass to condense and fit its shards together; the mirror formed anew in a blink.

I would bring Alyla into this laboratory. She was the obvious choice for observation and potential aid: The greatest number of years of life stretched ahead of her, fate permitting, and she would lose the most to dying of childbed fever. I would risk the Propriety Pledge for a chance of freeing her of the unchild.

Leaving the laboratory, I said, "Deepmand, take me to the Chandur residence."

We arrived in the late afternoon, and I hoped Harend Chandur would have returned home by now because I would rather deal with him than his unfaithful wife.

A young man answered the door, and my gowns left him speechless.

I asked, "Are you the son of Harend Chandur?"

"Nah-no! No, Lustrous Madam. I'm just Yash."

"I trust you are capable of finding me a parchment, ink, quill, and a room, where I may have a few quiet moments of study." Before broaching the topic of sleeping with Alyla, I would write down a secret that would relieve the family's financial difficulties. "You may also inform Harend Chandur that I am accepting his daughter's offer of hospitality."

The young man situated me in a room, where I sat on my ottoman in front of a desk. Faliti Chandur barged in, fist raised.

"What are you doing in my home, with our last skin of parchment? We can't afford to—"

"Spellsword Deepmand, kindly remove Faliti Chandur. I need a meditative atmosphere. Maid Janny, support me as I write."

Deepmand shut me in alone with Janny. Thumping and raised voices leaked in from the hall. Janny held my shoulder, and I gripped the quill, leaning forward over the parchment and closing my eyes.

I carried the quill into the laboratory, and my mirror showed an image of myself, leaning over the desk. Touching my slippers against the dais, I drifted into the mirror; the glass provided no obstacle, as if it were not there. My gowns hissed around the mirror's edges, and the temperature of the dream increased. I overlaid myself with my reflection, her arms merging with my dream body, which would bind my actions with those in the waking world. Where some people walked in their sleep, I could write.

My quill dipped in the reflection of the inkwell, where it would exist in the real world, and in minutes, I had filled the parchment with diagrams of diamond facets, along with written instructions on a cutting process. When awake, I wrote in a slovenly hand, yet in dream, my letters were small masterpieces.

I left the mirror and awoke to examine the true parchment. After correcting a few spots, where my ink had run out before I had predicted in the dream, I lifted my voice.

"I am finished, Deepmand."

He opened the door to admit Faliti Chandur, who entered red-faced and shouting. "You think you can do whatever you want because you're wealthy? I ask you, is it fair you ride in a carriage with golden wheels while my husband works all day to lose money, and my daughter bleeds away her bride price for every inch she swells?"

Harend Chandur had skulked into the room behind her. I extricated myself from the ottoman and, without meeting Faliti's eyes, gave the parchment to him.

"This details a diamond cut I have developed, which I call the 'round perfect.' These notations describe the new cutting method required. Harend Chandur, with this, your family will return to wealth."

"This is incredible. I've never seen such density of facets." His eyes widened as he examined the parchment, yet his gaze dropped, his face turning thoughtful. "But diamonds aren't important now, are they? I just want to know my daughter will be fine."

He handed the parchment back to me. Faliti snatched it from my hand.

"Don't be a fool, Harend."

"And," he said, attempting to meet Faliti's stare, "I want to know if the child my wife carries came from a god, or another man, because it didn't come from me."

The gravity of his meaning did not register in my mental logbook until his wife slapped him. She asked, "How dare you say that in front of her?"

He touched his face and began to blink. I feared he would cry, yet before that could happen, he left the room.

"I can save your daughter." I called after him. "I might be able to."

Faliti did not give Harend a second glance, and the disdain with which she treated him caused my skin to burn and itch. I found it difficult to moderate the tone of my voice.

"I know what you....You do not wish for Alyla to be pregnant. My magic may be able to help her."

"You are jealous of me, Resha. I know you are, and I don't trust your magic."

"I just need an hour alone with her."

"An hour? Alone with my daughter? Are you a girl kisser?"

"What? No! Pregnancy has clearly shrunk your brain."

Although a mother grew more forgetful when carrying a child, once the baby was born her intelligence rebounded even greater than before. This blessing of motherhood I might also lose.

Faliti must have doubted her own mental state. For the first time, I saw an expression of uncertainty above her cleft chin.

I said, "You poisoned Alyla with wormwood, yet she is still pregnant. My magic might be able to save her."

She gripped the parchment with both hands, her fingers tensing. "Use your magic, then. But I'll be there to watch you."

"I cannot permit that."

"And why not?"

I swallowed, looking to Deepmand for help. He locked his gaze elsewhere, on the front door and hallway. After licking my lips, I forced myself to speak.

"I would need to undress. So would she."

"You are a girl kisser!"

"No! I would commit no indecency."

"Don't try to justify your perversions. Get out of my house!"

My clouded mind had no capacity to deal with her accusations, and I felt overwhelmed.

Spellsword Deepmand said, "The elder enchantress is of unblemished character, even if her magic has unexpected requirements."

"Oh, and how often has she 'done her magic' on you?" Faliti whipped her eyes from Deepmand to me, and she held up the parchment. "Is that what this is? A bribe? A gift for a daughter's mother to keep quiet?"

In a way, I had hoped this favor would predispose them not to tell about my falling asleep with their daughter. I thought her rude for pointing it out.

My face had flushed, and I began to feel the lightness of a near faint. I could not convince Faliti with my fatigued mind, and I shuddered, taking the first step to leave.

Retreat would not help, I realized. I would have to convince someone, sometime. Leaving would admit guilt, would allow rumors that Faliti would be all too happy to spread.

I met Faliti's gaze, yet her angry stare stripped me of much-needed focus. Shifting my eyes to the wall beside her, I tried to organize my thoughts, although it felt like juggling hot sand.

"Alyla," I said. "She may lose more than her bride price. The childbirth may kill her."

"It better, after the grief she's put me through."

"What did you say? By the Fate Weaver, she's your daughter!"

"Better dead than giving birth to a bastard. She'd disgrace her brother."

"She may not give birth to anything living. It might not be—"

"And better than playing kiss-fanny with an enchantress old enough to be her mother." She threw the parchment at me but then picked it up again, clutching it to her breast.

"The child might not be a child, and I have to know. I have to see her." Heat and shame ignited inside me, and I no longer knew what I said.

"There won't be a child," Faliti said, "even if I have to tear it out of her."

"It, it's not what you suppose. She isn't pregnant with a baby."

"And just what else can you be pregnant with?"

"I don't know," I said.

"But you know you want my daughter. Leave, or I'll scream on the streets what you are."

"You too. There's no baby inside you."

"Are you blind?" She ran a hand down the slope of her belly.

"Have you quickened? Has Alyla?"

"I will, any day now. I've been expecting to. For some days."

"None of the women have. I can't believe they ever will."

The heat inside me mounted into a firestorm, and I had the ridiculous thought that my gowns would catch flame. I hung onto my cane, hoping I was not destined to fall to my knees in front of Faliti.

Sweat flooded in to douse my kiln of velvet, and all my strength and dignity also squeezed out of my pores. My knees wobbled; my shoulders sunk under the weight of sodden gowns.

Now Faliti would jeer at me. She would see I was as helpless as the girl who had fallen asleep in a field, under rain clouds. Any moment I would hear her chuckle and explode with laughter.

The silence of the room confused me, and I craned my neck upward. The tendrils of my headdress slid away from my eyes and revealed Faliti, clutching her belly. After blinking, I saw her eyes wide with the same fear I had seen in her daughter, the worry and uncertainty of all mothers.

"Fine," she said, "but I won't have you touching my daughter. Use your magic on me first."

"On you?"

"I don't want you to hurt Alyla."

I thought I remembered Faliti voicing a wish that her daughter would die, only a few minutes ago, and her protestation of concern baffled me. Then again, few things made sense to me while awake.

My plan had been to take Alyla into my dream. I wrinkled my brows, wondering why I should not take Faliti instead, except for the fact that this contemptible woman was the last one alive that I would wish to see me undressed. My gowns protected me from scorn, and stripping them away would reveal the full emptiness of my life.

My gaze settled on her belly, and I wondered if a heart beat inside a cluster of bones, as in the womb of Sri the Once Flawless. I had to know.

"Maid Janny, find a pallet. Spellsword Deepmand, you will stand guard outside the door."

VENOMOUS
-21-

"You will have to wear a blindfold," I said.

Faliti crossed her arms above the bulge of her abdomen. "Are you sure you're not a girl kisser?"

"All the nobility wear blindfolds, when I treat them in Mindvault Academy."

"Well, this is my house, and I won't let you do anything I can't see."

"Then, you must sleep." I waved to the cot, which Maid Janny had found.

"That's worse. I wouldn't even feel what you're doing to me."

"You have to, or the magic will not work." Actually, she would plummet into my dream regardless, yet closed eyes would not see me unadorned.

"How could my sleeping make a difference? Just put your magic in me."

My tongue slid over my palate toward my throat with my disgust. I imagined the other elder enchantresses learning how I had "put my magic" into people, in defiance of academy rules agreed to by all, to say nothing of the higher standards of faculty.

Janny had strung five clotheslines across the room and, after removing my golden hump, she began the process of undressing me, of untying and unbuttoning, pulling off layer upon layer of fabric. I had to concede that Janny had a certain strain of intelligence, as she never faltered in this task, retaining the knowledge of the exact order in which the gowns had to be removed. The complex sequence flummoxed me when awake.

"This is also necessary," I said to Faliti.

Faliti sat on the cot, observing. "By the Ever Always! Just like eating an artichoke. There's always another layer."

Janny said, "Except artichokes are less prickly."

My drooping eyelids decreased the effectiveness of my glare. I rested on my ottoman, as undressing took too long for me to stand, yet sitting increased the absurdity of resisting sleep.

I tried not to nod off in front of Faliti; the embarrassment of the thought alone burned my cheeks. Nonetheless, I found myself in my laboratory twice, although I left immediately.

Janny had removed my headdress, and Faliti must have seen my chin sag to my collar. I stole a glance and was surprised to see an expression on her face other than gloating.

Her brows high in curiosity, she asked, "You're preparing the magic? Is it almost ready?"

"No. Not yet." I touched my hair bun to check that no locks had slipped.

Faliti scowled at the gowns fluttering on the clotheslines, their enchanted fabrics twisting and coiling in the air current from my maid's scurrying. Janny had filled the five hanging cords with my honorary gowns, and now I wore the last two.

As Janny began unbuttoning my back, I held my eyes on the floor. "You must also disrobe, Faliti."

"Will the magic burn my clothes?"

Janny took my cane, and I stood, shrugging my shoulders from the gown then stepping out of the skirt. Only my innermost gown remained, the only one I liked independent of its usefulness in hiding me. Silk dyed purple shimmered with gloss between amethysts woven across my chest and sleeves. No one but Maid Janny had seen me in this creation, my own sleek design and jeweled secret, and dressed from foot to neck in flowing purple, I felt naked.

"The greater surface area for skin contact," I said, "the easier for me to draw you into...into my spells."

"I guess that'd make sense to someone." Faliti pulled off her blouse and unwound the long sheet of fabric that constituted her skirt.

Her nakedness took me by surprise. I found myself staring at breasts with stretch marks and veins made prominent by motherhood, the blood vessels branching out from areoles of enviable diameter and darkness.

"Try to kiss me," she said, "and I'll punch you in the mouth."

"You should lie on the cot and look away," I said as Janny tugged at the last lacings on my back.

"Why? You're looking at me."

I felt myself blushing, and I suspected I would have spiraled into a faint if not for the circulation of air so close to my skin. Squirming, I had no choice but to lift my arms for Janny to slide off my amethyst gown.

Faliti's eyes widened. "What're those?"

"My undergarments."

"They're so red. And is that silk?"

"What difference does it make? Lie down."

Faliti nodded to Maid Janny. "What about her?"

"She is pleasantly ignorable." I took Faliti by the arm. This all seemed unreal; sensations of floating and spinning left me shaky. I never held people like this, when they were conscious.

She lay on her side, and I nudged into her back, my legs pressed against hers. She said, "By the Ever Always! You're scrawny as a boy."

Faliti exaggerated, I reassured myself. I wrapped my arms around her warm sides to grip her belly, and she stiffened while I prepared myself for sleep.

"Will I feel anything?"

Her voice came from far away, and I did not answer as I had already reached the forty-third step. I glanced back to see the marble stairway stretching upward, and through the top archway, I could distinguish Faliti's black hair and massive shoulders. She had not tried to free herself or pull away yet. I hurried down the remaining steps, jumped, and towed her after me into the laboratory.

Although I appeared above the diamond dais in all twenty-seven gowns, Faliti came into being on the operations table naked, her arms and legs held in place by gold manacles. A blindfold wrapped around her head.

She gasped, no doubt from the coldness of the basalt stone. "What have you done to me? Resha, let me go!"

My voice resounded in the domed room. "Here, you will be silent."

Attracting the silver pillow to my hand, I touched her with it, and her struggling limbs went limp, her hands unclenching.

A copper cone whisked into my hand, the object modeled after those held to ears to amplify sound. I placed it on her belly, and then I Created a cloth with which to cover her breasts, as I found their size distracting.

Leaning my ear down to the narrow end of the cone, I waited for the spell to tell me the parentage of the child in her belly, if it was a child. A duke once had hired me to identify if the baby his wife carried belonged to him or to her lover. The test required a hair from the father, which I had neglected to take from Harend, yet I still listened to the disembodied child's voice as it spoke through the cone.

"I am a boy. For my father, no comparison present. For my mother, this is not a match."

My pulse accelerated. I had created the second test to ensure the spell worked, as I never had expected to find a child who was not related to the woman who carried him. The fact that the spell had recognized whatever she carried as a boy did not reassure me.

Gathering my courage, I summoned the blue diamonds and positioned them around Faliti's belly. As her tissues began to fade from sight, I forced myself not to look away, expecting too soon to gaze down at another unchild, something malformed to the point of being inside out.

The blue diamonds tumbled to the operating table, and Faliti's skin reappeared, hiding the womb from my sight. I had lost control of my spellcraft.

Such an embarrassment never happened, not to an elder enchantress. As my surprise receded, a sense of being watched prickled down my back, the same feeling I had experienced when in my laboratory with Sri. It reminded me of the moments in a dream before the realization struck that it was a nightmare, although over a decade had passed since I had experienced such a nocturnal grievance. I glanced at the walls, even upward at the skylight, yet I saw nothing but blackness, baubles, and prismatic stars.

Frowning, I decided that whoever was peering into my dream had annulled my detection spell. I had no intention of losing a battle of will here, however, and I hopped above the comatose Faliti to seize her abdomen. Gowns fanning around my levitating body, I Attracted the diamonds into the air then Repulsed them to their proper positions around her womb.

Membranes faded to reveal a white object that would have petrified me if I had not known what to expect. Even so, my abdominal muscles convulsed in disgust.

Multiple baby skeletons were bent and disfigured into the shape of one egg. Rows of ribs cluttered against foot bones; arm bones wrapped around pelvic bones, and wrist and finger bones filled in the gaps. Spines curved throughout the ovoid, except where a band of cartilage divided the bone egg lengthwise into halves. By my understanding of bone growth, I predicted the two halves would not fully merge and fuse until after birth, leaving soft spots like those on the skulls of human newborns.

Commanding myself to focus and not shrink back, I pushed the spell farther; the bones faded from sight, providing a glimpse of the insides of the unchild, of muscle tissue, violet gland sacs, and—

Magic from an external source invaded my dream. It felt like a pin stuck into the back of my spinal cord, a spell entering my laboratory and slipping into Faliti's body.

Her abdomen lurched, and something splattered my face. Bewildered, I wiped my chin to see translucent droplets on my hand darken into blood. I Repulsed the blue diamonds from Faliti, her belly blinking back into sight with a gash running from navel to groin.

Hysteria skittered through me as I felt myself crushed between confusion and horror. I did not know what had occurred, yet the color was draining from Faliti's skin, warning of massive internal bleeding. I had to concentrate, or this woman would die in my dream.

A platinum clamp flew into my hand. Waving it at her belly caused a dual Attraction between the edges of severed skin, closing the wound. And yet she was dying.

At my will, the blue diamonds flurried around her abdomen, revealing intestines and organs cut and pierced from bone shards that had lanced outward from her womb. I Attracted a bloodstone from a laboratory shelf, and combined with the silver clamp, it constricted all her abdominal arteries and veins to stop the bleeding. And yet she was dying.

Hands moving from one side of her belly to the other, I Attracted the bone shards back into the womb then confined them in a repaired birth sac. Whenever I found a major blood vessel torn, my magic bound its edges together.

Tracing and retracing her circulatory system, I convinced myself I had found all the leaks, and I Attracted my magic chisel then touched it to the bloodstone, which restored her blood flow.

And yet she was dying.

A jar glittering with sapphires floated into my hand. The spell stored within it began the process of finding all units of infection that had entered her blood from her cut intestines, crushing each contaminant with precise, paired Attractions.

The magic that held her body together would not persist if she left my dream. I had to stimulate her tissue to mend itself, and I beckoned flocks of silver pins toward me. When any two pins pointed to the same spot, they prompted multiplication of bodily units and the formation of connective tissue.

I arranged the first hundred pins in the air; the silver needles revolved around my fingers to point at the location of each blood vessel I had sealed with Attraction. Remembering the areas in need of mending was not a problem, yet as I had never before dealt with an injury involving so many organs, I ran out of pins at five hundred. And yet she was dying.

Faliti did not breathe Her blood did not flow, and her heart had stopped.

Turning her weightless, I lifted her, wrapped my arms around her. I Attracted my hands toward my chest and in doing so they smashed into her heart, forcing it to beat. My magic pulled air into her lungs, making her breathe. It wasn't working, and the only thing I could think to do in that emergency was more. The cartilage between her ribs cracked. Her body flopped in my grip. Keeping at it, I knew I had to save her. I would, accomplished elder enchantress as I was. No other possible outcome could be permitted.

And yet, Faliti was dead.

She had gone cold in my arms. I maintained my composure until I determined the cause: A toxin I had not looked for had paralyzed her lungs, its source the violet gland sacs in the womb.

My enchanted implements retreated to the shelves as a weight drove me to the ground, my gowns rippling outward in my collapse. I lost my grip on repressed revulsion and anxiety, a nausea rising from my quaking insides to my gasping chest. The bedlam of emotion advanced farther into my skull, where I felt my brain stem would rot, and I would never move again.

My error had killed her: I should have examined her vital signs every few minutes. I had to accept that either my bias against Faliti had undermined my attentiveness, or I was capable of miscalculating in my dream. Both possibilities disturbed me equally.

Worse than either thought, the "boy" in Faliti's womb had been deformed past humanity. A creature inverted, with bones on the outside and an interior filled with venom, had fractured and killed her. I would not wish that fate on any woman, not even Faliti, who had tormented me, and her husband.

A glance at the corpse on the operations table forced me to believe it had really happened. The thing inside her had possessed a magic bond with an entity outside my dream, a man or god, and whoever it was had peered into my laboratory, seen me prodding the unchild, and evoked death in Faliti.

All the women in Morimound likely carried such an unchild. For all I knew, the mothers had all died by now. If the Ever Thriving, Always Dying had generated the unchildren, then he had given not a boon but a blight. If a man and his magic were responsible, then Morimound was under siege.

I crawled to the diamond dais and fled the dream.

CURSED
-22-

Night Five and Day Six, Third Trimester

Maid Janny's fingers trembled on my gown laces, her eyes darting to the cot and Faliti's corpse.

I said, "Pay attention, you buffoon!"

Janny pinched her lips together. Upon leaving my dream, Faliti's abdomen had split open again. Not too much blood had trickled across the floorboards onto my gowns.

At last dressed, I waited for Janny to open the door. Then I swept past Spellsword Deepmand to find Harend Chandur sitting at the table, his hands clamped on his knees.

He leapt to his feet. "Where is Faliti?"

I ignored his question. "Check on Alyla expeditiously. Instantly. Now!"

After a moment of befuddlement, Harend ran up that atrocious ladder to the second story. I waited to hear him shriek, and I did not stop pressing my arms together until he returned to view.

"She's asleep."

"Asleep? Are you sure? Wake her."

Harend thumped out of sight, and my fingers gripped my face around my eyes. At last, I heard his voice again.

"She's feeling better. I think she's getting her appetite back. Is something wrong?"

He had witnessed me sighing, with my hand over my heart, or as near to that location as my gowns allowed. I took my cane from the crook of my arm, leaning on it and trying to think of a palliative way to tell him, yet nothing came to me.

"Faliti Chandur is dead. I could not save her."

No sooner did his mouth open in shock than I fled outside into the darkness of night. Sitting in my carriage, I failed to think of where I should go and soon found myself in my laboratory. Drifting from one black wall to another, I realized I could not risk drawing another woman into my dream, as it might elicit her death, yet outside my dreams, I was powerless.

Deepmand drove me to my manor, and I stumbled inside to spend a few hours sleeping in the silk harness.

I stood atop my laboratory, in chill night gusts below the red moon, and I wanted to weep. Every woman in Morimound might die from the unchild within her.

I tried to convince myself that they could not all expire, at least not all at once, yet the fatal spell I had sensed had been simple, merely one of activation. Many such spells could be cast at the same time, even by a mortal. I pondered if I could distinguish a spell cast by a man from the power of divinity but decided I would at least need to see it done again, to search for human variation, and I had no desire to provoke another death.

Waking up, I felt as weary as if I had not slept in days. I had a hard time seeing my breakfast, and when my eyes focused on broccoli, I gagged. The thought of wombs sloshing full of venom put me well out of appetite.

A shattering noise from the front of the house was followed by a tinkling. Servants ran down the hall. The sound repeated, and I realized I heard windows being smashed.

"What is happening, Mister Obenji?"

His brow drawn, he rushed out, Deepmand looking after him. More windows broke, and I thought I heard shouting.

Mister Obenji returned in a huff. "There are some men outside. I'll gather the help, and we'll keep them out of the manor. Dhatrod can run for the city guard. Not to worry, I'll handle everything."

Deepmand asked, "Is it a mob?"

"No. Not at all. All the same, I trust Elder Enchantress Hiresha would be most comfortable closer to the back of the manor."

"I should think not." I left the table, walking toward the breaking sounds. "There must be some mistake. The people of Morimound are reasonable."

Angry voices from outside filtered between the shards remaining in the crystal windows, and glass crunched as Deepmand strode in front of me. A young man had fallen below a window, gripping a cut on his forehead.

Mister Obenji strode toward him. "Are you hurt?"

"I don't think so, except for this blood."

A servant woman rushed forward to help, slipping on the glass. She pitched forward over her pregnant belly, before she thankfully recovered and righted herself.

"Careful! My girl, do you feel any pain?"

"I'm fine." She removed a scarf and pressed it against the young man's head to staunch the bleeding. "Just worried over Dhatrod."

"Avoid stepping on this glass. Remember that you carry a...something breakable."

A window down the hall exploded inward in a shower of crystal, and a stone clattered against the wall. I felt as bewildered, shocked, and sore as if the rock had been thrown at my stomach.

"Spellsword Deepmand, attend me on the balcony."

I walked upstairs and out to the marble balustrade. Men danced below me among the gardens; only, I began to suspect that they were not dancing but stomping flowers and kicking over statues. Several waved oil lamps in the direction of the front doors.

"Should I encourage them to leave, Elder Enchantress?"

I could form no answer, as a numbness overtook my mind and spread down my spine in a tingling. The people of Morimound could not be defacing my property. Their anger could not be meant for me, their benefactress, unless all these men had misunderstood Faliti's death. I tried to think whether news of it could have spread in the few hours of morning.

Voices shouted below. "Why should she have this, after all she's done to us?"

"She's no Flawless neither!"

"Look, there's the lily toad!"

"Kill her! It's the only way for our daughters."

Deepmand stepped in front of me and caught something, and I saw a brick in his gauntlet, encouraging me to wonder if it had been aimed at me. The brick crumbled in the spellsword's enchanted grip, its pieces raining on the men below the balcony.

The effect was a silencing one.

"I appreciate the gesture, Deepmand, even though it was unnecessary." No brick could have hurt me, due to the enchantment in my golden hump.

"Certainly, Elder Enchantress."

A familiar voice boomed over the estate grounds. "Stop, men of Morimound! This is not the way, for there is no guarantee the death of the apostate will appease the Ever Thriving, Always Dying."

Priest Abwar flounced down the path, his arms and green sleeves swinging about him as if he wished to communicate with those appendages alone.

"The apostate designed the Flood Wall, but our hands built it. By shutting out the sky-sent waters, we spurned the gift of death and rebirth. We defied a god."

His words gave me mental indigestion. Priest Abwar seemed to be calling me an "apostate," yet I did not understand how he could when he had named me the city's savior only days ago.

"The Ever Thriving, Always Dying cannot be controlled," he said. "His will is absolute, His design irresistible. When the floods could not reach us, He cursed the wombs of our women. None have quickened because they do not carry life. They carry the blessing of the Always Dying."

"Spellsword Deepmand, is he suggesting that my Flood Wall caused the mass pregnancies?"

"He might be, Elder Enchantress."

Priest Abwar turned to point downslope, to the base of the city; the back of his robes depicted the moon on a background of undyed white, the color of death. "No hope remains for our daughters and wives as long as one stone of the Flood Wall remains stacked upon another. Men of Morimound, tear down that wall!"

"Deepmand, did he tell them to dismantle the Flood Wall?"

"I regret that he did, Elder Enchantress."

"But they are all leaving. They are going to destroy it, and they mustn't. Tell them they mustn't."

"Halt!" Deepmand's bellow forced the men to glance back at me.

Although unaccustomed to the impropriety of shouting, I tried to speak so the men could hear me. "The summer rains will arrive next month. We require the Flood Wall to keep them out, or the city of Morimound may be inundated."

Most of the men's faces stayed blank, and I feared my voice had not carried. Abwar of the Ever Always lifted his hands, palms outward as if to block me from his sight.

"Do not listen to the apostate. Her magic tricked me into naming her the Flawless, and she has brought this evil upon us. Her hubris has polluted this city. Now, to the wall!"

The men returned the shout, "To the wall!" as they left the ruins of my gardens. My trembling legs could not support me, and I slumped onto the marble tiles, my gowns slowing my descent as they plumed upward, blocking my view of the world.

I did not much mind the damage to my estate, as it still had fewer flaws than I. A flood, however, would bring catastrophe, and I dreaded that Abwar of the Ever Always could be right in proclaiming I had caused the unchildren through my audacity in believing I could stop the Seventh Flood and avert the will of a god.

After flourishing for over a century, Morimound might have reached its prime. Perhaps I was doomed to witness its fall into squalor and desperation. By citywide flood, or by death of all our women from unchildren, the Seventh Age might end in a matter of months.

"I will see to repairing the grounds," Mister Obenji said, "and I'll pay guards to protect the manor."

"Deepmand, if you please. I feel I must retire to my room."

The spellsword lifted me to my feet. I teetered my way to the guestroom, to sleep and exert myself to understand how the men could so willingly invite their own destruction.

I reasoned those in the mob were affluent and not dwellers of Stilt Town, where waters had licked at house floorboards. To those in elevated brick homes, the threat of floods would seem distant, a stray historical fact, while the conditions of their female relatives obscured every thought.

I searched for any possible course of action. The city's only chance was that Abwar of the Ever Always was wrong, that the gods did not conspire our doom, and we faced only the designs of men.

If magic had created the unchildren then its users had employed a method unknown to me. My inquiry had to turn elsewhere, from method to motive. Someone might wish to bargain the lives of our women for a ransom of the city's diamonds, or another nation might plot to undermine Morimound. I loathed the idea of being in the power of foreigners, yet better them than a mishandling by gods.

In bitterness, I recalled that the Fate Weaver's priest had also prophesied the coming of the Seventh Flood. Morimound might be fated to fall.

LORDLY
-23-

Waking, I learned that Priest Salkant himself had arrived and now waited for me in the ballroom.

"You should have left him in one of the parlors, Mister Obenji."

"He claimed he was *meant* to meet you there, Elder Enchantress Hiresha."

I found the priest picking through his mess of grey hair and casting an appraising eye on the ballroom's chandeliers and vaulted windows. "Ah, Flawless Hiresha. Abwar of the Ever Always has withdrawn his support for you, which, to me, is the highest of recommendations."

"Perhaps he is right to doubt me."

"The Fate Weaver has selected your thread among thousands and blessed you with prosperity. The goddess does not choose idly." He waved from my gowns to the ballroom's blue satin curtains. "Now, Abwar rants about the pregnancies, and each web I read is chaotic. Should I worry?"

I tried to think of a reason not to confirm Priest Salkant's concerns but could not conceive of one. "The women, that is all the pregnant women of Morimound....It could be as the priest said."

He sighed. "She weaves as She wills."

"I am not yet ready to believe their futures will be snipped short. Morimound may have been infiltrated seven months ago by magic users. Find them, and we save the mothers." I massaged my temples, trying to loosen my thoughts. "Which nations would benefit from our downfall?"

Priest Salkant gripped his robes over his chest. "The realm of Nagra covets our gem trade. The people of Salarian depend on our rice fields and resent it. We've long skirmished with Rhiderac over water diversion for irrigation, and Pyridi's merchants must pay to travel over our roads to reach eastern markets."

"If I met with representatives from each nation, then I could determine if any played a role in the happenings here."

"Could you? How?"

"I can see guilt, if I know in whom to search."

"Goddess be praised! But you'll want to see more than the ambassadors, they're told nothing. We'll summon members from the power castes of each nation, and I know the perfect pretext. A ball hosted by an elder enchantress."

"A ball? In my manor?"

"What other purpose could this room have?"

I bit back the words "wedding reception." My gaze drew up inlaid columns to the ceiling's four sloped sides, which formed the underside of a pyramid painted with a day skyscape. The mosaic included a depiction of my floating laboratory; should I ever wed, I would permit the sun to rise in my dream.

"You may arrange a ball in my name," I said. "As long as the guests are reputable."

"They will all be wealthy, I assure you. The event can be held in two months, on the Day of Return."

I needed a moment to figure out why that would not do. "It must be sooner. The eighth month will mean early labor and likely death for the youngest mothers. Worse so for the eldest."

"Sooner then. The eve of Flood Moon. Now, if you will excuse me, Flawless Hiresha, I must see to the day's spinnings."

"I am not flawless," I said once he had left through the ballroom's triangular entranceway.

I returned to my room, sleeping to analyze what steps I could take in the interim. Preliminary reconnaissance of the ambassadors might prove useful, I determined, and from there, my attention shifted to the foppish ambassador of Jordania.

Although not from a suspect nation, he had requested a conference with me, for unsavory reasons, I had thought, yet his powdered face betrayed neither greed nor lust. Then I detected something far worse. When he had interposed himself before the front doors of my manor, his composed face had momentarily bent inward, nostrils flaring, lips twitching upward into the beginning of a snarl of murderous contempt.

The ambassador had suppressed all but the first traces of his expression, and no one could have noticed it at the time. Neither had I seen anything suspect in my prior evaluation of his statement concerning the "parade" of mothers. I had restricted my survey then, fearing to spot him winking in my general direction. Now I counted seven instances of loathing wriggling beneath the smooth control of his face.

While I observed him in the mirror and heard his words, a chill settled into my spine as if a maid had forgotten to tend the fire and I had awoken freezing in the drafty Academy.

"You do know," the ambassador had said, "that nothing good will come of those full bellies."

I had thought him facetious, yet I would not dismiss my concerns a second time. His conversation raced past in the mirror; leaning forward and gripping the glass, I noticed something unexpected: Each time the contempt had flickered into view, his eyes had rested on the Bright Palm, who had healed Sri the Once Flawless.

Another curiosity appeared between the corners of his curling lips, where his incisors shone with less luster than natural tooth enamel, and they clicked ever so softly on contact. I recognized the work of an artisan in Oasis City, who constructed false teeth for nobility who could not afford my regeneration services. His porcelain teeth, coupled with the menacing look toward the Bright Palm, were remarkable enough that I decided to search my mirror for an association, and I found a memory of Bright Palms chanting two days ago in the bazaar.

"...by three signs you will know him. The Lord of the Feast has no teeth to speak mercy...."

I scolded myself for confusing a fop with the most deadly of Feasters. The latter was known to have paralyzed town militias with waking nightmares, frightening families from the safety of their homes with visions of horror while hundreds of Feasters descended for a slaughter. I did not care to imagine the same happening to the city of Morimound. I must have erred, and the subsequent signs would confirm my mistake.

"...no ears to hear your pleas...."

The ambassador's hair covered any sign of ears, black locks falling straight down to sprawl over his shoulders. I would have expected the strands to displace themselves around the lobe of each ear, if he possessed any. This man had no ears, and my anxiousness hastened the jewels, which spun around the laboratory.

"...and a black triangle on his brow, where soul left body."

The powder lent his face the pallor of a frosted cake, and as his visage expanded to fill the entire mirror, I detected that he had applied twice as thick a layer of makeup to the region above his eyebrows, at the center of his forehead.

I reached into the mirror, and a sweep of my hand removed the powder, leaving me not with a memory, as I had never seen the skin of his face, but a prediction. A tattoo of a dark triangle pointed downward between his brows.

With a small degree of uncertainty, I believed I had met the Lord of the Feast. The thought of him here, in Morimound, stiffened me; he could attack any night, and I feared that only Bright Palms could resist him. The two sanctums in the city, which I had once considered too many, now seemed far too few.

His coat showed the stitching styles of two different tailors, and I suspected he had refitted it after stealing it from the true Jordanian ambassador; if anything, he was the ambassador of night. I had requested the help of a pathetic boy illusionist, and the Lord of the Feast had replied.

"I believe you requested my assistance," the frilled menace had said, "and I am at your service."

Accepting was out of the question. Salkant of the Fate Weaver had warned me against associations with Feasters, let alone their lord. If testimony of any dealings with him spread, my reputation would be obliterated, and the Oasis Empire might declare war on Morimound.

I wondered if the Lord of the Feast had been in Morimound before I arrived. He had to be here for a reason, possibly one tied to the mass pregnancies. However, his Feasting magic could only craft illusions, horrifying though they might be, and nothing so concrete and permanent as the unchildren. I wished I could know his purpose here, without meeting him.

His countenance yielded few answers. He never gestured, not once lifting his hands from his sides, and one might guess his arms paralyzed, or false, like his teeth, although I deduced he tensed his arm muscles to keep them as low as possible. His shoulders slumped as if his hands possessed an inordinate weight. They remained on his saddle horn when riding, and his horse did not even have a bridle or reins for him to grip. His gloved fingers could not all bend completely, and some were crooked as if once broken.

If he repressed animation in his arms then he stifled it in his face. He never smiled, although twice when speaking to me the skin lateral to his eyes began to wrinkle as if in mirth. At closer inspection of the moment he mentioned the "parade" of mothers at God's Eye Court, I spotted the center of his brows uplift an eighth of an inch, hinting at sorrow.

This twinge of emotion seemed to suggest he knew of the unchildren, perhaps even harbored qualms for the women who carried them, yet I reminded myself I could not converse with the person whose name mothers used to frighten their children. "The Lord of the Feast snatches little girls who don't milk the goats every morn'," I had once heard, as well as, "Lie and a monkey will have your eye, steal and the Lord of the Feast will make you a meal."

True, he did not measure up to the stories. He rode a brown horse, whereas in tales, the Lord of the Feast always charged in on the back of an eight-legged basilisk, and the man himself supposedly sported three heads, each of which devoured people whole.

This man inked his brows, and he wore a wig, evidenced by the locks on his head from two people with slightly different shades of black hair. Reaching into the mirror, I pulled the wig off while he stood frozen in my memory. I felt powerful doing it, leaving his scalp exposed with a presumed stubble of grey hair. Perhaps the Lord of the Feast was bald. I imagined ragged stumps of cartilage and skin in place of ears severed off by some past violence. His auditory canals were disconcerting holes on either side of his head.

Growing bold, I Attracted his false incisors out of his mouth. Now only his canines poked from the corners of his lips, increasing his likeness to a predator that hunted at sunset, specifically, a bat. I wondered if he had extracted his own teeth and cut off his ears for the inhuman visage, or if someone had done it to him. I did not see why he would have mangled his own fingers.

His magic would not affect the Bright Palms, and I imagined their placid expressions as they smashed his face with gauntlets, their fists imbued with magic toughness.

By telling me the inn where he stayed in the Island District, he had placed himself in my power. I could summon all the Bright Palms from the sanctums and surround him during the day, when his Feasters could not help him. Today, Elder Enchantress Hiresha could vanquish the Lord of the Feast.

I had no reason to delay in accosting him, yet delay I did, listening again to a memory of his words.

"You have the power to see everything, while I know everything but see nothing. Together, we have much to discuss."

The Bright Palms had offered no information about the pregnancies. Feasters could have noticed something at night, six months ago, during the citywide conception.

It mattered not. My associating with the one pubescent Feaster had strained Morimound's reputation, and the damage to the city would be exponentially worse if I was to be seen with the Lord of the Feast. We would be ruined as surely as all the mothers dying to the venom in their wombs.

I forced myself to rethink that last statement. The unchildren and the Lord of the Feast both posed potential threats to Morimound, of which the unmentionable things within the women were the most direct. Meeting with the Lord of the Feast would not in itself doom Morimound because I could claim I thought him merely an ambassador. He had disguised himself well as a fop.

However, even if he did know something that could help Sri the Once Flawless, Alyla, and the rest, I could not bargain with the Lord of the Feast. He would demand payment, perhaps in hostages, or influence in the city. He might know how to dispel the unchildren, or find the magic users who had fabricated them, yet I could not form covenants with a Feaster.

Neither could I accept the alternative, of shunning this line of inquiry. Doing so might very well mean hearing Alyla scream as bones shredded her insides, or listening to Sri's gasps as venom smothered her breaths.

I had to confront him, without accepting any of his terms. Rather, he would need to accept mine. The Lord of the Feast would assist me, today, or I would instruct the Bright Palms to execute him.

I would save my city, even if doing so risked its destruction.

GENTEEL
-24-

"I must suggest against this plan, Elder Enchantress."

"Spellsword Deepmand, runners have already been sent to the chantries. We will depart for the High and Dry Inn immediately after lunch."

"Elder Enchantress, there is something you must know. A possibility exists, that is…I might not be able to protect you from the Lord of the Feast."

I blinked in both directions down the hall in which Deepmand and I stood, and as far as my sleep-filled eyes could see, no one had overheard. Janny was preparing my meal, and I had told only the spellsword the nature of the man we would face.

"When the Feaster cut off my arm with illusion, I did not just see it happen. I felt it." Deepmand gripped the interlocking plates over his elbow. "It was not real, but it might well have been. This man, if he is who you think, will be much more dangerous."

"You forget we will be approaching by day." Strictly speaking, my research indicated that daylight might not save us, yet I felt Deepmand deserved some encouragement.

"They say the Lord of the Feast brings darkness to day. He has overcome the weaknesses of other Feasters."

I bit the inside of my cheek. "If he attempts spellcraft, then our screams will be heard by the Bright Palms, who will be close."

"But you will be closer. Elder Enchantress, you cannot leverage the Bright Palms against him because he will leverage your life."

"You presume, Spellsword Deepmand, I have something in this life that I should fear to lose."

He rested one hand on his turban, the gauntlet leaving a dent in the gilded fabric. His eyes swept over my gowns then down the long hall. "You have so much, Elder Enchantress."

"You have a family," I said. "If you think you cannot contribute to my safety, then you need not follow me into the inn. I will confront him alone."

The spellsword bowed his head while I swept to the dining table. Maid Janny set my goat milk and mango cubes before me, which I abstained from eating. Across the table, Sri the Once Flawless asked which of two scarves set off the color of her eyes, and Mister Obenji said something to her, although my drumming heart prevented me from concentrating on his words. She laughed and patted his bearded cheek.

I realized I might die today.

The peace and calmness following that thought surprised me, and I felt as if I had Lightened myself. In the next hour, I would learn if the thread of my life continued, or if it ended. Until I found out which, I was free from obligations. The many hands of the Fate Weaver cradled me.

On the carriage ride to the High and Dry Inn, I admired the rate of my heart, counting a hundred and thirty-five beats in a minute. Then I began to doubt myself, knowing I could never have made such a precise calculation when awake.

The carriage stopped at the inn, and I let myself out to find a group of five Bright Palms waiting beside a cart.

"We understand you wished to unburden your soul."

"Yes, a smidgen of unburdening is just what I needed today. Mister Obenji will be leading a procession of men here carrying expensive furniture. They may not come all at once, so I will thank you to be patient."

"You should have told us to bring the cart to your manor."

"I do believe you are right. Thoughtlessness is no doubt a side effect of an over-burdened soul. Now, if you will excuse me."

I strode toward the inn door; Maid Janny hustled beside me, carrying my ottoman. She glanced back at Deepmand.

"Why is Gautam staying at the carriage?"

"He will assist the Bright Palms."

"He's looking after us like a hound with a bur in his backside."

"This is no time for your vulgarity." I stopped before the inn door, waiting for someone to open it for me.

With a gleam and a thump, Deepmand landed next to the door. "My place in life is by your side, Elder Enchantress, until life does end."

His words produced a tremor through my chest, and I hoped he would come to no harm.

The door opened from the inside, and a man in an orange suit beckoned. His face appeared splattered with a fleshy paste, his nose swollen and purplish, and the missing two fingers on his upraised hand confirmed him as a leper. More surprising still, above his shoulder protruded the jeweled hilt of a sword, which appeared disconcertingly familiar.

Deepmand preceded me inside the inn, where two other lepers with swords and bright clothes led us with uncertain gaits into a parlor. One had silver triangles tied to his face, where he should have had a nose. The arms of the last man ended in moveable stumps, all his fingers gone. I did not know whether to laugh at the fingerless swordsman or be horrified.

"What's going on?" Janny craned her neck to see around the ottoman.

The Lord of the Feast sat on a couch, his suit and vest the red of aerated blood, lace spilling from his jeweled cuffs and surging from his collar in a silk spume.

As I entered the room, he rose, only returning to his seat when I had positioned myself on my ottoman. His expression was neutral, his voice controlled.

"Enchantress Hiresha, you've come at the perfect moment."

He slouched, arms limp at his sides. Beside him, a woman wore a low cut dress that revealed no bosom but ridges of ribs under sallow skin, gaunt as if she had nearly died of a wasting sickness. She lifted a cup to his lips, and he drank a steaming black liquid with an affected sigh.

"Once brewed," he said, "the bitter bean is an antidote to drowsiness. It may be the greatest necessity you've never tried."

The emaciated woman sipped from a second cup then lifted it in offering to me. I would not have expected the

Lord of the Feast to invite me for a cup of bitter bean, and I might have doubted my assessment of him if not for the curious leper guards and the bony faces and twig arms of the women in the room; the four starving figures reminded me of the physique of the Feaster boy I had interrogated.

"I will not partake," I said.

"It's not poisoned." He glanced at the painfully undernourished woman who had tasted the drink. "She's a dear heart but couldn't survive a drop of nightshade."

The woman looked like a skeleton wearing a skin suit. She revolted me, as did all the presumed Feasters, with their dull, sunken gazes of fright. Among them, the Lord of the Feast appeared healthy, even with his snowy face and seemingly paralyzed arms.

Waving away the cup, I said, "Bitter bean only puts me to sleep."

"You don't say?" He swallowed from his cup, which the woman then lowered in order to dab his mouth with a napkin. "Then you're better off without. I'm convinced it's no good for me, it's too delightful."

The lepers with swords disturbed me, yet I worried more that the Lord of the Feast plotted to delay until the Bright Palms outside departed. My heart fluttered, beating two hundred and three times a minute, and I noticed I could count the silver links on his pocket-watch chain: thirty-seven. I also identified the twelve varieties of flower embroidered on his vest, from camassia to wisteria, a feat I should not have been able to achieve while awake.

"I did not come to dither," I said. "I know who you are."

"You do? Then please remind me, it's been days since I introduced myself."

A.E. MARLING

"You are the Lord of the Feast."

Maid Janny gasped, and a rustle of my gowns told me she hid in my silken train.

His brows rose in surprise at my denunciation, yet as they stayed lofted for more than a second, I could tell it was feigned. "Do I have a surplus of heads? Do I stand thirteen feet tall? No, I am merely 'Tethiel.' That is, until I lift my hands."

One of his gloved fingers twitched, and the woman beside him winced. She was afraid, and I believed I should be as well, yet I still felt as if the thread of my fate thrummed under a goddess's touch.

Deepmand drew his scimitar over his shoulder, although his blanched face and bloodshot eyes suggested that only the stiffness of his armor kept his hands from shaking. The leper dandies reached for their blades, the fingerless one locking his wrist into a gauntlet attached to his hilt.

"Don't bother, my hearts," the Lord of the Feast said. "The spellsword could cut through you like wicker. But he won't. He's too wise, which is more than I can say for the Bright Palms outside. My dear Enchantress Hiresha, discovering me has only confirmed my good opinion of you. But one could interpret the presence of the Bright Palms as a discourtesy."

"They will only accost you," I said, "if you fail to tell me what you know of the mass pregnancies."

"By threatening me, you're doing just what I would do. You've disappointed me tremendously."

"Father." A leper limped into the room, toward the couch and the Lord of the Feast. "They are loading furniture."

"Your furniture?" The Lord of the Feast gazed at me with blue eyes, which burned like icicles across my skin. "You haven't told the Bright Palms about me."

"I will, unless you speak substance."

"And what will you tell them? That I'm serving cups of bitters?"

"I will tell them of whom they must dispose."

"And 'whom' is that?"

I had to stand up to him and stop his circuitous speech. After the Bright Palms ran out of furniture to load, they would leave. "You. They will kill you."

"Did you hear that, my hearts? Was it not a well-spoken threat?"

The Feasters grinned, and one leper spoke in a hoarse voice. "Not veiled in the least, Father."

"How charming," he said. "A man can never tell how much a woman cares about him until she threatens his life."

"You are mocking me," I said.

"I mock your faux pas," he said, his tone still impossibly even and collected. "Only threaten those you know, or you may not hit upon what they most fear. You see, those five automatons outside could not catch me, should I ride away on Eyebiter, and even if they could, they still would not kill me."

I peered at his face for signs of trepidation or dishonesty, but only his left cheek quirked, hinting at amusement. He had to be a master at self-suppression.

"The Bright Palms would never let you live," I said.

"They may be heartless, misinformed fools, but they mean well," he said, "and it'll not be a better man who kills me, but a worse one. My living harms fewer than my death."

"The argument of a carrion bird."

"Enchantress Hiresha, have you ever considered why Feasters—why my children—never break into homes? Never cast through windows?"

"The implication is that you forbid them?" I considered it remarkable how fast I had thought of that reply.

"I care for my children too much to give them what they want. But on the night of my death, my sons and daughters will celebrate by breathing terror through keyholes and killing thousands in their beds."

I was sure of it now: He was delaying, while my heart hammered my ribs at an unsustainable pace, and heat built inside my gowns to the point where I clung to consciousness.

"Maid Janny, pick up the ottoman. Unless this fop speaks of the pregnancies, we are leaving."

Before my gowns could finish sliding off my seat, Janny hefted it and ran out of the inn.

The Lord of the Feast stood. "Before going, you should know that though I am safe from the Bright Palms, these, my seven dearest children, would be strangled. If they come to harm, then tomorrow, on the capital building in every nation, words painted in blood will tell how enchantresses cannot cast spells when awake. That they sleep naked with every sword they enchant."

My heart stopped mid beat, and for two-thirds of a second, I feared it would never start again. Then it bludgeoned my insides while my mind reeled, scrambling for a clue as to how he could have learned of our shame. I felt as if he had robbed my thoughts.

He continued. "Each department chair in the Mindvault Academy will receive a letter detailing how you broke the Propriety Pledge, resulting in the death of one Faliti Chandur."

I faced him with open mouth and tearing eyes, wishing he could have done something more civil, such as threatened my life.

"Don't look so surprised. I have many children, who smell fear in many fascinating flavors." His tongue peeked out to touch his upper lip, which was painted a deep red. "I feel I've forgotten something. What was it? Ah yes. Without my intervention, the women of Morimound will birth fiends that will enslave this city for twenty generations."

A jolt ran down my spine while tears mixed with sweat in my eyes. "What will they birth? How must I stop it?"

The Lord of the Feast nodded to the woman beside him, and her rat-bone hands drew a folded handkerchief from his coat pocket then lifted it toward my damp face. Spellsword Deepmand held up a gauntlet to block her from touching me.

The crimson-suited lord closed his eyes, for a moment. "The Bright Palms are moving away from the inn. You should go."

I wiped my face with my gloves. "I cannot depart until I know how to save my people."

"Elder Enchantress, we should leave."

"Listen to your spellsword. He is wise with fear."

I needed the Lord of the Feast's information concerning the mass pregnancies. I wanted it more than fistfuls of rubies. However, I had a hard time focusing on him, as my heart had beat so much adrenaline into my blood that my vision blurred, and I could not risk crossing him further, not when he knew so much about enchantresses.

On the way out of the parlor, I stumbled over my gowns and would have fallen on my head if not for the cane. When I reached the carriage and found myself still alive, I did not faint. I merely fell asleep extremely fast.

In my laboratory, I realized that my heart had almost exploded, and I had nothing to show for it. I wanted to believe the Lord of the Feast had bluffed his way out of my threat by denying that the Bright Palms could kill him, yet I had not spotted evidence of the lie and still could not in the mirror.

He might have spoken true, and if so, my errors in judgment had offended the one person who seemed to know anything about these pregnancies.

CRUMBLING
-25-

"You faced the Lord of the Feast and didn't scream or nothing." Maid Janny padded my brow with a damp cloth. "Are you made of marble?"

"I believe I did sweat," I said.

"No more than normal."

My less-than-erudite statement left no doubt that fatigue once again clogged my mind. I staggered into my manor to see a servant woman stooping over her belly to sweep crystal from the broken windows.

"My girl, did I not tell you to leave those shards alone?"

"I'm sorry. I didn't know you wanted me to."

Now that I squinted at the woman, I noticed her sickly complexion and spindly limbs, which seemed inadequate to support herself without the help of the broom. She was Alyla, whose mother I had killed.

After swallowing twice, I said, "Alyla. Ah, what are you doing here?"

"Our house was empty, except for Yash, and mother never liked me being alone with him." She held the broom handle before her as if she could hide behind it. "I guess we weren't alone. Mother was still there, in a way."

"Has the bricker laid her in the floor yet?"

I regretted my words as soon as tears welled over her lashes to roll down her cheeks. She wobbled her head from side to side.

"We couldn't pay him, the bricker said he wouldn't do it for less than five silvers. It'd be a bigger job, he said, because of her tummy."

"Mister Obenji will attend to the arrangements." I reached out to pat Alyla's arm for comfort, yet I was uncertain that would be proper, as her mother had died because of my negligence. I cringed; feeling like an inch-long splinter had been shoved under my thumbnail.

"I'm so glad my brother isn't here to see this." Her tears dribbled onto her belly.

Maid Janny stepped up to her and hugged the girl, making the motion seem natural and easy. Of course, Janny had an unfair advantage over me: I could not hug anyone in these gowns.

I offered what support I could by gripping the sleeve of Alyla's blouse. The gesture seemed wrong, somehow. "You may stay here, of course. However, keep away from those shards. If you slipped and fell on your baby, er, I mean, I do not like to think what could happen."

"I will! Thank you, I will! Oh, should I call you 'Miss Flawless?'"

"Absolutely not," I said. "Wait, where is your father?"

"He's down in Stilt Town."

"Why is he not with you?"

"He said...what he said was he had to break your wall."

"The Flood Wall?"

A memory smashed into me of Abwar of the Ever Always leading a mob downhill, and I wondered if it had happened yesterday or today. I wished to believe the mob had since come to its senses and dispersed.

"Deepmand, can you see the Flood Wall from here?"

"I admit a suspicious amount of dust in that direction, Elder Enchantress."

"Drive me there. Morimound cannot lose its greatest defense."

On the ride downhill, I dreamed of my meeting with the Lord of the Feast. He had mentioned that the mass pregnancies would lead to the enslavement of Morimound, for hundreds of years, which sounded like the doing of a god. I hoped he was mistaken about that or had lied. I might not be able to detect his prevarications due to the control he kept over his face: Not once had I spotted signs of fear, even during mention of the Bright Palms.

Stilt Town swarmed with men, and ladders piled against the Flood Wall. Pick-axes swung, and hammers broke off stones piece by piece, which were then stacked into baskets on pulleys. I could not believe what I was seeing. Morimound was destroying its one hope; without the wall, the Seventh Flood would come in only a matter of time, maybe as soon as next month. I tried to tell the men this, in a calm and dignified tone.

"Morimound faces sufficient disaster in the mass pregnancies. We must not remove the Flood Wall."

Few heeded me, amid the shouts of, "For your daughters!" and "Unwall the wall!" Mud prevented me from leaving the carriage, as did my shaking muscles and lightheadedness; the exertions of my heart at the morning's meeting had left me exhausted.

I needed the city guard to stop the disassembling, yet most of them manned the pick-axes and carried away baskets of rubble. Neither could I gather much support from the acolytes; many gathered around Abwar of the Ever Always as he sacrificed oxen, goats, chickens, and even pet dogs. The bloodied mud surrounding him sickened me.

Dark stains and grime covered his green and white robes. "The wall is spittle in the face of the Ever Thriving, Always Dying! We are not above His will! Forgiveness will come only when the wall is ground to gravel."

The possibility that my wall had angered a god heated me into a stupor. An irrational fear grew in me that I would sweat until my tissues shriveled to nothing, like the fleshless Feasters I had witnessed today.

Even after I regained my aplomb, the guards would not listen to me, and neither would the civilians, perhaps for good reason. I pictured the Loom of Life, where a black thread of my fate severed all the other strands in Morimound's weave. My wall might have doomed the city, as could my dealings with the Lord of the Feast.

I knew I could concede nothing to him, should we ever meet again. If we did reconvene then I would have another chance to detect his lies, and I could not afford to miss any information that might save Morimound's women. In addition, I wished to test whether I would have the same physical response: A surfeit of adrenaline had evoked greater wakefulness than I had ever felt outside my dreams.

"Elder Enchantress," Deepmand said from the carriage door, "I must insist we return to the manor before sunset."

His concern was reasonable, as encountering the Lord of the Feast at night would place me entirely in his power. His presence in Morimound unnerved me to no end; every dusk would be like sleeping on an executioner's block, wondering if the axe would fall and he would attack the city.

More Bright Palms could counter him, yet summoning them would require time and—given his reaction today—would likely infuriate him.

As the carriage skated over the city streets, I watched the sky. It changed to pink, and I began to resent the pedestrians slowing me. Children flocked across the street, playing a game in which they touched a brick from each age in the city's history. Dots of glaze marked the clay blocks, with blue for the Seventh Age, green for the Sixth, and so on. The children scrambled everywhere to find the older bricks, which bore marks of red and black.

I shook my cane out of the window. "Go home. Your mothers will be worried."

Women at a well set down their urns of water to shriek at me. "There she is!"

At first, I thought they approached to thank me, or compliment me, yet they beat the sides of the carriage with their fists and shouted without any social nicety.

"What have you done to us, Enchantress?"

"Do we carry the seed of the Always Dying?" A woman clawed at her own belly, weeping. "Can you tell us that much?"

I cowered as far back in my carriage as the silk harnesses would allow, unable to say anything.

By the time we crossed into the Island District, the sky had darkened to red, and the lanes had all but cleared. We raced through parks alongside flowers closing their petals for the evening, and I discovered my left hand to have a death grip on my cane.

The sun had dipped out of sight behind the banyan trees, yet I still believed we would reach the manor before it set. A cadence of hooves on bricks behind the carriage prefaced a rider passing us, yet I did not recognize the implications of the man until I saw his lurid red coat.

REFORMED

-26-

"Enchantress Hiresha, I request your presence in my realm." The Lord of the Feast leaned from his saddle toward my carriage window. "I must show you something."

My heart began to race, and I banged my cane against the carriage roof to urge Deepmand to drive the horses to a gallop.

The Lord of the Feast said, "Can you outrun your fears?"

The thudding of my blood began to clear my mind, and I remembered that Feasters grew more dangerous if one fled from their magic. I glanced at the sunset, wanting to think that the Lord of the Feast could not cast during both day and night, despite what rumor told. I wished to disbelieve it so much.

In trying to escape, I might die, yet by following the Lord of the Feast, I endangered many. I did not know which peril should be preferred, yet I had to choose.

"Spellsword Deepmand, slow the team to a walk."

The fop's horse lessened his pace as well, and the animal gazed in at me with a single black eye.

I straightened myself, pulling my arms from their harnesses. "I cannot follow you into your realm. My place is in Morimound."

"It's not far." He nodded to the purpling sky. "Just ten minutes away."

With deep breaths, I hoped to keep my heart rate below the point where my teeth throbbed from excessive blood pressure. Being under the stars beside the Lord of the Feast was the most frightening experience I could imagine, yet after his threats in the inn, I believed a refusal might endanger more than merely myself.

By agreeing, I reasoned, I might gain some concessions. "First, tell me why I should trust you."

"I keep all my promises." The corners of his eyes creased in amusement. "A man's death threats are only as good as his word."

"Then, will you swear to my safety in the night?"

"My children will not harm you, except with my leave."

"That is no assurance at all!"

"The key to keeping one's word is to never give it."

I wished for my magic. If I could enchant when awake then I could protect myself by Lightening him to the weight of cattail fluff and letting the wind carry him away.

"Spellsword," the Lord of the Feast said, "I believe there is a perfectly dreadful fountain on your next left. Be a good heart and drive to it."

Over the clop of hooves, I heard Maid Janny weeping and Deepmand trying to comfort her. The carriage stopped near the sound of water trickling. When my hand opened the carriage door, I noticed my fingers did not shake; I had settled into the serenity of knowing that my fate this night had been decided by a goddess before my life's first breath.

In the fountain, water flowed between miniature ziggurats and down hundreds of tiny blocks representing Morimound homes. It really was dreadful. Strangler fig trees surrounded the fountain, their trunks a mesh of root branches as if normal trees had partially melted, oozing down and spilling over each other.

The Lord of the Feast took a long step down from his saddle, without using his hands. The horse snapped his yellow teeth in my direction in a carnivorous manner then bent down to drink from the fountain.

I began, "Lord of the Feast—"

"Never call me that." His hands tensed into fists. In the blue light of my earrings, his coat had turned dark. "Not unless that is what you want to see. My name is Tethiel."

I was not about to call him by his first name, as a lady should only assent to that for the man she had married. "Well then...before your interruption, I wished to note that you once claimed we had much to discuss. Did you lie?"

"Not in the slightest. Oh ho!" His chin dropped to regard a moth that had landed on his coat's carnation. As its wings fluttered, their eyespots blinked at me in a most forward manner.

"Your magic could not have caused the mass pregnancies," I said. "They must concern you in some other way."

I followed his glance upward, after the moth, to find the sky sprinkled with stars. The muscles between my shoulder blades tensed.

"If you think about it," he said, his face solidifying back to a blank expression, "the worst a Feaster will ever do is scare someone to death. Morimound faces something less pleasant."

"The unchildren." I gripped the ruffles of fabric over my throat. "Are they the progeny of a divine?"

"I would humor you, Enchantress Hiresha, but I'm supposed to be angry right now."

If he was angry, I could see no trace of it in his calm demeanor. "Because of your mood, the women's lives will all be risked?"

The left corner of his painted lips dropped a seventh of an inch in sadness. "Enchantress Hiresha, nothing I do will be for the sake of your people, or you."

I had guessed his motives self-interested, yet to hear him say it outright in no way encouraged me. He would demand something, some boon in return for his aid, and I could only wait and worry what it might be.

My blue glow turned his powdered face to the color of a frozen corpse's, which spoke. "And here they are. Pall, Wane, Gorge, show the enchantress your mettle."

Shadows stood around the fountain, despite a lack of anything to cast them. One shadow sharpened in focus to become a handsome man in dandy clothes, who darted to Deepmand's side to kiss his bearded cheek, and when the spellsword swiveled in his armor to seize him, the man back-flipped into the darkness.

Another man wearing only velvet pants strode forward, his muscles threatening to tear open the skin of his chest and shoulders. If I was not mistaken, more muscle groups bulged in his arms than existed in humans. Behind this brute, a man-shaped creature with an exoskeleton of silver walked toward me like a metal insect, his face jutting with gold fangs and antennae, his jeweled sword locked in the grasp of his gauntlet hand.

The sword and attached gauntlet forced my mind into contortions; I had seen both early today, on a decrepit leper who should have had barely the strength to lift a sword, let alone march while covered in silver. I recognized also the other two leprous dandies by their swords, although their once-halting movements had become smooth and confident, the stances of weapons masters.

The rumors had not lied. The magic of Feasting had cured the lepers, at least in appearance.

They grinned at me with their youthful, unblemished faces. I forced myself to overcome shock and sniff at the one who had kissed Deepmand, to indicate that his lewd display had not impressed me.

Earlier, the jeweled hilt of one sword had struck me as familiar, and I now saw why. The dandies flourished swords with sophisticated silver and gold etchings that glittered along their lengths. I recognized interlocking hexagonal patterns, along with stylized broken shields, and a panorama of the mountains south of Morimound.

"I enchanted those two swords for Bright Palms, and that one for a prince."

The first two swordsmen stuck out their tongues at the one with the prince's sword. For the silver insect, this involved a muscular pink appendage with spikes coiling in the air.

Seeing my enchanted swords in the hands of Feasters shocked me; I had eschewed empowering weapons and armor, whenever possible, because nothing better came of such immature devices than killing idiots in war. Now my swords might dismember my own people, perhaps even Deepmand and Maid Janny.

"Exquisite," the Lord of the Feast said. "Weapon crafting is not even your specialty, yet you surpass all other enchantresses. The lightness of these swords is a great help to my hearts."

I decided he was not entirely devoid of discernment. "My swords better utilize positional weight change. However, do not ask me to enchant any for you, as Academy edicts would force my refusal."

Pleading crept into my voice because the Mindvault Academy maintained records of all enchanted items, and any constructed outside of legality might be traced, giving the Lord of the Feast proof of my complicity and even more leverage over me.

"No," he said, "that would take the delight from finding them."

His words sickened me as I realized he must have an even more deplorable task for me planned.

The dandy brute said, "Bet the lady would like seeing me cut a tree in half."

He began to puff out his chest, breathing in the night air. His skin inflated, his abdominal muscles lost behind a potbelly filled with swirling darkness.

"No, Gorge," the Lord of the Feast said. "Purge yourself. Now."

The dandy leaned over, and shadows spewed out his mouth. The grove turned frigid, and I rubbed my gloved hands together.

"Restraint," the Lord of the Feast said. "Always restraint."

His horse half-kneeled and half-squatted, allowing him to step into the saddle without using his hands, and by this time I felt too overwhelmed to be further surprised.

"Enchantress Hiresha, I no longer feel safe in your city."

"You no longer feel safe?"

"I will be gone with the dawn."

Cracks of panic spread over my poise. He would leave me with no more knowledge of how to help the women. "Will you return?"

The Lord of the Feast peered down at me, and I feared he would give me an ultimatum, a task I could not accept in exchange for assistance I could not refuse. I hoped he would divulge it now, to end the suspense of not knowing what would be asked.

"The bone children were not created by a god," he said, "but by a man who would become one."

His horse reared, and he galloped off into the night. Shadows obscured the swordsmen, and the dandies disappeared as suddenly as they had come. My servants and I were alone in the dark grove.

Relief welled through me, even as my drowsiness returned to bow me over, and I hobbled back into the carriage. Maid Janny huddled inside, her hands pressed to her ears, and her eyes squeezed shut.

If the Lord of the Feast was not wrong then I could find this man, the mortal god. Evidence of him might reveal itself at my estate ball. I might save my city without further need of the Lord of the Feast; I hoped the threads of our fates would never cross again because, in a flash of mind-wracking pain, I realized what he quite probably desired.

He did not want me to enchant swords but to enchant him. Tales that I had regenerated nobility would have reached his notice, and he must have concluded I could replace his severed ears and teeth. I could even remove the tattoo on his brow, permitting him to better disguise himself, to escape the Bright Palms and to sow horror.

Acceptance of such a bargain would bring my ruin.

Once he committed another atrocity and the Bright Palms identified him, they would know what I had done. The world would realize I had assisted the Lord of the Feast, and all my enchantress colleagues would know I had ruinously broken the Propriety Pledge alongside him.

IMPENDING
-27-

Day Seventeen, Third Trimester

Alyla's complexion had improved over the last week and a half. She reclined on a chair, stroking her abdomen. "I was thinking of naming her 'Neema.'"

The fork spearing my quartered floret of broccoli quivered, and I had to set it on the table. "You might not want to name your, ah...after all, what if the baby is a boy?"

"I always wanted a girl," Alyla said. "I could sew her the most darling little dresses. Would Mister Obenji take me to the bazaar if I asked him? To look for cloth?"

"Absolutely not," I said.

Her father had not returned for her, and I had begun to wonder if something unfortunate had happened to him.

My appetite perished as a quavering spread outward from my stomach. When I rose from the table, Maid Janny placed my teacup in my hand.

"You should drink more, you only took three sips."

"Tea is insufferable in this weather."

"Don't try that excuse. This kettle was chilled."

"I cannot drink all this. I am too busy to stop every fifteen minutes to ask for a chamber pot."

As I set down the teacup, I realized the indelicacy of my last statement. Thinking had become even more impossible as late-spring rains had exacerbated the heat with humidity. Taking off my gowns would bring inordinate relief, yet I would never—not when they were all I had accumulated in life.

Through a haze of awareness, I saw Mister Obenji bow. "Elder Enchantress Hiresha, I am assured the new windows will arrive before the ball. Also per your request, I have interviewed several promising young men to play the parts of women servants and guests. They will appear feminine, but not pregnant."

"Yes. Wait, did you ask me a question?" His words and their meaning wriggled from my grasp like oiled slugs, and I had already forgotten everything he had said.

He glanced to Deepmand before answering. "Of course. I asked if you could speak with the chef today, and I am thankful to hear you can."

I was annoyed at myself for agreeing to meet with the chef. Before heading to the kitchens, I checked on Sri the Once Flawless. She was sitting up in bed, the sheets jutting outward from her midsection as if she clutched a pillow.

"If you must confine me here," she said, "then promise to send Mister Obenji. I have not seen him for twenty hours."

"He is heavily occupied," I said.

"You are cruel, Hiresha."

Janny asked, "Have you been practicing?"

In reply, Sri winked.

My tongue curled in disgust. "It is unseemly for elders to woo."

Sri smiled, unabashed. "When I see Pallam Obenji twirl his cloud-white mustache, one side at a time, my heart feels like it will stop. It's never too late for romance."

"Maybe your heart will stop," I said, "if you continue to excite yourself with this nonsense."

"Have you noticed how he wears several rings on each hand, two on each of his little fingers? But you must have. At first, I thought to ask him not to be so ostentatious, but I think I will love him best just the way he is."

"Unless you have pains or emissions to report, I will leave."

Sri replied with no more than a sigh as she plied her needle to embroider blue thread into black cloth.

In the kitchen, only one oven burned, yet its heat combined with a sticky, suffocating scent of dough forced me to lift my gloved hand to hide my gagging. I never remembered feeling so nauseated by baking.

The chef waddled to me, a papyrus in one hand, his other tugging on the few remaining tufts of his hair. "Mister Obenji gave me a list of sixteen ingredients. Sixteen! I cannot orchestrate appetizers and seven-course meals for eighty people with sixteen ingredients."

"I should think that many courses would be redundant," I said.

"Fate Weaver, bite me! Just two spices on the list, chili peppers and garlic, and only muddies eat garlic."

"Garlic has numerous health benefits, and flax seeds are a spice."

"They taste like wood pulp."

"The objective of dining is nutrition, not taste."

The chef clutched the lobes of fat on either side of his neck. "You have no respect for art."

"I should have warned Mister Obenji against hiring an obese chef. You are clearly not objective toward food."

Maid Janny muttered, "Then you're clearly not objective toward gems, dressed like a royal treasury."

"Your extrapolations are unpardonable, Maid Janny."

"Excuse me, Madam Enchantress."

This new voice came from a one-armed man loading barrels into the larder, and I recognized him as the wine merchant. His remaining arm waved to the jewels on my gowns.

"Such masterful cuts! I was a gemcutter once, you know. They said I was the greatest in Morimound."

"Not with one arm." He could never have held the chisel and the mallet.

That arm dropped to his side. "My chisel slipped on the hundred and forty-seventh cut of a paragon diamond. I ask you, is it right that a man's livelihood should be ended because of something that happened in a split second?"

"Of course it is right." I thought of a fist-sized diamond, a faceted miracle sent by the gods and destroyed by a man's blunder. "If you marred a paragon diamond, then they should have cut off more than your arm."

His face turned as red as his nose. Veins descended his brows like bolts of blue lightning.

Spellsword Deepmand lifted a gilded gauntlet toward the merchant. "The elder enchantress meant no judgment. She merely has strong feelings toward gemstones."

By Deepmand's tone, I realized I must have said something offensive and unbecoming to my station. Inwardly, I groaned, wishing that caution outpaced my tongue. Embarrassed, I could do no more than nod to the merchant in apology before leaving the kitchens.

Outside, I oversaw the replanting of the gardens. Alyla and estate servants joined me in walking the grounds.

"These purple flowers do not quite match the hue of beryl jewels," I said. "I suppose I must be satisfied."

"I think it's pretty." Alyla bent forward to sniff the hydrangea.

"Careful," I said to her. "And, confound this heat!"

My head pounded, and I rubbed my temples, my fingers damp with sweat inside their gloves. Even with four servants waving fans at me, I sizzled in air choked with water vapor.

Although rain clouds gathered on the horizon, they would only increase the heat's stickiness. The storms terrorized me, each a reminder of the Flood Wall being deconstructed below. I could only hope that the Ever Always would have mercy and withhold his rainstorms next month.

"Oh, my!" Alyla said, accepting a bouquet of the purple hydrangeas from a servant.

"Flowers are a horrible gift," I said. "They only wilt and die."

Seeing Deepmand wince made me realize, to my shame, that I had erred again.

"But they're lovely now," Alyla said. "Thank—"

One moment, the girl was speaking, and in the next, I found myself in my laboratory.

A.E. MARLING

Unsettled in the break of continuity, I checked my latest memory. My mirror showed my eyes fluttering as I slumped, my chin hitting my cane.

I, Elder Enchantress, had fainted. Perhaps no one would notice, if I returned quickly.

The diamonds on the dais below my slippers separated as I Burdened myself, the jewels' sparkling formations stretching downward. With a snap, they returned to their place, and I remained in the laboratory. Consciousness eluded me.

Anxiety pained my insides as if I had swallowed gemstones with sharp edges. I worried that my gowns might be the death of me. Any water I Created in dream would have no bearing on the real world, as I could not add or subtract matter from reality but only change its weight and how it was bound together. An Attraction could save me if I gathered water vapor near my unconscious body into my mouth.

Selectively targeting airborne water with a spell that crossed the dream threshold would tax my abilities. I Created a silver ladle in preparation to hold the enchantment, yet in my desperation, I feared heat stroke might damage my brain before I could construct the requisite magic.

My amethyst flashed with people calling my name. I had a sense that my real gowns had become sodden, and I left the silver ladle floating to try fleeing the dream once more.

I awoke as water gushed over my head, and I lifted my drenched headdress to see Maid Janny reach for another bucket.

"Enough!" I said. "Enough!"

"Open your mouth," she said as she hurled the water at me.

Spluttering, I accepted help to my feet but had to bend over just as fast to vomit. Fortunately, Janny had a bucket in hand.

My gowns automatically Burdened dirt and water, which wicked off them. Soon I had dried enough that the weight of the water no longer immobilized me, and Janny led me into the manor for some shade and rest.

As I settled my arms into the silk harness, I noticed Janny taking the key out of the door. She closed it behind her and locked me inside.

Her shout carried through the keyhole. "You're not coming out until you promise to drink more."

"This is preposterous!" I sat up and drummed my palms against the door. "You cannot trap me in here. All the mothers' lives depend on me. Open this door. Deepmand!"

With no rescue forthcoming and not about to comply with Janny's duress, I settled back to sleep. I had procrastinated on something unsavory for far too long and now would attend to it.

Under the jewel stars shining through the laboratory skylight, I rotated my mirror parallel to the floor and gazed down to see a dream memory. A reflection of myself labored over the dying Faliti, her belly half-translucent from the enchantment of my blue diamonds. During the procedure, I had manipulated and scanned the interior of the unchild but had sequestered it, rather than spending time analyzing its organs.

I wanted to banish the memory from my dream, yet I forced myself to peer inside it, to count the clusters of venom sacs surrounding the thing's beating heart. I identified the toxin as similar to that found in the bite of a coral snake, for which I had an antidote shelved and ready: an enchanted powder of emerald would neutralize the venom.

Within the unchild, the brain connected neither to brainstem nor to its internal muscles; this abomination would have no self-control. I found this curious yet not unanticipated. The muscles within the unchild had contracted at the moment when magic had invaded my dream from an outside source. A row of canine teeth had protruded on both sides of the oval of bone, digging into the womb for traction, while the halves of its shell had separated enough to revolve. Sharp bone edged the narrow ends, and one side of the ovoid had cut one way into Faliti, the opposing side slashing the other.

The sight gouged my insides with fear, hurting me as if I too carried an unchild.

The bone ovoid had shattered, the forces applied by its muscles and the womb greater than what the undeveloped bones could withstand. I had no doubt that by the end of the third trimester, the stronger bones of the unchild and its more complete mineralization of cartilage would allow it to slash its way out of the abdomen.

The old and the young need not have the strength to give birth; the unchildren would birth themselves, ripping out of their mothers and leaving them to die in blood.

My arm sliced through the air as I exiled the unchild from my dream. I felt foul, shriveled, and dead, mummified in my gowns.

The Lord of the Feast had claimed we would become slaves. I began to believe him because any man responsible for the unchildren would have dominance over Morimound; we could not resist his will in anything, or he would maul all our women, from the inside. The Seventh Flood could sweep over the city in seconds.

Whoever he was, this man wished Morimound's devastation. He hated the city, and I would find him at the ball among the foreigners. I would have to find him. Only, I was no longer certain I could control him.

UNINVITED
-28-

Night Thirty-Seven, Third Trimester

My life would culminate tonight.

My disease of somnolence had led me to the Mindvault Academy, where I had studied flatworms and salamanders, learning regeneration to finance studies of my unrelenting desire for sleep. Although I had eased others of their relentless weariness, mine had proven unresponsive because I had not been destined to leave the Academy yet. On the semester breaks I had surveyed midwives and assisted ailing mothers, hoping that one day I might journey on the same path of life.

The Fate Weaver had molded my thread into the pattern needed to save Morimound. She had given me knowledge and magic, and I had to believe they would be enough to free Morimound's women of the unchildren.

The last guest had arrived at my manor. The sun had set, the doors locked and bolted. I strode among the dignitaries of other realms, my gowns fluctuating in small air currents and appearing to grab at any who strayed too close.

I was flustered with the foreigners crowding my rooms and lounging on my furniture. Anything they scratched, I would have to replace.

The men wore gossamer linen or flowing robes embroidered with dancing monkeys. Plants from Nagra's magical gardens interwove their collars and sleeves, fat flowers sickening me with their weight of perfume.

Their wives were no better, some infested with jewelry childishly modeled after insects. Other women boasted vines that curled around their fingers and held their drinks for them.

I had a boy at my side with an effeminate face, and he wore the dressings of a proper woman, complete with interlocking designs of henna up his arms and legs, bracelets and anklets jangling, gems braided into his hair, and his brows painted violet and tufted after the elegance of purple-crested lourie birds.

I asked the guests, "Are the women of Morimound not beautiful?"

My sagging eyelids opened long enough for me to catch the reactions toward my womanly boy. Later, I would analyze their responses in my laboratory for surprise, suspicion, and animosity, as the guilty party would expect every woman to be pregnant. A few other boys sashayed about in blouses and skirts to emulate the wives of Morimound's higher society.

My eyes shut and refused to open; I wondered how I could stay awake another moment into the night. My gowns prevented me from pinching myself to alertness.

"Elder Enchantress Hiresha." Mister Obenji's voice sounded next my ear. "There is a gentleman outside. He claims to have arrived late."

I forced open one eyelid. "You told me all the guests were present."

A.E. MARLING

"I did. And you previously admonished me to refuse this individual's entry to the estate."

"If he was not invited then he has no business here. Direct him to wait out the night in the gardener's shed."

"He protests an oversight, that you must have meant to invite him. An Ambassador Tethiel, and his daughter."

The name connected in my mind with a jolt, and my heart lurched into an escalation of beats. I bowed my head, my headdress hiding what must have been a horrified expression. I followed Mister Obenji's feet into the hall, Deepmand behind us.

"Mister Obenji," Deepmand said once we had reached the gold-leaf stairs above the door, "if I could have a word alone with the elder enchantress."

The aged servant left, while Maid Janny stayed and was duly ignored.

"Elder Enchantress," Deepmand said softly, "you must not allow *him* into your manor."

"I would be better to refuse and anger him?"

"You and your guests could be harmed."

My thoughts were quickening, and I felt almost awake. "He could frighten them from outside just as readily. His illusions penetrate walls."

"Appeasement encourages more demands."

"The women of Morimound cannot afford more enemies."

He held his voice respectfully quiet. "When will you refuse him, Elder Enchantress? If not now?"

My answer terrified me too much to be spoken aloud: When the unchildren are gone and my city is safe. I wondered if I would truly accept any demand to achieve those results.

I started down the stairs, yet Maid Janny backed away. "Not going down, no thanks, not if he's there. I'll be in the kitchen, comforting the wine barrels."

With her gone, I had to slide open the door's viewing window myself, and the exterior of its silver bars reflected crimson from the glare of an ostentatious coat. The Lord of the Feast waited on my doorstep, and he must have recognized my eyes.

"Enchantress Hiresha, allow me to present the debutante Physis, my daughter. May we come in?"

A woman sparkling with spinel jewels had her arm locked around his, her low-cut, jeweled gown shamelessly derivative of enchantress fashion. Her features reminded me of the Feaster woman who had sat in the High and Dry Inn's parlor couch, as if the two were sisters—one stricken by a lifetime of poverty and hunger, the other boasting the curvaceous health and confident gaze of a woman in her prime.

"I cannot invite into my home people of your sort."

"You have nothing new to fear," he said. "Physis has already played the mouse inside the Mindvault Academy."

With two fingers, she pulled down the corners of her full, crimson lips for an exaggerated frown; her teeth were painfully white and appeared subtly too sharp. "You wear such a sorry face, Elder, in your sleep."

I happened to know I did frown in my sleep, in concentration. My insides twisted at the thought of a Feaster leering over me in bed. I recognized that elements of her face were similar to the novice Kally, who had gone missing from the Academy and was assumed to have made the mistake of throwing herself off a cliff. She could have crept the halls at night and spied on me for years, concealed as long as she had controlled her urge to Feast.

Nonetheless, I said, "You have no place at this ball."

He said, "We could always find another way to amuse ourselves in this city, at night."

I imagined him slipping illusions of snakes down chimneys, maybe even tricking people to think their homes were shaking and collapsing down onto them. I glanced past the gilded stairs, toward the ballroom. "Would you promise to harm no one? And none of the furnishings."

"My word is worth the lives of many men," he said, "and I swear we'll harm no one. Unless we must."

Closing the peephole, I leaned my brow against the door. Deepmand made no move to unlock it, and I had to shove the bar open myself.

"You may enter," I said.

The lady Feaster lifted a corner of her skirt with two fingers and walked inside with a deftness she had lacked during the day. I accompanied her and the Lord of the Feast to the ballroom, gnawing my lip as I remembered stories of Feasters causing mayhem at nightly gatherings. It was a small consolation to know that "Physis" had never harmed me in the Academy.

After Mister Obenji had introduced them to the guests, the Lord of the Feast turned to his companion.

"Now, my daughter, mingle but no *dining*."

She leaned closer to him, running her long red nails over his throat. "Get stabbed and die, Father."

The lady Feaster swept over the reflective marble floor, guests parting around her then trailing behind like papyrus scrolls caught in a winter gust.

The Lord of the Feast stepped beside me. "Is it not grand for one's children to have your well-being foremost in their thoughts?"

"I would not know."

I strode away from him, toward a dais fashioned after the one in my laboratory, although this one merely had clay tiles shaped in diamond designs. Standing atop the platform, I cleared my throat because, with the Lord of the Feast here, I had wakened enough to remember what I should have said at dinner.

Deepmand clapped his gauntlets together, and the smashing clang drew all eyes to me.

"I welcome you to Sunchase Hall, on the eve of the Flood Moon. Morimound will observe a month of silence in remembrance, rain being the loudest sound in the streets. Tonight, however, we will have music."

While musicians plucked out some manner of racket, attention drifted from me and chatter resumed. A guest sauntered to the Lord of the Feast. "Ambassador, am I to understand your carriage broke?"

I worried how this conversation would progress.

"Were you trapped out at night?" asked one woman. "I'd be deathly scared."

"I was deathly bored," the Lord of the Feast said in his restrained tone, "and uncertain whether attending a ball would worsen that condition. Of course, I found myself surrounded by Feasters, which settled the matter. Nobody is more tedious than those who talk of nothing but their last meal."

Instead of recoiling in terror, the women tittered, and the men slapped Tethiel's back. I told myself not to be surprised that his flippancy tickled their infantile minds.

Although I tried to ignore the Lord of the Feast's chatting, I could not take my eyes from the lady Feaster; men seemed unable to escape her, and clusters of them begged her to dance. Perhaps they misinterpreted her hungry smile and brazen stare. She might subliminally elicit a fight-or-flight impulse, which their base minds misinterpreted as arousal.

Her ostensibly enchanted gown no doubt drew them: Its jewels changed colors as she moved, from red to green to blue to black. The gems cycled hues in the opposite direction she spun, making them appear to be bright insects scuttling over her silk.

The neglected women clustered, whispering and smiling behind their hands while flicking their eyes to the Lord of the Feast. They touched their scarab amulets out of nervousness, some giggling, and approached him in groups. I wondered at their attraction; the curiosity and uniqueness of his mannerisms apparently overcame their inadequate minds.

"He rode in after dark," one woman said as her group passed me on the way to him.

"And he didn't look at all frightened. My Brendock would've soiled his robes."

"He couldn't be a Feaster, could he?"

"What a dreadful thought! I hope I'm the first he asks to dance."

I judged that while the possibility of his being a Feaster appealed to the women, any certainty of the truth would repel them. Snorting at their childishness, I glanced at the Lord of the Feast. He possessed more than a fearless gaze, I granted. Slack shoulders aside, his features brought to mind portraits of kings, not the overfed and inbred variety but the pedigree who conquered lands with bands of dauntless followers and proclaimed themselves sovereign.

As two groups of women closed in on the Lord of the Feast, he protected himself by stepping to the center of a group of men and directed their conversation toward me.

"The Enchantress Hiresha surely can tell us," he said. "Is it true 'Morimound' means 'Hill of the Dead?'"

"Yes," I said. "In reverence to those whose lives ended in the six floods."

His voice remained unassuming. "My children tell me you bury your dead within the walls of your homes."

"Because we are civilized," I said. "Rain torrents unearth any buried in the ground, and only heathens use pyres."

"Still," he said, "the perfume of the dead must linger."

"It is the scent of mourning."

"That strikes even me as rather macabre."

From atop my dais, I scowled down at the Lord of the Feast and the surrounding foreigners. His circle included a Morimound merchant, who had already inebriated himself. The man kissed the boy mimicking his wife with entirely too much enthusiasm.

The Lord of the Feast interrupted this offensive display. "Do you ever fear the deceased will break through the bricks and rise up in your homes? I'm sure to have such a nightmare."

"Do not answer him," I said. "You will ask no more questions of that nature, Ambassador."

"As you wish."

A woman cleared her throat in prelude to introducing herself to him, yet he continued to speak to me.

"I also know, Enchantress, the meaning of your name. 'Hiresha' is 'the queen of gems.'"

The Lord of the Feast surprised me not insignificantly, as few enough people in Morimound considered the meaning behind my name, and never foreigners. He must have had his Feasters creep around until they found its meaning.

"My father was a diamond polisher," I said by way of explanation.

The sweating head of the Morimound merchant wobbled and rolled as he tried to focus on my gowns. "Whysh no diamondsh? Lots o' color. Lots and lotsh. Too goodsh for diamonsh?"

"These yellow and green jewels are diamonds, as are these blue ones." I touched my earrings.

"Yesh, but you aresh the Flawlesh. You should haves flawlesh diamonsh."

"I am merely an enchantress. And the color impurities grant the jewels metallic properties, increasing their enchantability."

"Diamonds are like people," the Lord of the Feast said, "only the flawed can be flawless."

I glared at him. "Why must everything you say be nonsensical and offensive?"

"The truth, I fear, is ever thus."

He appeared oblivious to his rudeness in distracting me. I should have been attending to the expressions of my guests.

A foreigner coughed into his hand before speaking. "Madam Enchantress, I have never heard of blue diamonds. Yellow ones, yes, but not blue."

"They are rarer," I said, scanning faces in the crowd. Salkant of the Fate Weaver detached himself from an adjacent circle of conversation and began listening to the group gathered around me. The priest had attended alone, without a woman mimic, as his wife had died in childbirth years ago.

"Is blue the rarest color?"

"No," I answered the foreigner. "Diamonds are the tears of the Ever Always, the hardest substance on Loam. They fall from the sky—"

Priest Salkant lifted an arm then made a fist. "And should falling diamonds pierce to the center of the world, the Fate Weaver would crush them in one of Her eight divine hands."

"The force would turn a diamond pink." I finished for him.

I had slept with a diamond in my hand, trying to change it to pink with massive internal Attraction. Sadly, my grip was weaker than a god's.

"Silver diamonds are rarer than pink," Priest Salkant said.

"True," I said, giving up on checking faces for the moment, "yet I theorize that if the goddess holds a diamond longer, if more of her force channels into the jewel, it will redden. A red diamond would be the rarest."

"Enchantress Hiresha, my heart," the Lord of the Feast said, "when you speak of jewels, your eyes shine like diamonds."

I turned, not wishing him to stare into my eyes. "That is impossible. Human eyes can never attain a diamond's luster."

No one before had ever compared my brown eyes to diamonds. Brown diamonds did exist, and I felt an urge for a mirror, to compare the hues.

A woman nodded to the Lord of the Feast and whispered to her friend, loud enough for everyone to hear. "If I had as many jewels and silks, he'd be fawning over me."

"A lace chaser, to be sure," the other hussy said.

They could have only meant to provoke him and draw his attention, and I hoped he would acquiesce and stopped pestering me. I worried what people would say if he stayed nearby the entire night.

"In distant lands," the Lord of the Feast said to me, as if the women had not even spoken, "they believe when a dragon swallows a diamond, the furnace in its gullet bakes the gem red."

"I had not heard of that." I felt close to exploding with exasperation.

Forcing my gaze away from the Lord of the Feast, I examined those dancing with the boys dressed as women. My heart beat at over twice its normal rate, and I could read some facial expressions, although none were incriminating.

My attention continued to slide to the lady Feaster, at how the jewels on her gown sparked and shifted colors as she spun from the arms of one man to another. The gems had to be an illusion. She licked her lips at some of her partners; instead of repelling them, her vile behavior lured more.

I wondered how the men would react if they knew they were dancing with something of more bones than flesh. They lifted her with ease yet gave no sign they clutched the sharp ridges of her ribcage, nor did they shrink back from the touch of her skeletal hand. To them, the illusion had to be compelling.

For a moment, I allowed myself to imagine that the same magic would banish my sleepiness, would turn me into the same affable dance partner. Swallowing, I set aside the idle thought.

My silence had caused the guests to disperse, and apart from Deepmand, the tiles surrounding me were empty space. The Lord of the Feast strode into the clearing to avoid a crowd of women. He said, "My daughter is well behaved tonight."

I lowered my voice, hoping the other guests would not step closer to hear. "Have you not even a spicule of shame?"

He whispered, "I try not to indulge in shame."

"There lies the weakness of your character."

"Then I wish I was weaker."

"You mean, you 'wish you were.'" I made no attempt to hide my smugness at correcting the Lord of the Feast. My satisfaction diminished when he gave no sign of embarrassment. I realized that most everyone was watching, although at least they stood too far away to hear us.

"We do all have our failings. And yours, Enchantress Hiresha, is dishonesty."

"I have no such problem."

"Then why do you insist everyone call you 'elder?' You do the word injustice."

I had expected to be offended, yet not in this manner. He had no right to speak to me this way. Although I might be younger than I preferred people to treat me, the matter did not concern him.

"'Elder,'" I said, "is merely a title. Of deference, as unfamiliar as the term may be to you."

The pale blue of his eyes, I decided, most closely matched the absorption spectrum of aquamarine: not a particularly valuable variety of beryl jewel, I took pleasure in noting.

I swerved my attention back to the dancers, feeling increasingly agitated at the sight of so many engaged in this ritualized vulgarity. Whenever the lady Feaster held up her hand in protestation that she must rest to catch her breath, ten men pleaded for her next dance.

Worse still, the Lord of the Feast remained uncomfortably close to my dais, and the guests might misconstrue that I wanted him there. The thought locked my throat with humiliation. I braced myself to tell him to remove himself from my person, yet he spoke first.

"No point in putting it off any longer. We must dance."

HESITANT
-29-

"Dancing is a pointless activity," I said.

"Making it a necessity."

He spoke the ridiculous statement with the utmost seriousness. My heart rate surged, and all the heat of those in the room, along with the humidity, threatened to broil me. I remembered Deepmand's admonishment that every time I acceded to a request, I would have more difficulty refusing the next, yet I feared to give the Lord of the Feast a direct refusal.

"This room is thronged with women. Why would you ask me to dance?"

"Because no one else has."

"If you must stack nonsense onto falsehood, dance with your 'daughter.' You deserve her."

"Physis does whatever I say. Naturally, I can't abide her."

"I—I cannot dance." My composure sifted out of my wringing hands. "I must watch the guests, for signs of wrongdoing, you understand."

"Oh, for the would-be god? He won't be here."

I inhaled through my nose with such force that my head stung. "What? He must be."

"Scant chance of that. Too few of your people."

"He cannot be from Morimound."

"Why would he be a god of another city when he could have his own?"

I controlled my breaths, and the Fate Weaver spared me from heat stroke. Keeping my voice low, I asked, "How can you be sure he thinks of himself as a god?"

"That would make delightful dancing conversation."

The Lord of the Feast wanted to be seen dancing with me, I was certain, so he could later threaten scandal by revealing his identity. He must wish to control me, to train me to go along with his increasingly degrading requests. I wanted to hear him say so directly.

"I have difficulty imagining a man in your position, and physical limitations..." I glanced at his lifeless arms. "...dancing. There must be a reason."

He shrugged, the gesture exaggerated because his shoulders started and ended slumped. "After losing everything, one must either find enjoyment or die. And death is too easy."

His words rankled me, because I doubted he knew anything of true loss. He had immense power, in the waking world.

"These gowns prohibit my dancing," I said. "And how would you partake without lifting your hands?"

"A thing isn't worth doing unless it's impossible."

"Your self-conflicting statements demean the air with which they are spoken," I said. "It is impossible, and you need not have asked."

"I believe I could lift one hand and maintain control." He raised his voice and said, "And you needn't wear all those ridiculous gowns."

"Excuse me?"

I grew dismayed at the number of guests swiveling an ear toward us. If only I would turn to stone then I could be rid of the twisting feeling inside me. More than anything I wished to be gone, yet I could not flee my own ball.

"Your gowns are overdone. And I say that as a man with rubies on his shoes."

"I have never been so offended!"

"I am sorry," he said, "to hear it. You should have been offended more often."

"Well! Those are spinels on your shoes, not rubies."

I stomped off the dais with as much force as my slippers would allow, leaving the Lord of the Feast to the mob of foolish women. I wished I could banish him from my ball.

As I drew closer to the edge of the ballroom, my vision fogged as my heart slowed; I had spent so long beside the Lord of the Feast that I must have expended most of my adrenaline.

I found one of my mimic women, yet I could not remember to whom I had already introduced her...or him, rather. With no other choice but to risk appearing foolish, I presented him to everyone again; I hoped the words coming out of my mouth conveyed some manner of meaning because I was losing all awareness of them.

My cane slipped on the smooth tiles, and I stumbled. I accepted the first hand that offered assistance, yet as the gloved, misshapen fingers closed on mine, a chill shot up my arm.

The Lord of the Feast lifted me with one of his hands. "A gift for you, Enchantress Hiresha."

My pulse thumped in my ears, and the world snapped into focus with the shock of seeing that hand reach into his coat pocket. Having one arm raised strained him visibly; his other arm remained thrust downward, his shoulders trembling, and his porcelain teeth clicked against each other.

"In—in thanks—for you opening your lovely home to us." A gold chain snaked out of his coat, ending with a red jewel. "The king of gems, for its queen."

Although rubies were commonly referred to as "the king of gems," a glance told me the red jewel did not reflect enough light in the green part of the spectrum to be one. I was more concerned with all the eyes darting between us; the lady Feaster grinned with unmasked delight.

I could not accept a gift from the Lord of the Feast, in front of so many witnesses, least of all a jeweled necklace. Morimound men gave such jewelry to those they wished to wed.

As the jewel—a topaz, I judged—dangled before me, the white glove above it darkened. Blackness like spilled ink soaked out of his fingers. Although the guests might ignore it as a trick of the light for a few more seconds, I knew that his magic stirred. I needed to snatch the topaz, before his hand became something terrifying.

Deepmand gripped the hilt of his scimitar. The lady Feaster inhaled, the gowns over her belly beginning to expand. Her jewels darkened to onyx.

The Lord of the Feast likely did not understand the implications of a jeweled necklace. Even so, refusing meant risking the lives of everyone in my manor, as well as all the women of Morimound. I still needed his knowledge.

His black fingertips narrowed and elongated.

If gaining his aid meant accepting his every whim then I could not refuse him anything. I would have to dance with him. I would have to follow him to bed to regenerate him and perhaps even to commit further improprieties. He claimed that my enemy would enslave the city, yet he could do the same, through me. Once the world saw Morimound as his ally and despised us, we would depend on his Feasters for protection, or die when he abandoned us.

I would have to deny him sometime, and to do otherwise here would infect me with regret. I only hoped that he spared Alyla and Sri, who were hidden away in the manor's family rooms.

My tongue as dry as chalk, I struggled to form words. "You are wel—welcome to my home, Ambassador, yet I cannot accept this gift. It is inappropriate."

His hand dropped, and as the blackness seeped out of sight, I had to blink fast to avoid crying in relief.

I checked his face for anger. If anything, his brows crept upward in amusement.

"Many women wear such necklaces in Morimound," he said. "Or is the stone flawed?"

My voice was a whisper. "In Morimound, jeweled necklaces are engagement presents."

"What! You're sure? Pox me, of course you'd be sure, and I see my children have played a prank."

He glanced to a doorway, where the lady Feaster and her spinel gown slipped out of sight.

"I hope you will forgive them, Enchantress Hiresha. My children live in such misery, I can hardly begrudge them their mischief."

"Then you make yourself complicit, Ambassador. I bid you goodnight."

I had borne far too many shocks for one evening and needed rest.

"Should you search, you won't find me in the city," he said. "I will be gone with the dawn."

"That is the most pleasant thing you have said all evening."

My exhaustion caught up with me, my consciousness shrinking and darkening. Even as I strode out of the ballroom and into a hall, I felt myself sliding backward toward dream. I shouted, yet my words came out a mumble.

"Deepmand...take...sleep."

Servants and the spellsword assisted me to my room. I knew I had forgotten to say goodnight to my other guests, and a lady Feaster was still loose in my halls. Drowsiness pulled me down, preventing me from doing anything but descending the stair into dream.

By custom, my guests would stay until daybreak. If one of them had showed any confusion over the women mimics, I would catch him before he left.

CLANDESTINE

-30-

Night Thirty-Eight, Third Trimester

The Lord of the Feast had been right.

Search as I might, I found nothing in the miens of the foreigners to suggest that one was the magic user responsible for the unchildren. I was no closer to the truth than when I had begun.

Slipping out of sleep, I said, "I need...the ambassador."

Maintaining consciousness was a struggle. Drained, I felt I had not slept in weeks, and I continued to feel that way, even while sleeping through morning and into the day.

Maid Janny helped me eat, as I was unable to focus on my fork long enough to track its progress to my mouth. Nausea gurgled and fermented within me, from the stress of knowing I would have to seek out the Lord of the Feast. I could not wait for him to return in another month: Alyla and Sri would die by then in premature labor to the unchildren.

"There, there." Janny wiped my chin and gave me water with which to rinse my stinging mouth. "My enchantress will be better soon. I know she will."

I passed my time in the laboratory crafting jewels, even chancing upon a snow diamond. I cut it into a white stone of fifty-eight facets. While polishing topazes, I realized that the jewel the Lord of the Feast had tried to give me had been darker than pink topaz but lacked the orange undertones of red gems of that class. I wished I could have held it, to determine its relative weight; the stone might have been a variety of zircon, if it had been real and not illusion.

The indicator amethyst flashed, and I woke up, expecting to find Deepmand or Mister Obenji in my room with a lamp. Instead, the room was dark.

I waited for my earrings to rouse themselves. Their blue light shoved shadows into the corners as I searched for the one who had spoken my name.

"Hiresha."

The room burst with red and green light: Jewels on a scandalous gown blazed. I saw the lady Feaster grinning with fang teeth, ribbons of energy flowing from her hands in pulsing coils of color.

Surprise wrung all the air from my lungs, and I flailed, trying to free my arms from the harness.

"Shhhh!" Ropes of crimson power reached from her palms to caress my throat. "I am an invitation from the Father."

"An invitation?" I gasped for breath. "From the Lord of the Feast?"

"Yes, and he would love you to call him that to his face." She lowered herself against the door, sniffing close to the keyhole. "Whisper it in his ear, and then lift his hands to your breasts."

"I should think not!" Feasters were the most improper group of degenerates I had ever encountered, even more so than actors.

She opened the door and beckoned me to follow her into the hall. Instead of walking, she floated a foot above the ground.

"No proper enchantress can do that," I said. "Not in this world."

"Goody for me, I chose the stronger magic."

As she spoke, her glow faded, and the hall's shadows enlarged to cover her. Guards patrolled my manor at night, yet the Feaster guided me around the first two.

"Take off your earrings," she said from the darkness as another guard neared. "Oh, you're hopeless."

I scurried around the corner, yet twenty feet of gowns still trailed behind.

The guard called out. "Elder Flawless? Er, Older Enchantress? No, wait, er...."

"'Elder Enchantress,'" I said.

After he apologized and clomped away, the Feaster reappeared and led me outside the manor, into the rain. Her feet floated above the gravel path, gown fluttering. I frowned at her pretentiousness.

I asked, "Did you stay here? I mean, during the day."

"I'm good at finding dark places to hide."

The raindrops that fell on her chest shone with red light, glowing as they ran down her cleavage. If there was one thing worse than a Feaster, it was a gorgeous one. With my attention focused on her contours, I tried to bring to mind the gaunt figure last seen at the inn. I could not recollect her. This woman bore no trace to that woman, and of the two, the illusion before me seemed more real.

"You no longer have guest rights at my home," I said. I would prefer to find a nest of cobras in my wine cellar.

"Can't take those back, you silly prig." Physis pinched me, her nails sparking and popping with orange light. She motioned to a gazebo. "Wait in there."

Rubbing where she had shocked me, I trudged toward the gazebo. My gowns had begun to weigh down with rain. Droplets ran between my fingers; I had forgotten my gloves. I wished to go back for them, although that was out of the question. As I neared a garden statue, I noticed that it was not a statue but the dandy brute.

"Oh," I said, with all the eloquence I could gather.

He crossed his arms above abdominal muscles that bulged in twelve places, and water glistened like glass beads over his sofa-sized chest. I felt him staring after me as I scurried into the gazebo. The empty interior permitted me to drag inside the full train of my sopping gowns. Rain pelted the roof and formed curtains of droplets. I was rather exposed, without my gloves on, and for modesty's sake I hid my hands in my draping sleeves.

Two figures stepped into the gazebo, splashing in the puddles my gowns had shed. A swordsman pulled a cloak from the shoulders of the Lord of the Feast then left us alone.

"You promised to leave the city," I said, "yet here you are."

"I did leave, Enchantress Hiresha. Then I returned." His eyes gleamed in the blue light. "Time is dwindling. You discovered me with little trouble, and now you will ferret out the would-be god. I'll put you on his trail."

His confidence emboldened me to envision all the women with unencumbered bellies, free of unchildren. Anticipation of their safety fluttered up my spine.

I pulled my mind away from the future to the present danger clad before me in lace. "First, Ambassador...But I can hardly call you that, can I?"

"My name is Tethiel."

"And your last name? Your family name?"

"I no longer have one."

"How does a man lose his family name?"

"The same way he loses anything," he said. "By trying to save it."

His nonsense displeased me, although I was sorry to hear he had lost his family name. I recalled him saying last night that he had lost everything, and I wondered if this was what he meant.

Having but one name always made me feel impoverished. As a woman of Morimound, I had lost my family name at birth, and I would gain one only after marriage.

"Before we proceed," I said, "I wish to know the cost of your assistance."

"I never mentioned a price."

"You said you were not here for our sakes." I fought to hold my voice calm. "I believe you covet my regeneration services, and, if true, you will admit it now."

The Lord of the Feast glanced at one of the gazebo's benches, in which I had no chance of sitting. He remained standing.

"I do want to be whole," he said, "that's why I adopted Physis. Once she learned what you did in the Academy, what was involved, I realized it was impossible." .

Regenerating teeth and ears was easy enough. Instead of blurting that out, I lifted a brow.

"You would have to share my dream," he said, "and my nightmares would shatter your mind."

I very much doubted that, and he would be in my dream, not the other way around. Again, I was proud of how I held my tongue.

"You disagree?" He peered into my face.

My expression must have given away my thoughts. I felt compelled to speak, as if the Fate Weaver tugged on my life's thread.

"As novices, we defeat all our nightmares."

"But not mine." He gazed into my eyes now, and I had to look away. "You do not fear death, but that's not enough. No, quite impossible."

That the Lord of the Feast would have nightmares had never occurred to me. I exhaled a long breath, knowing I could keep my dignity and still save the mothers.

He turned away, facing the wall of rain. "I only want one thing. For you to find the man, so I may kill him."

Whether conscious of it or not, he had hidden his face from me at this critical moment. He might have just lied.

I asked, "What would you gain from his death?"

"This city is ripe with fear." He breathed as if savoring the rain-scented air. "And none of it was caused by me. I can't have someone more terrifying than I. It would ruin my reputation."

A spasm in my chest sent air bursting out my mouth. I thought I had sneezed, yet I could not recall my sneezes carrying such a high, ringing tone. No, I had laughed. The Lord of the Feast had tricked me into laughing over this serious matter. His manipulative rudeness had coerced me into neglecting the decorum of my offices.

"Your antics are inexcusable," I said, "and I insist you apologize."

"Do you?"

"Laughter is audible complicity, and you are wrong to evoke it in others."

"This is not a ballroom, Enchantress Hiresha. No one is judging you."

His words blended into the downpour. I glanced outside the gazebo but saw no trace of Feasters, or anyone else. I did feel quite isolated.

"We must always judge ourselves," I said.

"I leave self-judgment to the experts."

His right hand opened, and something glittered between two broken fingers. My eyes widened as I realized he held the red jewel from last night, although without its chain.

"But I will admit one thing," he said, "that I appreciate gems only as much as an illiterate appreciates illuminated books. Their language is lost on me, but to you, they speak."

My breath caught as the jewel dropped from his trembling fingers onto a wooden seat. He did not appear to have noticed his mistake.

"I also admit a certain clumsiness. Things slip from my grasp, and I forget about them. Truly negligent, wouldn't you say?"

I nodded, unable to find words. The jewel rested on the edge of a wooden slat, and I worried it would fall out of reach between the boards.

He stepped over my train of gowns to the other side of the gazebo, facing away from the gem. "Enchantress Hiresha, I will give you time to gather your...thoughts. Then we will speak of business."

I gazed from the back of his jacket to the shining stone on the bench. Last night, I had refused the jewel because it had been attached to an engagement necklace and because many would have witnessed my accepting a gift from the Lord of the Feast. Neither concern applied here.

Certainly, I could not allow such a jewel to be found on my person. I resolved it would not. After determining the composition of the gemstone, I would discard it.

Taking a step, I reached down with a naked hand and picked up the jewel.

My intake of breath betrayed my surprise at finding its relative weight less than a zircon's. I would have thought this a topaz, if not for the sharpness of its facet edges.

The lighting had turned the jewel dusky, and as it rolled across my palm, reflected sparks danced over my fingers. Its brilliance prickled my skin and stood my hairs on end, and the sound of the rain faded, the world dropping away to leave me alone with this jewel.

I thought I knew what this was, what it could be, if only it was not another illusion. I hoped beyond measure it was real.

My fingers closed over it, gripping the jewel so its tip dug into my palm. I hid my hand in my sleeve and waited for my mind to descend back to the realm of Morimound and the mass pregnancies. The Lord of the Feast turned, and our eyes met. I spoke first.

"You will dispose of the malefactor, once I find him?"

"One second after I lift my hands, he'll be highly distracted. You might even say terminally distracted."

"One second? You are certain about the interval? Sufficient, I should think. Very sufficient. Very...."

The chatter petered out as I wrested back control over my tongue. His words had shocked me, yet they also had consoled, in a way, because I had worried what I would do once I had caught the would-be god, afraid he would threaten the lives of the women carrying unchildren. He would not do much threatening in one second.

An inconsistency occurred to me. "Are you worried about the fanfare? You will have helped save a city. Would that not damage your 'reputation?'"

"If there is any fanfare, it will be yours."

After the word "fanfare," his chest had shuddered a miniscule distance, his ragged breathing evincing sadness. I wondered if he was sorry he could not partake in any celebration, or if something else grieved him.

"What do you mean by, 'if there is fanfare?'"

"My magic is not like yours, Enchantress Hiresha. No good can come from it." His stare never left my eyes, and he blinked only rarely, no more than once every ten seconds. "Should I try to help people, I would only harm."

"If there is no good reason to use your magic, why ever did you learn it?"

One fold of lace about his neck trembled, likely disturbed as he swallowed, an indicator of intense emotion.

A.E. MARLING

"That," he said, "I have not told even my children."

I could scarcely conceive of something so shameful that he would fear to speak of it to night-crawling degenerates. "Are you certain your magic can do no good? If by eliminating one man you can free a city from—"

"I can't dwell on any good it might do. Better for all to act selfishly. I will snuff out the Soultrapper because it benefits me and my adoptive family. Both causes, I assure you, acceptably undeserving."

"The Soultrapper?"

"Ah, yes. What do you know of Soultrappers?"

INHUMAN
-31-

"The treatise on Soultrappers was speculative, and, I had hoped, incorrect." Grimacing, I thought back to my general education course on the magics. "The manuscript claimed they imprison the soul of the dying in his or her own corpse. As the soul tries harder and harder to liberate itself from the decaying prison, the resulting soul pressure is appropriated to empower the spells of Soultrappers."

"I've never heard it called 'soul pressure' before," he said.

"Regardless, I fail to see the relevancy. Soultrappers control minds, not create unchildren."

"They corrupt minds, as well as other flesh."

The thought of a Soultrapper's magic festering in so many wombs spread a feeling of rottenness within me like black mold creeping over the inside of a yam. At the same time, both my empty hand and the one clamping the jewel tingled with the excitement of finally progressing; with the help of the Lord of the Feast, I would free Morimound from the Soultrapper.

"He must be very powerful," I said. "To have corrupted so many."

"Not yet. He will be, once the Bone Orbs are born."

"Bone Orbs?"

"That is what you found in the woman, was it not? A sphere made of a child's bones?"

"Yes. Why would their birth give more power?"

I thought of the presence I had felt as I examined Faliti. The Soultrapper had been watching me, had activated the unchild—the "Bone Orb"—to kill Faliti, as he would kill all the women unless we followed his commands. If anything, his influence would decrease when the Bone Orbs were born.

The unchild had contained a brain, I remembered, although one not connected to its nervous system. The brain would not serve any function, if the Soultrapper had created the Bone Orb as a weapon.

I wondered why the Bone Orb had resembled a child at all, with its shell of infant skelature, its own heart and brain. Venom sacs alone would have sufficed for lethality.

As those facts turned over in my mind, another thought occurred to me and my arms began to tremble, a cold sweat leaking from my palms. The jewel slipped an inch in my grasp. I had not eaten properly in several days, and I felt the deficiency, as though there was nothing beneath my skin to prevent my shriveling inward and collapsing.

"The Bone Orbs," I said, "they couldn't have souls, not like true children? You don't think the Soultrapper is using them as prisons?"

"Murdering is dangerous, corpses are cumbersome. Better to grow your own cages, and trick souls to enter them."

The feeling of hollowness spread upward from my chest, and the gazebo's pillars began to move and orbit me, the rain blurring between them. The Lord of the Feast smeared into a shadow stretching over my vision.

"But, there are so many," I said. "So many. They can't all hold souls."

I thought of the souls of children trapped in Bone Orbs, unable to move anything, ever, not a limb, not a finger. If they did not have a firm grasp of the wrongness yet, they would once born. Their lives would be a void. A prisoner in solitary confinement could at least reach out and touch the walls around him, hear his own cries, yet the unchildren would have nothing in the blackness except loneliness and desperation for escape.

"That is why I must kill the Soultrapper now," he said, "before the Bone Orbs are born and he gains the power of a god."

I had feared for the women's lives, yet the true danger was worse than I had ever imagined. My world felt as numb and dark as the consciousnesses of those imprisoned souls.

Realizing I was fainting, I first tightened the hand that had held my jewel, although I could not feel it now. My chin lifted upward, my eyes snapping open as I pitched face-first toward the floor.

The Lord of the Feast reached to catch my fall with one hand, and his fingers blackened and transfigured into things resembling claws, their razor points slashing through my sleeves and sinking into my arm to scrape the bone.

Pain whipped up my shoulder, my arm jerking away as white light flashed through my eyes.

"Hiresha!" He had let go of me, leaving me swaying on my feet, each fiber of my arm throbbing. "It was only—"

"Illusion." I stared down at my unripped sleeves, my arm unharmed. It had felt real, and I could see why his magic was deadly: Too much pain and terror could stop a heart.

A.E. MARLING

"I shouldn't have tried to help you." He frowned down at his clenched fists, which dribbled with blackness.

Worrying I might have dropped the red jewel, I opened my hand. The gemstone glittered alongside a triangular indentation in my skin. I snapped my fingers closed and spoke.

"We must locate the Soultrapper. Tell me how Bone Orbs are made."

"My children never discovered that."

"You said the Soultrapper was not strong yet. Therefore, he could not have used a spell with an area of effect. I believe he touched each of the women."

"Magic is always most potent on the touch," he said. "Even Feasters of small appetites can engulf a man if they catch him sleeping."

"Caught in bed or not, over fifty thousand women could not be touched by any small number of Soultrappers."

"There is never more than one in a city, though he may have followers," he said. "Enchantress Hiresha, your servants are searching for you."

Over his shoulder and through the rain, flickers lighted windows of the manor then winked out of sight, reappearing in the next room. The Lord of the Feast had not turned his head, and I wondered how he had known of the flurry of activity.

When the servants failed to find me, they would turn their attention outside, and I had no desire to see the Feasters confront Mister Obenji, Maid Janny, and especially not Deepmand. I would have to finish this conference quickly.

I asked, "The followers do not share the Soultrapper's magic?"

"They would be powerless, snared by dreams of power. The first of the Soultrapper's worshipers. When you search for him, look for a man of no great importance who nonetheless views others with a possessive eye and a sense of entitlement."

"Are you suggesting I examine every man in the city? Does it even have to be a man?"

A few lights had paused in the manor, at windows facing us. I worried that someone had seen the glow of my earrings in the gazebo.

"We have never found a woman Soultrapper," he said. "You should also know that it is a messy magic. A Soultrapper must use his own blood to inscribe a glyph onto a dying man, binding soul to corpse and corpse to Soultrapper."

I rolled the jewel between two fingers. "Thus, a Soultrapper would be comfortable shedding blood."

"His own blood," he said.

"I still do not see how he could have created so many Bone Orbs. Can you tell me nothing more?"

"Only that you must find him soon, and without further help. I'll be gone with the dawn. When you're sure of the Soultrapper, speak to Physis."

"I do not want her in my home."

A man shouted my name from a manor window, calling out for me as if for a runaway child. I believed it was Mister Obenji, and I would have some firm words with him.

"Physis will wait outside, at night," the Lord of the Feast said, and he moved away from the gazebo entrance and bowed his head, inviting me to leave first. "I wish you productive dreams, Enchantress Hiresha."

Still not knowing an adequate way of addressing him, I merely nodded and stepped past him. He did not move as my gowns rippled over his boots.

I stopped at the threshold of the gazebo, gazing out into the rainy night; in the light of my earrings, the droplets shone like falling sapphires. Each bead of water was distinct, yet I knew my mind would fog as soon as I left the Lord of the Feast and my adrenaline waned. I would plunge into weariness, unlikely to flounder to my feet until evening tomorrow.

"It is almost worse," I said, "to have flashes of clarity. When I sleep. And right now. Without them, I would not know how much I was missing."

He did not speak, although his eyes never left my face.

I held the jewel before me, between two fingers, its pavilion side up, and a raindrop shattered on its point. Despite all the time in my hand, the gem had remained cool. I wondered if it could be what I hoped: a red diamond.

It would mean I held the same jewel as had a goddess.

My fingers curled around it, bringing it to my chest. I glanced again at the Lord of the Feast, yet the intensity of his eyes forced me to look away.

"Your guards," I said, "does your magic truly cure them of leprosy? At least, would a person believe herself cured of her ailments, at night?"

The question shamed me, yet even if Feasting magic only helped the diseased at night, that still amounted to something. I could think of nothing I would not give for eight hours of lucid thinking, in which to converse naturally, in which to experience the world.

"How long have you wondered this, Enchantress Hiresha?"

My voice quavered. "For—for years."

Muscles in his face trembled as if starting to form into a cohesive emotion, yet he swallowed it down, and it was gone. "Then know, the beginning of the Feast is the beginning of regret."

I strode out of the gazebo, chin lifted so the rain would hide my tears. He had warned me against it. If even Tethiel could not recommend his magic then I would find no solace as a Feaster. He could have increased his influence over me by saying otherwise, by leading me on into shadows, yet he had not. My chest ached, although I could not say whether the feeling was relief from temptation, or despair of escape.

"Thank you," I said over my shoulder, yet I was not sure he heard me. I thought of him gazing after me as the path crossed through the manicured bushes.

My world contracted, my awareness narrowing to a simple desire not to wander into a lily pond. Curtains of sparkling droplets fogged into a wet darkness. I yelped when a hand seized my shoulder; I had not even seen the man coming.

"Elder Enchantress, what warp in fate's weave drew you out here?"

The bearded man wore a drenched shift and nightcap; an enormous scimitar was balanced on his shoulder. I had to blink twice more before I accepted this unarmored man as Deepmand: Only a spellsword could activate the Lightening enchantment in that scimitar.

I clutched the jewel out of sight. "You need not concern yourself with what I was doing."

His voice raised, his hands clenching. "How can I protect you, if you wander into the night?"

"I question that you can protect me at all. A Feaster was in my chambers."

"A Feaster? The lady Feaster you invited inside?"

"I do not like your tone, Spellsword Deepmand. And do you feel that your raiment befits a representative of the Mindvault Academy?"

His wet shift clung to his legs, and black hair bristled outward from his calves. Without his armor, he was diminished, appearing too similar to a man for my liking.

"You spoke with the Lord of the Feast, didn't you?" Deepmand glanced into the garden shadows with a sneer. "Elder Enchantress, you must have a guard of Bright Palms, or he'll be the death of you and this city."

I was no mood to be berated by anyone half-naked and hairy. "Deepmand, I will accept your advice the moment you provide an alternate method of curing Morimound."

On unsteady feet, I hobbled past him into the manor. Once dry and secure in my room, I freefell into sleep. I arose in my laboratory, with the red jewel lifted before my eyes.

A trigonal stone, the four major facets of its crown were curved to lend gentleness to the cut. With an average width of five eighths of an inch, it made for an impressive jewel, despite the subdued and off-white lighting of my laboratory.

A sapphire bobbed above the operations table, glowing, as did all the jewels I had Created. I Attracted it to my other hand and scraped it with the red jewel. A white groove etched down the side of the sapphire, and my hands trembled so much that I lost hold of Tethiel's gift; it dropped a foot and a half before I Attracted it back to my fingertips.

The red jewel was harder than corundum. I checked it for enchantment yet found nothing. This could be a diamond, and not just a false one Created in dream but a blessing of gods—a wonder, a treasure beyond price—which I could carry with me in reality.

One more test would prove it. My breath came in short gulps as I Attracted to my hand a silver diamond from a shelf. I activated it, and a ray of pure white light shot upward, extending through the skylight and into the night.

I moved the red jewel into the beam; the light bent as it entered a glassy facet. In that instant, I knew. The ray had refracted within the jewel to the characteristic angle of a diamond.

The red diamond shone with the color of rose petals held up to the sun. As more and more light pooled in the jewel, its facets lit the laboratory walls with triangle patterns, all spinning as the jewel revolved in the air between my fingers.

My dream city might forever stay locked in night, yet I felt in this moment the warmth of basking in summer's grandest day.

AFFLICTED
-32-

Day Thirty-Nine, Third Trimester

Drowsiness paralyzed me, and I was too tired to swallow whatever foul-smelling ooze Maid Janny spooned into my mouth.

"Even babes eat applesauce," she said. "Perhaps you'd rather have broccoli ground into a green paste."

I mumbled something then succumbed to sleep.

In my laboratory, finding the magic user seemed more impossible now than ever. I had expected Tethiel's information to lead directly to the source of the mass pregnancies.

Between examining the faces in my mirror of tailors and jewelers and other men whose professions allowed them to touch large numbers of women, I stole glances at the red diamond. I could improve its cut: Additional facets would throw more light back at the viewer's eye, at the cost of shearing off pieces of jewel from its pavilion end.

I resisted the alterations, knowing I would only have one opportunity to perfect the stone, and the moment could be better savored once Morimound's women were safe. Not to mention, the thought of diminishing the diamond in any way upset me more than cutting a gemstone ever had.

I forced my attention from the red diamond long enough to decide that the key to finding the Soultrapper lay in understanding the Bone Orbs and their creation. Summoning a replica unchild from memory, I scowled as it levitated above my operations table. When I had encountered the one unchild, yellow bands of cartilage had circumscribed each interlocking bone. The Bone Orbs would enlarge over time, and their external skeleton would replace the cartilage, bones fusing together to form something that looked like an eggshell with one groove running from end to end.

My prediction grew in front of me, leg bones twisting to fit between stretching ribs. I had a sense that I gazed upon some nefarious puzzle box of ivory: If I could find the right bone in the white jumble then I could open it and free my city.

A band of cartilage had divided the orb into halves, and the one I had witnessed had revolved along its yellow axis to cut Faliti. That young unchild had fractured. A quick prediction told me that most unchildren would grow solid enough to kill their mothers and birth themselves, without breaking, before the end of the month. Tethiel had not lied about running out of time.

I awoke struggling with my harness. The haze of my consciousness melded with my anxiety, producing a near delirium.

"Maid Janny! Maid Janny!"

"My, my," she said, unthreading my arms from the silk bindings, "you look all caught up, like a fly in a web."

"Not a fly."

"A butterfly then, by your color. Or a moth. Or a pack of moths and butterflies stitched together."

"Take me to Sri and Alyla," I said.

Janny guided me down corridors that I no longer recognized, into a guest room. I needed several seconds to reassure myself that the blurry figure in the bed was Sri and the one sitting on a nearby couch was Alyla. A third woman stood next to Alyla, a servant I had ordered to accompany the girl, as I deemed the risk too great for one so frail to move about the grounds alone. The sight of her and Sri alive reassured me, and I focused on Sri's long white hair, finding the Once Flawless sleeping with her mouth open.

"You were sick in your room for two days," came a girl's voice, confusing me until I localized the sound as originating from Alyla. "Are you feeling better?"

"No."

My eyes had steadied on Alyla, who sat on the heavily pillowed couch with a book propped on her belly, and I imagined the Bone Orb inside her revolving, blood spreading down her sides and over the cushions. I squeezed my eyes shut.

"I have a present for you," Alyla said, blushing down at the book in front of her. Without lifting her eyes, she held out a shawl embroidered with an iris, in purple thread. "Do you like it? This flower won't wilt."

"I regret saying that about the flower," I said. "How did you know that purple was my favorite color?"

My purple dress was buried under a menagerie of hues. The gown would be complemented well by my red diamond, a great loss to the global aesthetic that I would always have to hide the jewel.

In a rush of ear-popping panic, I realized I did not know where the diamond was. I opened one hand and found it empty. In my second hand, the jewel glittered in the moment before my fingers snapped closed again. The relief was startling.

Alyla glanced at the embroidered iris, her eyes shying away. "Mister Obenji told me I could pick anything I wanted, and the lady said purple was the most expensive."

I reached out for the shawl but stopped short of taking it. "I cannot wear that."

"Oh." Her face fell. "I suppose it doesn't have any gold embroidery, or silver lace."

A vague understanding that I had offended Alyla induced me to try to say something placating. "It is only that the shawl has no meaning."

She rubbed from her eye something that might have been a tear. I must have said the wrong thing again.

"I'm so sorry," Alyla said. "I only wanted to give you something, Miss Elder Enchantress. You've been so good for taking me in."

Trying to help her understand, I pointed to my gowns. "I wear only achievements. Each of these means something. The maroon one is most hours slept in a day. The teal is highest leap. The black with gold thread is greatest force of Attraction."

Maid Janny snickered. "What was that last one?"

I spoke over her. "You are not at fault that your gift is meaningless."

Alyla sobbed and kept repeating herself. "I'm so sorry. I'm so sorry."

I felt like crying, too, and wondered if I should keep silent forever lest I again offend someone as sweet as she.

My struggle to think how to comfort her was eroded by thoughts of the Bone Orbs ripping from her and Sri, the unchildren tumbling out to roll over my ornate rugs. I clenched my red diamond until it cut skin, knowing that Alyla's small size would throw her into labor prematurely. She would die of childbed fever, or of womb lacerations, and if I tried to help, then the Soultrapper might very well kill her in the same way he had her mother.

This conversation might be the last Alyla heard before contractions wracked her.

I snatched the shawl and handed it to Maid Janny. "Find a place for it. I will wear it. I thank you, Alyla, for the beautiful gift."

Lifting one of my sleeves, I dabbed the tears from her face. Her sobs decreased in force, and she tried to smile for me.

"Maid Janny," I said, "I will take my lunch in this room."

"Would you mean dinner? It's quarter past nine."

"When I say I want lunch, you will serve it. No matter the time."

Janny left me with Alyla and Sri, who had yet to wake. I sneaked a hand in to check Sri's pulse, and she still lived.

A servant woman in the room spoke to Alyla. "You must read for the elder enchantress. You have such a pretty voice."

Alyla gazed down at the book that balanced on her belly. She cleared her throat but did not speak.

"I should like for you to read," I said.

She closed the book. "I heard something in the bazaar, something an acolyte said."

The servant woman touched her arm. "I told you not to believe him."

Alyla twined her fingers together. "He said the Ever Always planted death in us. That we won't have baby girls after all."

My left hand clutched my right, which in turn held the red diamond. I lifted both hands to press them against my mouth, unable to say anything.

"Is that why mother died?" Alyla dragged her tear-stained eyes upward to meet mine.

Pushing through the pain in my chest, I said, "No, it is not that."

"Then will I have my baby girl? I've picked the loveliest name."

I thought of the perfect names I had chosen for my own children: Chrysoprase, Beryl, Carnelian, and Agate. Images of the four doors to their rooms closed in my mind and locked; the jewels fixed into the wood were all dim in a dark hall.

"Save that name," I said. "For your next child. You are young, and you will have more, I promise you will. Only, not yet."

"Then...." Alyla cradled her belly. "It's a stillbirth?"

My tongue fretted forward and back against my teeth. I could not tell them about the Bone Orbs. I never could. "I will try to make everything right, yet please, do not inquire how."

The servant woman took Alyla's hand, and I observed how the maid by turns clung to her fingers and patted them. I wondered if I should do the same to Alyla's opposite hand or if that would have a counterbalancing effect.

A snort drew my attention to the bed. Sri the Once Flawless lifted her head. "Mister Obenji is coming!"

I said, "Exactly how do you purport to know that?"

"I heard him, of course." She tried to lift herself to a sitting position but could not manage it. The pregnant servant rushed to help her.

"Careful," I said to her. "And, Lady Sri, you could not have heard him. There was nothing to hear."

Even as I said it, I glanced over the ruffles on my shoulder to see Mister Obenji speaking to Maid Janny. I moved into the room a bit more to gain the space to turn around, and then I left for the hall to listen.

Janny was holding a tray with a saucer and sliced oranges. "She's the bravest woman alive and good at heart. But she's never happy. By my reckoning, everyone should have at least one day of happiness."

Mister Obenji looked past Janny to see me. "Elder Enchantress Hiresha, I give thanks to the Ever Always for your recovery."

"I was not sick. I merely stayed in bed until evening."

While I ate, Sri tittered over Mister Obenji. "Did you see, Hiresha? He's wearing the turban I embroidered for him."

Mister Obenji's white mustache bent upward in his smile. "The lady Sri could've been a master tailor."

"Any needlework at all is exemplary," I said, "considering her arthritic hands."

He cast a concerned eye at me, making me wonder if I should apologize. He salvaged the situation for me by clasping her lumpy fingers and saying, "Lady Sri has lovely hands."

Meanwhile, Alyla was hugging the servant woman, and although I thought I should say something more to her, I needed all my focus to feed myself and stay upright. My drowsiness weighed on my head like a lead skullcap.

After finishing my saucer of milk and cubed mangos, my tongue felt swollen and slimy, and my stomach roiled. "Maid Janny, you have served me spoiled milk."

"If it had spoiled," she said, "wouldn't you have tasted it?"

"I cannot be expected to taste everything I eat."

My stomach heaved, and bitterness spread up my throat. I stumbled from the ottoman and fell on my side, which was a blessing: A bedstead hid me from view when I vomited.

"I think I am less than well," I said as Janny helped me to my feet. I had never had so much difficulty digesting, although I had never been under such stress.

We passed servants in the hall who scurried to clean up the mess, and my next awareness was of Janny securing my arms in the harness.

"Mustn't sleep," I mumbled while slipping into my dream.

Surrounded by shelves full of glowing baubles, I decided I must investigate my nausea before a lack of nutrients endangered my health. I replicated myself, the copy standing before me in only petticoats.

"Lie down, Elder Enchantress," I said to her.

She complied. The golden manacles on the operations table retracted, as I saw no need to secure myself. The blue diamonds spun around my hands, subdividing her as I searched her liver and kidneys for signs of poisoning. Her organs were healthy and shapely.

I asked her, "Have you experienced any other symptoms?"

"My breasts ache," she said.

Now that she mentioned it, I supposed my breasts tingled on touch; I had not noticed because I had more important things to do than acknowledge bodily sensations.

The symptoms of nausea combined with tender breasts caused my mind to recoil. I thought I knew what this indicated, yet, no, it could not be that. The idea was too monstrous.

The blue diamonds sped to reveal the replica's womb.

"I have disquieting news," I said to the other me. "We are pregnant."

WINNOWED
-33-

The embryo inside me was not my child; my copper-cone bauble told me as much. A Bone Orb was growing in my womb.

The size of a tick, the unchild resembled a sphere, a blob of flesh that had invaded me by unnatural means. It had yet to develop any bone shell, and its heart had not begun beating, meaning I had carried it for no more than a month. I had not noted any change in my monthly emission, as I never had one; magic in a white-sapphire anklet arrested my cycle. Fertility was a nuisance before it was needed.

I felt unclean and angry beyond measure that this intruder would defile the place meant for my children. A golden knife whisked from a shelf to my hand. I had resolved to craft an enchantment to excise the trespasser from my body.

The red diamond would serve as the receptacle for the magic, both because of its availability and because of its capacity for complex spellcraft. Into the diamond, I copied the knife's enchantment, which caused units within the body to disintegrate through self-suicide, and I tuned its specificity to the unchild's tissue signatures.

While I worked, I grew aware of a presence, the same I had felt before the unchild had shattered in Faliti. The Soultrapper watched me.

He could not harm me, I told myself: The unchild had not yet developed any venom. Still, my spellcraft felt rushed, and I forced myself to slow down and concentrate. To the enchantment of disintegration, I added one that neutralized the venom in other Bone Orbs as well as one designed to reabsorb the bone found in the womb. The latter two effects would not apply to me, yet they might prove useful, should I ever use this enchantment to cure another woman of her unchild. I would not dare to do so while the Soultrapper lived, as he could command the Bone Orb to revolve and shred her womb.

The red diamond now glowed, as did the other objects on the shelves and the jewels floating about the laboratory. Unlike them, the red diamond was real and would carry its enchantment to the waking world, although there it would not glimmer.

I judged the enchantment would dismantle the final vestiges of my unchild in fifty hours. Relieved, I noticed that I no longer felt I was being watched. Whether or not the Soultrapper had understood what I had done, he would likely sense the loss of one of his unchildren. He must realize he had erred in infecting me, as not only had I developed an enchantment to annul a Bone Orb, but I also knew that the Soultrapper had touched me.

Now, he could not escape.

Only ten people had touched me in Morimound, and the Soultrapper was one of them. Tethiel had said a woman Soultrapper had never been found, and I ruled out the four females who had presumed themselves on my person.

Six men remained: Deepmand, Priest Salkant, Priest Abwar, Harend Chandur, Mister Obenji, and Tethiel. The

Lord of the Feast had gripped my arm last night, yet the unchild had been developing inside me for approximately a month. I studied the expressions of the others as they viewed the pregnant women.

The glee evident in Abwar of the Ever Always most concerned me. I did not enjoy the prospect that a respected priest could be responsible for the mass pregnancies.

Fondling, slapping, pinching, Priest Abwar touched most everyone around him as he waddled about in his green and white robes. When he spoke of the Ever Always causing the pregnancies, his enormous tongue heaved from one side to the other of his smiling mouth, and speaking of sacrificing to honor his goddess lifted his whole face in a grin like an enchantress receiving a shipment of jewels and gold.

The sacrifices he had performed had bloodied the ziggurat steps, and I remembered Tethiel saying a Soultrapper would have no fear of blood. The priest did dread something, however, as his face pinched together in terror for fractions of a second. He was neither pregnant nor in danger of dying in a flood, since he lived up high on the Island District, and I wondered if his fear was that he would be discovered a Soultrapper.

I could be mistaken. Priest Abwar's terror might derive from something else—perhaps his god—and he tended to show the most delight at mention of the sacrifices, again implying a penchant for blood but not necessarily for Soultrapping. I had to be certain, before requesting Tethiel to strike.

INCRIMINATING
-34-

Day Forty, Third Trimester

Awakening to morning beaming through windows, I left my room to find Deepmand. "Prepare the carriage. We will pay a visit to the Priest of the Ever Always."

An aftertaste of nausea made breakfasting difficult, yet after the half-portions I felt revitalized. I would soon determine if Abwar of the Ever Always was the Soultrapper, and, pending confirmation, I would bid Tethiel to cut the priest's thread from the fabric of life. All the grief and worry caused by the mass pregnancies would be recompensed.

"Elder Enchantress Hiresha," Mister Obenji said, "Lady Sri wished you to speak with her."

Determined to leave as soon as I had dealt with the Once Flawless, I entered the sickroom to find Sri on her side, her gasps short and shallow. "So little breath fits inside me nowadays," she said. "I think I'm being crushed from the inside."

"All mothers feel such, and your age worsens it."

"Sometimes I forget how old I am." Her thick-jointed fingers ran over the sheet covering her mound of a belly, and I tried not to think of the Bone Orb. "It was foolish, yet I had hoped to be a mother."

"I predict you would have made a good one." She would have done better than I, certainly.

"Now I understand I'm to be a mother of death. I'm afraid, Hiresha. Afraid I'm the cause, that the Ever Always blighted us because of me."

"This is not the work of a god."

Sri clawed at her hair, distraught. "I disgraced us! Shamed the God's Eye Court with my thoughts of nudes!"

"Thoughts of what?"

"I was fated to be weak. All through the court proceedings, I imagined the handsome petitioners undressing themselves. Sometimes I stayed up nights thinking about them dancing, their bronze skin oiled and gleaming, and when they touched—"

"How thoroughly indecorous!"

"Only I should have been punished. Alyla and the rest shouldn't have to die."

"I will not permit that to happen." I took her hand, as I had seen the servant do to reassure Alyla. Sri's arm felt far too light. "I will undo the mass pregnancies."

"But how can you? They're the work of a god."

"They are not," I said. "And neither are they the result of your scandalous thoughts."

"I wish I could believe that."

"Your belief is not required, for it to be true."

"Then," Sri asked, "you can cure me?"

"Once I find the source of the pregnancies, I will cure them all at once."

The Bone Orbs all connected to the Soultrapper, or to an object of magic focus he possessed, and if I could bring this keystone into my dream then I could commandeer his magic to channel the red diamond's enchantment into each woman.

She closed her eyes, holding her distended belly. "I'm not sure I understand. Instead, I will trust you. I am glad I wrote you to come to Morimound."

Her confidence only worsened my nervousness. I could disappoint so many.

Leaving my manor, I learned from an acolyte that Abwar of the Ever Always still oversaw the destruction of the Flood Wall. On the way to him downhill, we stopped at the bazaar, as I needed a chain to safely wear and hide the red diamond. The merchant stalls bustled, although few spoke; this was the Flood Moon, a time for whispers, which gave the market a ghostly feel. A staggering brightness burned down in-between the clouds looming on every horizon.

I found a chain of gold that held an opal of similar size to the red diamond, and Maid Janny paid for it. The merchant weighed the coin in his hand and grinned, leaning toward me to whisper.

"I like to think you'll enchant that, Lady Flawless. It's the best gold of the Skiarri Mountains."

"Do not call me the Flawless." At any other time, I would not exchange whispers with a man, yet Flood Moon tradition demanded it. "You trade with the Skiarri Mountains? Did they have a warm spring?"

"A real melter." Half his face and neck tightened with concern. "I worry we'll be missing your Flood Wall all too soon."

I feared the same. If higher than average temperatures in the mountains liquefied too much snow then the rivers would overflow.

On the way back to the carriage, I heard a muffled chiming behind me, and I needed two seconds to interpret the noise as an enchantment triggering in my golden hump. That sound meant something had been accelerating downward, toward my head.

Deepmand clanked around to look above me, where a brick slid forward and back in the air like a falling leaf. The enchantment had Lightened the brick and saved my life. Maid Janny puffed out her cheeks and blew the brick away.

The spellsword Lightened himself and leaped upward, turning as he did to scan the surrounding buildings. He must not have seen anything of note because once he touched down he jumped a second time to survey.

The sight of a man in gilded plate armor hopping about had stilled the bazaar. Everyone watched Deepmand and me, some with suspicion, which I felt was unfair, given that a brick could have recently crushed my head.

Deepmand spoke in a growl. "Couldn't spot the thrower. Wait here, Elder Enchantress."

While he tromped away to question a few onlookers, Maid Janny cupped a hand to my ear.

"Did someone just try to murder you?"

"Do not be ridiculous. A brick merely slipped loose from a wall."

"Must've been one slippery brick. The walls aren't that close."

The spellsword returned with a scowl, and the way his eyes shot over the onlookers convinced me that he believed someone had thrown the brick. I found the concept unpleasant to the extreme, that one of my own people would attack me when I was working so hard to save them.

In the carriage, I stripped my gloves then reached into my mouth to remove the red diamond, which I had hidden under my tongue. With the jewel and chain in one hand, I descended to my laboratory.

Using a chisel spell of Repulsion, I broke the opal from the gold chain, and Attracted its clasps to fit around the red diamond. The necklace floated from my palm to wrap around my neck.

I disliked having to wear the red diamond on a necklace because any who saw it might falsely believe me engaged; however, a bracelet would risk displaying the jewel far too often, and I could not allow any to deduce who had given me the jewel. An anklet would provide an excellent place of hiding, yet foot jewelry was never more than trinkets; I could not insult the gods who had created the red diamond by shackling it so far from my heart.

I had considered implanting the jewel into my flesh, the most conducive spot being my breast, yet the whole premise struck me as lacking a certain refinement. A necklace would serve because none would ever see the stone, except for perhaps Janny, who hardly counted.

The necklace's clasp sealed as I enchanted the gold chain, Attracting the metal to itself and making it next to unbreakable. The removal of my head would be required before someone could steal the red diamond. While I found this concept not altogether agreeable, at least the diamond was safe.

I opened my eyes and shoved the red diamond necklace under the ruffles around my neck. Relieved, I gazed outside the carriage window of Stilt Town, where men covered with mud clanged their pickaxes against the Flood Wall in a horrifying racket. Sections of the wall had been demolished, revealing stretches of skyline and black clouds dragging rain. I imagined water surging through the rents in the mortar, lifting nearby shacks off their wooden posts and sweeping the splintering wreckage into Morimound, to smash apart buildings and drown children.

Seeing the breaches in the wall felt like pieces of tissue carved out of my intestines. Salkant of the Fate Weaver might have wished for his prediction of the Seventh Flood to come true, yet Priest Abwar risked actualizing it. I remembered he had announced the scheme the day after I discovered the Bone Orb in Faliti, and now I wondered if he might have wished to distract me from the true threat of his Soultrapping.

Deepmand opened the carriage door to a view of Priest Abwar, his robes wet and dark up to the thigh; water trickled into Stilt Town from a break in the wall. Dots of brown mud and perhaps dried blood splattered up to his bulging paunch.

"Can you feel the will of the god between your toes? This water was sent by the Ever Thriving, Always Dying, and only by placing our fragile bodies in His merciless hands may we earn mercy." The priest whispered as loudly as most men spoke. "Quickly now, remove the last impediments."

A.E. MARLING

He rolled his hands in the air, beckoning men to pry up the stones at foot level. As they did, water flowed over Priest Abwar's sandals.

I lowered myself to the carriage step but would go no farther. Water stinking of ox dung spread under the carriage.

Deepmand splashed his way to the priest and tapped his shoulder with a gold-plated finger.

UNAWARES
-35-

"The apostate." Priest Abwar had turned to me. "I'm surprised to see you down here with us simple, god-fearing men."

I could not reply to him from this distance, out of respect for the Flood Moon and the drowned ancestors. The priest tromped forward, splattering my gowns with mud.

"As little as you deserve your position," he said, "you can still service me and satisfy the god."

I whispered with a hiss. "Exactly what are you suggesting?"

"Priest Salkant has the backbone of a stick insect and won't consent to the sacrifices. He says it would damage our reputation and decrease trade, but what good is reputation if everyone dies to a god's culling scythe?"

"Reputation is more valuable than life," I said. "If Salkant of the Fate Weaver forbids you from doing something, he must have reason."

He gestured with raised fists. "I must appease the Ever Always, before the women birth His judgment of death. I've torn down your abominable wall and sacrificed a hundred oxen. It is not enough. I must give the god people."

I blinked three times. "How does one 'give' the god a person?"

"By chanting as their blood flows down the ziggurat steps."

"You do not mean...you cannot mean—Oh, how monstrous!"

"Not at all. It's an honor to die to save your nation from flood, and our ancestors approved of the ritual. The city has a rich history of priests preventing floods with human sacrifice."

Aghast, I struggled to find the breath even to whisper. "I do not recall ever reading of that."

"Salkant has cobwebs for guts, but with the support of the Flawless, I could do what needs doing."

I had no intention of accommodating Priest Abwar, yet his willingness to harm others increased my resolve to test him for being the Soultrapper. "You will have my support, if you can produce two outcomes. First, I wish to know more of Bone Orbs. What can you tell me of them?"

"Bone Orbs? You did say, 'Bone Orbs?' Yes, well, of course I know of Bone Orbs. They're the lumps where broken bones don't heal properly."

I had forced my sleepy eyes open to watch his reactions, although I would have to wait to evaluate them. By his words, he seemed to know nothing of the unchildren, yet words could be false.

"Very good," I said. "Second, you must cut your palm. The waters of the Ever Always should taste your blood."

"My—my blood?"

Soultrappers bled themselves, Tethiel had said, and I wished to observe the ease with which the priest shed his own blood. He had little problem with the blood of others, as the dark crusts on his sleeves attested, not to mention the rust-colored grime under his fingernails.

"The Ever Thriving, Always Dying," he said, "would have no wish to see my blood. I embody Him, and to cut myself would be to cut His divine personage."

"Nevertheless, I refuse to condone human sacrifice, unless you begin with your blood. A prodigious gout of it."

I was grateful to Tethiel for reassuring me that no god had created the unchildren, freeing me from considering the option of human sacrifice. Now, I would condemn it in any event.

Priest Abwar lifted a knife to his palm then lowered it again to sharpen it against a whetstone on his belt. He dropped the knife into the mud and cursed.

"Arse worms!"

Wiping the blade against his robes, he rested the edge on his palm. I believe his hand trembled. He closed his eyes and eased the blade forward and back as if cutting a piece of lettuce.

I was not sure if he had pierced his skin until three red drops rolled down his wrist, their color contrasting with the sudden paleness of his face. His arms drooped to his sides, and his three chins rolled upward as he tilted. Only when he had impacted into the mud and speckled me did I realize he had fainted.

"Spellsword Deepmand, my business here is finished. Inform the acolytes that it will not be human sacrifice that saves our city. It will be me."

In carriage and in dream, I confirmed that the priest's terror at cutting himself had not been feigned. I might have interpreted this fear as worry that I would discover his identity as the Soultrapper, yet his eyes had not dilated and demonstrated similar fright when I had mentioned the Bone Orbs.

Glee had elevated Priest Abwar's face at the proposition of human sacrifice. As noxious as the idea seemed to me, I believed he relished killing and bloodletting others.

My search was for another variety of despicable. After Burdening the grime from my gowns, I decided that Abwar of the Ever Always was probably not the Soultrapper: By demolishing the Flood Wall, he endangered not only the citizens of Morimound but the Bone Orbs as well. The Soultrapper would wish the mothers protected, a position upheld by Salkant of the Fate Weaver.

Salkant's command of the pregnancies would explain why his daughter had avoided the condition. My mirror scrutinized him. He gave both women and men calculating glances out of the corners of his eyes. When he regarded me, I read veneration in his face. That was reasonable enough, given my station, yet he unsettled me by having to repress expressions of eagerness at the mention of the Seventh Flood. He hoped it would come; he wished for a catastrophe that would kill the greater majority of the Morimound people.

Priest Salkant had predicted the Seventh Flood, and he would have an interest in seeing his prophecy occur. He might have gone as far as to cause the disaster himself, by implanting the city's women with Bone Orbs.

I wondered if I now had sufficient cause to summon Tethiel, or if I should wait for additional proof. Not knowing how Priest Salkant could have touched so many women still galled me. I could mention "Bone Orbs" in front of him to see how he reacted, yet he struck me as a more calculating person than Abwar of the Ever Always; he might assume my motive and harm me to guard his secret. Deepmand might not be able to protect me from the Soultrapper's magic.

Tethiel commanded power, illusion or not, and I wanted him by my side when I confronted the true Soultrapper. The more I thought about Tethiel, the more advantages I saw in contacting him tonight; with him accompanying me, I could think with clarity. If Priest Salkant revealed himself as the Soultrapper then justice would fall on him in one second.

Once I left my carriage, the balcony over the front door of my manor sheltered me from a downpour. Amid the rush of water, I heard a splashing and crunch of gravel, no doubt from a gardener running to escape the rain.

Two servants paused in opening the manor door to glance behind me, and I sensed Deepmand Lightening his scimitar. Not knowing why he would activate the enchantment, I twisted and leaned to see past my golden hump.

An acolyte approached at an irreverent speed, and I worried he would not be able to stop himself before colliding with me. Only then did I notice the glint of a dagger in his hand, and I had no time to ponder what impropriety he hoped to commit.

The scimitar swooped down, Burdening as it dropped through the acolyte. I flinched as Deepmand attacked and was relieved to see that the scimitar had encountered no resistance in its swing. He must have missed.

Maid Janny was screaming, and the acolyte now rested on the ground in a most extraordinary position. One arm, his

A.E. MARLING

head, and half his torso lay perpendicular to the remainder of his body. A red substance mixed with the rainwater as it spread from him, seeping into the gravel.

An open-mouthed moment elapsed before I realized that Deepmand had not, in fact, missed. I did the sensible thing and advanced a few more steps toward the door, pulling my gowns away from the blood. After discerning that a minimum of splatter had reached me, I lifted my chin to the spellsword.

"That was rather brash, Deepmand. I was hardly in any danger." I had my own defensive enchantments, after all.

He peered at the surrounding gardens then glanced from his bloodied scimitar to my golden hump, which would have protected me from the attack. He might have known as much.

"My apologies, Elder Enchantress. There could've been more than one assassin." His words ground against each other with tension, almost in a growl.

"No, I am sorry, Deepmand. You acted rightly. I only find the suddenness of a surprise attack most unsettling, and I could have wished to question him."

Although Deepmand had defended me from highway robbers before, this occasioned the first definite attempt on my life, and I admitted a measure of satisfaction that someone deemed me important enough to assassinate. This acolyte must have been one of the Soultrapper's followers, sent out of fear that I would soon expose him.

I was on the brink of discovering the Soultrapper.

"Mistress Enchantress," a servant asked, "are you well?"

Realizing I grinned down at the corpse in an unseemly manner, I corrected my expression. "Maid Janny, turn over the portion of the body with the head. I wish to see his face."

Janny had pulled her bonnet down over her eyes. She did nothing more productive than weep.

I said, "Oh, you are quite useless."

Spellsword Deepmand nudged over the corpse with his scimitar, and I saw the dead man wore a surprised expression. I did not recognize him yet, although I noticed his robes bore the eight-sided stylized depiction of the Fate Weaver, with her spider body adorned with human face and hands.

Inside my manor, I wasted no time in falling asleep. I confirmed in dream that I had never before seen this acolyte; in addition, his face portrayed less hatred than I would have expected for an act of blind passion. Rather, he seemed focused on the goal of ending my life, suggesting he might have acted under orders.

I decided his vestments of the Fate Weaver did not necessarily implicate Priest Salkant. The assassin might have stolen his garb, or his membership in the order might be supplanted by his pact with the Soultrapper. Still, this bore mentioning to Tethiel, and I hoped to see him imminently.

Upon waking, I took a mid-afternoon lunch with Alyla. She waited until after I had finished eating before she spoke. "Dhatrod told me someone tried to hurt you."

"Clearly that someone failed, and nothing more needs to be said concerning it."

I could not help but glance at her navel; previously an indentation, it now thrust outward. She scratched at her new stretch marks.

The sun would have to set before I could contact Tethiel through the Feaster Physis, and I passed the time sleeping. Although I considered drawing a replica of the assassin's face, to be dispersed across the city to find his associates, that might frighten the Soultrapper into unwanted action. He might prepare to defend himself by attempting to harvest the Bone Orbs before they fully solidified.

Better, I decided, to surprise the Soultrapper. Of course, sending a follower to kill me showed desperation on his part; he might already be preparing for my arrival, and each hour I delayed benefited him.

Soultrappers could control minds, I reminded myself, and the assassin perhaps did not attack me out of free will. He might not even have had an obvious connection to the Soultrapper, who might thus still feel secure. I might still have time.

A flashing amethyst beckoned me to wake, and I found Mister Obenji leaning over me. He still wore the turban that Sri the Once Flawless had embroidered with the symbol of the gods divine: the Weaver's octagon, enclosed by a solar eclipse.

"Is it night yet?" Yet, even as I asked, I saw that daylight shone in from the window.

"Elder Enchantress Hiresha, the Ambassador Tethiel awaits you in the pink parlor."

HOPEFUL
-36-

Pink topazes were rare, and I had given one of the more distinguished parlors a theme of corresponding color, envisioning pleasant hours would elapse there with other mothers as our children played under the tables draped with lace and clambered up pink ottomans to wallow in pink pillows on pink couches.

As I strode into the parlor, I realized the bright color complimented Tethiel's crimson jacket and the doilies were reminiscent of his lacey cuffs; however, both his foppish attire and the feminine atmosphere of the parlor jarred with his profession. I chided myself for rushing here instead of meeting him in a more somber room.

"You," I said, "always claim to leave the city with the dawn. Yet you always return."

"Then I am dependable in my inconsistency."

He had risen as I entered the room, and he resumed his seat only after Maid Janny situated me on an ottoman. She laid out a tea tray and poured two cups, flinching as she set Tethiel's in front of him on a doily.

She muttered, "Oh my! Oh my!" then scurried from the parlor. Decency demanded the door be left open, although she retreated out of earshot down the hall, to stand beside Deepmand.

A.E. MARLING

Tethiel regarded me, and I wondered if he searched for the red diamond among my gowns. The jewel nestled hidden against my left breast, its glassy edges sharp against my skin but reassuring.

I asked, "How did you learn of my interest in red diamonds? I only mentioned them at the ball, and you had one already."

"Consider it an unfortunate guess."

"A fortunate one, you mean."

"I mean what I say, Enchantress Hiresha."

The tea in my cup scarcely trembled as I lifted it to my lips. Tethiel made no motion toward his saucer, and I realized he would not; with his fingers bent as if by torture and hands thrust downward to hold in his magic, he could not feed himself. In sipping the tea, I had blundered and flaunted my advantages like someone dancing in front of a one-legged veteran.

Tethiel was even more dependent on others than I.

"My maid could be called back," I said, realizing as I did that Janny would quail from the task, "to help you with...to assist you—"

"I am content to savor its fragrance." Steam wafted from the cup toward his face.

In the strong light, I noted his features followed the golden ratio: Everything pleasing to the eye in nature adhered to this proportion, from the branching of veins in aspen leaves to the spiral of seashells. It was the first rule of gem crafting. The perfect proportion governed each facet of his face, his chin exactly the correct amount larger than the space between his brows, his lips just more than half again as wide as his nose.

At the ball, the women would not have understood why they thought Tethiel attractive. I found comfort in knowing that beauty could be quantified by numbers. Of course, his alluring proportions had no effect on me, certainly not with his face powdered.

He said, "I am pleased to find you so composed, hours after your attempted murder."

"And how would you have learned of that?"

"Your servants are most trustworthy. The one who sold the news spoke nothing but truth."

I chuckled for a moment then caught myself, following the indiscretion with a remonstrative scowl. He of all people should not go around hoodwinking people into laughter.

Tethiel sat on the edge of a couch, his hands dangling off the front of the pink cushion. "The Soultrapper must fear you will find him, to have played out his hand like this."

"I agree. The acolyte wore the symbol of Priest Salkant."

"That you were attacked by an acolyte confirms the Soultrapper is not a priest."

I asked, "How does that make any manner of sense?"

"The Soultrapper meant to distract you, and to test your magic. He could not be wise to your full ability."

"The Soultrapper meant to kill me, and we should not dismiss the priest. He has influence and the greatest means."

"For those reasons, we must rule him out. Soultrappers seek power and devotion, and the priests already have both."

A.E. MARLING

"Historically, those with power are the hungriest for more."

"The price of magic puts most men off their appetite. Enchantress Hiresha, yours is a beautiful and gentle power, and thus an exception." The late-afternoon sun broke through the clouds and shone through the window behind Tethiel, brightening the lace around his neck and granting his wig a luster similar to jet. "Most magics demand sacrifices that repel all but the desperate. A Soultrapper must listen to the screams of imprisoned spirits, for as long as he lives, which is only as long as he escapes the notice of someone stronger. The priests have hundreds of servants, can eat five meals a day, and bed anyone they wish. They have too much to lose."

"The priests would not be 'bedding' just anyone. One of them is married."

"You would sooner accuse them of Soultrapping than dalliance?"

"I...." The priests represented gods, and the thought of them engaging in any wrongdoing was beyond disturbing; Tethiel's refusal to accept them as Soultrappers felt as relieving as a steam bath on a cold day. "I will defer to your expertise in the depraved."

"At last, you give me my due credit."

Tethiel had clenched his hands on the couch when he had mentioned magics and their sacrifices. I recalled him speaking of his nightmares, and his death grip on the pink cushion struck me as tragic.

"I still wish to know," I said, "why you became a Feaster."

For a quarter-second, sadness frayed the edges of his composed face. "That would cast me in the most unfavorable light. At my age, good lighting is of the utmost importance."

"I already know who you are. What could be worse?"

"Very little, I will grant. But this Soultrapper is, and I do so ever wish you'll point him out. I feel I must Feast soon." His fingers dug deeper into the pink cushions.

"Unfortunately, if the Soultrapper cannot be a priest then, well, the last option is a past acquaintance," I said slowly, unwillingly. Although Alyla had said her father had gone to dismantle my wall, I had yet to see him down there. "Harend Chandur by name. He is disaffected, yet I hate to think of him as a Soultrapper. No, I do not envision him being one. He could never have touched so many women."

"Then why suspect him?"

Harend Chandur had touched me, and someone who had done that had impregnated me with an unchild, a condition from which I was only now recovering. "I would prefer not to say."

"You must be certain. Morimound will have no second chances, and neither will I. Should I Feast on the wrong man, the Soultrapper may sense it, and he will waste no time in harvesting the Bone Orbs. On his guard, he may kill me as I kill him. Then my children would commence a gluttonous festival."

At that, I mistakenly breathed in a sip of tea. After coughing twice in as ladylike a manner as I could into my napkin, I said, "Something connects all the Bone Orbs to the Soultrapper, and if I could find that focus, my enchantment would unmake all his spirit prisons."

"The Soultrapper himself is the focus, his blood and his body."

"Then after you kill him, I will have to..." I coughed again but a foul taste remained in my mouth. "...well, the essential point is that the body must be retained."

Sadness flickered across Tethiel's face once again, this time accompanied by his mouth pinching into a crescent of disgust. I found it comforting that he sympathized with me for having to sleep with a corpse.

A new thought occurred to me, one that pained me as if I had swallowed a handful of needles. "I can undo the Bone Orbs, yet what of the souls inside them?"

"Do souls not enter the body at birth?"

"No, at quickening. That time has passed, and the orbs must contain souls."

"Then, Enchantress Hiresha, what do you believe happens to people after they die?"

A coldness itched its way up my throat and welled behind my eyes. "Spirits journey to find the cavern of the Fate Weaver, where they view the synthesis of every being's threads in the grand pattern of the Loom of Life."

"Then there is your answer," he said.

"I feel there must be more I can accomplish for them. Spirits should have lives."

"They will have freedom, because of you. You will also stop the Soultrapper from imprisoning anyone else."

"Will I? I still have no idea how he imprisoned so many. The Soultrapper must have touched each woman, yet he could never have done so."

"Enchantress Hiresha, my heart, I believe you've solved it. The Soultrapper touched each woman, without touching her."

"This is no time for your self-contradicting statements."

"Truth only comes from contradiction."

"Nothing comes from the impossible."

"Clearly, this is possible."

I snorted in irritation. "How then could a Soultrapper touch each woman, yet at the same time, not touch her?"

"That you must discover. I see no possibilities, so I will defer to your ability to create miracles." He rose to his feet, and I saw his fingers had left ten indentations in the couch. "With your permission, Enchantress Hiresha, I will now depart."

"To leave the city, only to return in a few days?"

"That would be most foolish, since I expect you to unmask the Soultrapper tomorrow."

He left in a streak of red satin. I folded my hands over my chest, above the red diamond, wondering if he could be right.

No one else had ever had such confidence in me, not since my falling asleep over the spindle had frustrated my mother to despair. Enchantresses in the Academy aspired to my position and deferred to my judgment, yet they had also witnessed my failures to cure myself of sleep; they would not imagine me capable of overcoming a cataclysm on the scale of a Seventh Flood.

Excitement hummed through me even as drowsiness bowed me forward. I struggled for a moment with the quandary of touching without touching, yet my heart rate was slowing, my mind sinking into a morass of fatigue. Perhaps Tethiel was right; maybe I could unravel the puzzle in my laboratory.

Maid Janny chattered as she helped me to my feet. "Don't know how you abide him. His face never moves, must be like talking to a corpse."

"He has expressions," I said. "You merely have to look closely."

"You're not buzzed with him, are you? I'm beginning to worry."

"I will not even pretend to know what you mean."

"Are you flipped over him? Roasted? Bunny-eyed? Jelly-kneed?"

"How absurd! Maid Janny, you are most respectable with your mouth closed. Remember that."

She pestered me with a few more concerned noises as she guided me into my room. Secure in my sleep harness, I descended the hundred steps so I could identify the Soultrapper.

EXPOSED
-37-

In magic, touch created the strongest link between arcane practitioner and recipient, allowing for the most complex and potent of spells. This bond had persisted in the growing unchildren, and I had witnessed the Soultrapper exploit it to shatter the Bone Orb in Faliti and spy on me as I cured myself of the unnatural pregnancy.

The strength of the touch lay in proximity, given that distance tended to dilute spell power. The nearness of the magic user's soul might be the causative agent, yet that explanation was insufficient because I knew enchantresses could lie close to someone but fail to draw him or her into dream if clothing separated the two. The touch of flesh upon flesh had to matter.

I sat floating in the air, one arm crossed over my chest, the other propping up my chin. Green light shone down on me, and then orange, as first a glowing emerald then a fire opal passed overhead.

Neither could flesh alone explain it, I knew. I could not take a lock of someone's hair and sleep with it, expecting to capture its owner's entity in my dream, yet I could craft an enchantment by touching a jewel then giving the jewel to another. Intermediaries could exist.

Soultrappers would not work with jewels but in corrupted flesh. Tethiel had said they branded a dying man with their own blood to create a spirit prison, and I wondered if they could achieve a similar effect by entrusting their blood to a follower, who would use it to paint a glyph.

Marking so many women could never have escaped notice. In the Third and Fourth Ages of the city, blood from animal sacrifices had been applied to the sick and to newlyweds. Such rituals had long since fallen out of favor.

Assuming that the followers could somehow have written fifty thousand glyphs without anyone observing them, which I deemed impossible, I estimated they would need at least five drops of blood for each woman. This Soultrapper would have had to leech all the blood from his body twice over to account for the pregnancies.

I doubted both that the Soultrapper possessed sufficient followers for this feat and that he could store his blood long enough to accumulate the needed gallons, over several siphonings. Even cooled by ice chips, blood tissue would degrade.

To avoid such prohibitive quantities, I wondered if the Soultrapper could have applied the same blood to different women at different times. Again, blood seemed less than conducive to this function because of its tendency to dry and clot, yet I imagined him distributing some part of himself that would pass from the hands of one woman to another, touching them all indirectly.

Salkant of the Fate Weaver was missing the tips of four fingers, ostensibly from spider bites, yet a man had attacked me today wearing the robes of one of his acolytes. I imagined Priest Salkant cutting off his own fingers and inserting them into thimble-sized reliquaries, which his acolytes would press against each woman before reading her fate in a web.

Jewels raced over the walls of the laboratory and up into its dome, their speed embodying my anticipation. I could tell I was close to viewing the Soultrapper's face; soon I could point to one man and name him responsible.

No precedent existed for acolytes of the Fate Weaver to touch women with talismans or finger-sized objects. Even if Priest Salkant had invented one, application of four dismembered fingers would have taken a month or more, given the number of women; in the God's Eye Court, I had noted the conceptions tended to center around one week for all but those of wealthy families, who had begun gestation a month later, on average.

The disparity in conception times could be explained, if the four dismembered fingers were applied later to those living on the Island District, perhaps to delay suspicion in the authorities, yet I could not believe this method could affect so many women within a span of a week. If women had stood in long lines to receive the "blessing" of the Fate Weaver, acolytes of the other god would have squealed to me about it.

Given that a task could not be done fast enough with four vectors, the obvious solution would be to create more of them, or in this case, subdivide the fingers. I cringed, imagining the fingertips dissected into pieces then disseminated among the women, and I wondered at the method of dispersal. All the women I had examined in the court had been pregnant, and to achieve that degree of morbidity, the pieces had to have reached them through a means in which all women engaged.

All women ate, and I considered the possibility of minute quantities of the fingers implanted into foods, poisoning the women with pregnancy. This method had the advantage of explaining the disparity among the rich, as they would eat different foods.

I steepled my hands in concentration then twined my fingers at the thought that my womb too had begun to foster an unchild, meaning I might have consumed a sliver of a human fingertip. The concept of having inadvertently been a cannibal gave me no little displeasure.

The piece of the Soultrapper would need to be infinitesimal, both for reasons of covertness and because there was only so much of him; however, the smaller the piece, the greater the chance it would be digested before its magic took effect. The Soultrapper's magic corrupted the flesh, not strengthened it, and the ingested-finger theory began to seem less probable, unless the modicum had a means of protecting itself.

This gave me an idea. I replicated myself and gestured for my mirror image to lie on the operations table; she did so, wearing only her red undergarments. Blue diamonds flurried around my fingertips, and I used their enchantment to bisect her stomach at intervals of one thousandths of an inch.

Even though I had expected it, I gasped when I found a morsel of the Soultrapper imbedded in my stomach lining. Two-sevenths the size of a grain of sand, a mote of bone floated in a cyst in the wrinkled mucous membrane, shielded in a bubble of inflamed tissue.

The bone mote contained units with formative fiber matching those of the unchildren. More than that, I sensed the Soultrapper peering at me; he no doubt knew I scrutinized a piece of him.

"How much," the replica asked, "do we think he perceives of our laboratory?"

He likely only received a vague sensation of my attention. I refrained from saying this aloud for the sake of my replica, as I was not in the habit of responding to myself.

The red diamond lifted itself out from my collar to my hand. I expanded its enchantment to search out traces of the Soultrapper throughout my body then eradicate them. Having a piece of him inside me made me feel filthier than if I had eaten all the dust in the Academy, which I had calculated at never less than a total of seventy pounds.

This bone mote was the seed, the connection between Soultrapper and each woman that initiated the Bone Orbs. By cutting out a piece of himself and tricking us to eat it, he had touched us without touching.

"What about Tethiel?" The replica gazed up at me with my own eyes. "Do we trust him?"

Irritated that I would interrupt myself, I waved my hand, and the replica vanished. I refocused on the trails of inference, knowing with every moment that I converged on pinpointing the Soultrapper.

If I had swallowed the bone mote in a bolus of food then I might have expected to find it transported into my circuitous intestine before it touched my flesh and formed a cyst. I had begun to suspect that it was not eaten but drunk. Most women in the city ate rice, yet not from the same seller, removing any ready method for the Soultrapper to pollute the grain with his bones.

A.E. MARLING

The city had three water reservoirs, which pumped into a hundred and thirty-five public wells. With the help of followers, the Soultrapper might have visited all the wells in one day, lowering into the flows presumably empty urns that instead contained thousands upon thousands of bone motes.

Even with the diminutive size of the motes, the total volume of bone required staggered me. Some motes would dissolve in stomach acid before touching, and many would be drunk instead by men and animals. Allowing for a wide margin of loss, I estimated that at least six pounds of bone would be needed, far more than a few finger bones, closer to the combined weight of the bones of a hand, the arm attached to it, four ribs, and one foot.

In fact, I knew exactly which bones had been sacrificed because an image of the Soultrapper now stood in my mirror. Reviewing my memories had revealed him in less than a second.

Anlash Niklia, wine merchant of the "Liquid Diamond" vintage, had hefted wine barrels with his one arm the night I first saw him. The arm appeared to be compensating for the missing one with a length that bordered on grotesque, his fingertips reaching within an inch of his knees. He favored his right foot, and his left never flexed, and the boot struck the brick street with a subtle "clack" of woodenness. His potbelly hung out of his open vest, and on occasion, the vest slid back on a hairless chest and revealed scars on either side of his bulging navel: The jagged white lines provided evidence of his self-inflicted rib amputation.

He had flinched in fear at his first sight of Spellsword Deepmand, causing his hand to slip on a barrel; a brass hoop had slit his thumb, from which he had sucked the leaking blood. That alone would have convinced me he shared none of Priest Abwar's hemophobia, even without the fan of white scars on his palm, from repeated, self-inflicted cuts.

The merchant had done more than bloodletting. I imagined him deep in a wine cellar, sweat trickling through tangled clumps of his oiled hair as he sawed off his own foot; he would have screamed and used a torch to cauterize the wound. Extraction of his ribs would have been even more agonizing and laborious; he must have lain in a puddle of his own blood, strapped to a table and struggling against the pain and the desire to faint, as his followers bent over him with serrated knives.

Anlash Niklia had admitted that he missed a cut on a paragon diamond, and his arm had been removed in punishment. He must have recovered the limb and kept the bones, storing them until he could find a use for them.

I had first encountered him in the crowd hunting the Feaster. His black eyes had glinted from within flabby skin as he snatched glances at the night's shadows. Only now did I appreciate his enmity at the mention of the Feaster boy: He must have understood that the Lord of the Feast wished to hunt him down and kill him.

He had warned me of the herbalist who was overdosing the women. By arresting the herbalist, I had saved lives but I had also protected the Bone Orbs the mothers carried; without knowing it, I had done a service for the Soultrapper.

In exchange for the information he provided about the herbalist, I had agreed to purchase Anlash Niklia's wine. He might have defiled most of the women in Morimound by poisoning wells with bone motes, yet he had needed to deal in wine to blight the daughters living in the Island District, who drank water from private, guarded wells. This explained why the wealthy women had grown pregnant later; the Soultrapper had needed time to sell his Liquid Diamond wine to the various houses.

I had served his wine at my ball, yet I had not drunk any there, only touching it to my lips at the toast. Salkant of the Fate Weaver had unwittingly inoculated me by insisting I taste the "second best wine in Morimound," the label of which I now read in my mirror as Liquid Diamond. Maid Janny had swigged wine that day but just the priest's estate vintage, only later indulging in the Soultrapper's concoction at my ball. If she was pregnant now, it was merely by days.

Priest Salkant only drank his own wine; by extension, he served nothing else to his daughter, who had thereby escaped the epidemic. Many women living in Stilt Town were too poor to buy wine and too far from the public wells, thus avoiding pregnancy by drawing water from rain barrels or straight from holes dug in the mud.

No doubt remained in my mind that I had identified the Soultrapper. I scowled at him in my mirror, wishing to replicate him so I could Repulse and Attract his heart into two pieces, or Burden him until his remaining bones shattered.

I never permitted myself to indulge in Creating replicas of people for gratification in my dream. I would have to content myself with watching Tethiel annihilate the Soultrapper's mind with waking nightmares.

At last, the Lord of the Feast would lift his hands.

DESTROYED
-38-

Day Forty-One, Third Trimester

"You should allow me to execute him, Elder Enchantress," Deepmand said. "The less we involve the Lord of the Feast, the better."

"Tethiel has promised to neutralize him in one second. The Soultrapper will not realize what is happening until it is too late."

"I could behead him in one swing."

"His disembodied head would have several seconds before it lost consciousness. During that interval, he could kill women out of spite."

"Those without bodies tend not to be in the right state of mind to cast spells."

"You mock me, Spellsword Deepmand. I should not have informed you of anything."

Deepmand's tone suggested he expected me to change my mind now, when awake, something he should know I dared not do. Whereas my thoughts flowed like a river in dream, they now trickled in a desert of drowsiness. I struggled simply to string words together, and analyzing the merit of his argument was quite beyond me.

"I meant no offense, Elder Enchantress. I am only concerned for you, and the rest of us. Remember, this is the Lord of the Feast."

"I am no forgetful invalid, thank you very much."

"Elder Enchantress, I could brain the Soultrapper." Five plated fingers closed on the scimitar hilt over his shoulder. "Split his skull in half."

"Kindly do not ask me to change my plan again, Deepmand. If not for Tethiel, I would never have located the Soultrapper even if he leapt up and down, waving his single arm in front of my face."

The spellsword's face changed in a peculiar way, although I could derive no insight from it yet.

A servant knelt before me. "Mistress, a man in funny clothes is in the west gardens. Said he was waiting for you."

"Unless you are a certified clothes judge, your opinions are best withheld," I said, irritated. "However, you may take me to him."

While I walked into the gardens, four servants held a canvas sheet above me with poles to shield me from the downpour. So little light penetrated the rain clouds that my earrings shone, and when I found Tethiel in the gazebo, I was reminded of the night he had given me the red diamond.

Tethiel stood as my gowns squeezed into the gazebo's arched entrance. When my servants had departed from earshot, he said, "By your glowing face, Enchantress Hiresha, I judge the night a success."

"The Soultrapper is Anlash Niklia," I said in a whisper, out of respect for the Flood Moon. "He ground his own bones into powder then sprinkled them into the city's wells and his fine wines."

"A wine merchant? And instead of blood glyphs, he bound with bone. Promising. Most promising." His lips spread halfway to a red grin of hunger.

"Will you confront him in the bazaar, or at night?"

"People feel too safe during the day for my tastes, and the overcast will make spellwork more manageable. Go to him now in the bazaar. I'll follow on Eyebiter."

"I will depart without delay."

"Before you do, Enchantress Hiresha, I would ask you for a promise."

I felt a crushing sensation. Tethiel had said he would not ask anything of me, and I feared he would renege on his word and demand I sleep with him. To regenerate his teeth...or something equally scandalous.

"You must promise," he said, "not to betray my presence to the Soultrapper until I strike."

I exhaled in relief. "Is that all?"

"If the Soultrapper is on his guard, he may realize I attack him only with illusion. He might resist long enough to scourge me with his magic."

"Or long enough to activate the Bone Orbs and mutilate the women."

Sadness tempered hunger, at the edges of Tethiel's face. "You will promise, then?"

"I wonder that you even asked. Of course, I promise. And...I wanted you to know something."

My direct address had almost been of his first name, which would have been most improper. Now, uncertainty fluttered through me about my phrasing, or even what I wanted to say.

"I think that I wish to thank you."

"You may thank me when all is done, Enchantress Hiresha."

Not knowing how to thank him for more, for saving Morimound, for the red diamond, I trod out of the gazebo. My servants covered me from the rain on the way to the carriage.

The patter of hooves on brick streets accompanied by the louder sound of the rain lulled me to sleep. To pass the time in my laboratory, I considered Deepmand's offer to decapitate the Soultrapper. The suggestion was impractical, as the Soultrapper would see the scimitar drawn, and I was uncertain he could not activate the Bone Orbs all at once, with one thought. No, we needed Tethiel to cast a nightmare of instant death.

Deepmand's peculiar expression, when I had mentioned Tethiel's invaluable assistance, had been of fright and betrayal. He had no right to look at me that way after we had discovered the Soultrapper and would free the city within hours, and I felt wronged by his lack of confidence.

I blinked awake, seeing the carriage door open and Deepmand's beard dripping in the rain. Striding out, I gazed around the bazaar for sight of Tethiel.

A man rode toward me, with another on horseback beside him, yet both these horses had black coats, while Tethiel's mount had been brown. The cloaked men dismounted.

"We speak for the Father."

One lifted his hood, revealing the pockmarks and scabbed skin of a leper, and I recognized him as one of Tethiel's dandies, although he now only wore a plain leather vest.

I peered through the bursts of rain. "He is close?"

"Close enough. The Father can't let himself be seen by the Trapper."

The second leper said, "He has to be sure, before he lifts the black chalice. He wants you to scare the Trapper into admitting he's who he is."

"I thought Tethiel trusted my judgment," I said. "Tell him to strike the moment I speak to a wine merchant."

"No. You're to scare the Trapper."

This made a measure of sense, as Tethiel's Feasting would perform better if the Soultrapper was frightened, yet I had thought Tethiel wished to attack at the first available moment. I had not expected to have to converse with the Soultrapper, and I found my stomach tightening and my breathing sharp.

Deepmand pointed across the bazaar, and I dragged myself between the merchant stalls. The rain began to weigh down my gowns.

Maid Janny said, "What's going on?"

"You have nothing to fear," I said.

"Great. Now I'm terrified."

I spotted a banner reading, "Taste Liquid Diamond," and another, "Anlash's Fine Wines, A Life-Changing Experience." His arrogance disgusted me.

The one-armed merchant sat in a rope chair, while two assistants—two followers—lounged on barrels. At the sight of me heading toward him, he started, then tried to hide the reaction by rising to his feet.

"Madam Enchantress, a rare pleasure. I trust my wines have satisfied you?"

The sight of him filled me with revulsion. He lifted his single, overlong arm in greeting. His beady black eyes squinted out at me from between drapes of hair as oily and slick as seaweed, and raindrops skidded down his oiled potbelly and between breasts more voluminous than mine.

I said, "I know what you are, Anlash Niklia. I pronounce you under arrest for the death of Faliti Chandur and the endangerment of every woman in Morimound. Your execution will be summary."

"I—you must've drunk too much of my stock. I don't know what you're talking about."

His face flashed with shock, and his eyes darted to Deepmand in fear.

The whispers died out in the bazaar, and merchant and customers alike looked up from wares as I shouted.

"Anlash Niklia, tell me you are not a Soultrapper!"

"I'm not a Soultrapper. Whatever that is, I'm not one. I'm just a vintner."

His eyes held mine the whole time, to see if I had spotted his lie. I had: Both sides of his mouth turned down in a facial shrug, indicating no confidence in his words; his remaining arm reached toward his neck in a sign of desperation, and his voice dropped in pitch, whereas in a nervous but innocent man, it would have climbed.

"You lie." I raised my voice high enough that Tethiel would have to hear me. "You are a Soultrapper!"

"Nah-no-no! I'm not even a gemcutter now. I have no magic. If Soultrappers have magic."

I wondered why Tethiel waited. Behind me, one of the cloaked lepers spoke.

"Threaten the roach."

"Let's see how he squeaks," the second one said.

My vision had begun to swim and not merely from the rain. This encounter was not going as I had planned: Tethiel should have attacked, and any threatening move made overtly against the Soultrapper might frighten him into slaughtering the city's women. I did not wish to follow the advice of the dandies behind me, yet I did not see what choice I had.

"Spellsword Deepmand...."

"Elder Enchantress?"

I leaned both hands on my cane, feeling unstable and close to tipping over sideways in front of all the onlookers in the bazaar. Within moments, I might see the Soultrapper kill every woman in Morimound. I could not order the spellsword to decapitate him, yet I had to do something. I glanced around once more for Tethiel on his horse, and after seeing nothing, I screamed at Deepmand.

"Seize him!"

Lightening his armor, the spellsword launched himself through the air. His gilded gauntlet clamped onto the Soultrapper's throat, lifting him off his feet.

The Soultrapper opened his mouth, and a wail filled the bazaar. I dropped my cane to cover my ears while the shriek echoed from every direction, a high sound of sudden pain rising from many throats. All around me, women gripped their bellies and collapsed.

I too clutched my abdomen, anguished in knowing the worst was happening. Tethiel had to strike now, before the Soultrapper killed the rest of the women, and I glanced about for signs of illusions descending from the clouds, of nightmares running across the bazaar. I saw nothing but stunned citizens gaping at the sprawled women, where blood spread over rain puddles.

Lifting my chin, I screamed at the sky. "Kill him!"

"You really mustn't," the Soultrapper said, his voice now relaxed, almost a purr. "Or Morimound will lose all its women."

"They," I asked, "they're not all dying?"

"If I die, they all die."

He spoke the truth. I could not believe it, yet I could see he did. The Soultrapper had not killed all the women, only those nearest, I presumed; the Fate Weaver had spared the rest so far.

My chest stung as if I had inhaled a fume of burning poison ivy; I had not anticipated that killing the Soultrapper would activate the Bone Orbs. I had not, because that meant we had no way to stop him; it meant that Tethiel, who knew so much about Soultrappers, had engineered a plan that could never succeed. Killing the Soultrapper would only mean killing half the populace of Morimound, all in one second.

The day's drowning heat fled from me, and I felt frozen. Tethiel could destroy Morimound in a second, through the Soultrapper, yet he would never do that. I could not believe he would do it; I had seen sadness in his face. He must have been delayed, maybe attacked elsewhere. I could not think that Morimound was in the chokehold of not only one man but two.

I glanced over my shoulder, and past the golden hump, I saw the two dandies dragging Maid Janny away, an arm stump pressed over her mouth and a knife over her throat. One leper hushed me with a finger to his flaking lips, and then he drew a thumb over his throat.

"No!" I called after them, although I could not say if to entreat them to release Janny, or for the Lord of the Feast not to strike.

Turning back to the Soultrapper, I saw Deepmand lift his scimitar and rest its blade between the folds of the Soultrapper's chins. The spellsword glanced to me, for orders.

I said nothing, knowing nothing that could save Morimound now. Despair lanced through me in a line of pain from throat to hip. I had failed once again.

The Soultrapper touched the spellsword's neck.

Deepmand gasped and flinched away, a welt erupting on his skin. It seeped with bodily fluids with such violence that it hissed. The scimitar dropped from Deepmand's hand to smash against the wet bricks, and the rest of him followed it, his arms slackening and his massive torso tipping back like a leaning tower; he landed with a crash.

I watched dumbfounded as Deepmand shriveled, and he aged two decades in seconds, his eyes clouding, his cheeks collapsing into the hollows of his face. Brown steam hissed from the chinks of his armor with a stench both sulfurous and rotten like a bloated goat I had once found by the riverbank.

A.E. MARLING

"Anger me and he dies, Enchantress," the Soultrapper said. He bit his thumb then traced a symbol of blood on Deepmand's forehead, a glyph.

I waited for Deepmand to stand, for his gaping eyes to show some sign of life. He was a spellsword of the Mindvault Academy and my protector; he was my strength. If he yet breathed, I could not see it. If he yet lived, the Soultrapper's spell held him at the brink of death.

I sank to my knees; the weight of my saturated gowns bore me down, and the knowledge of my failure paralyzed me. Deepmand's gilded plates now looked less like armor than a sarcophagus.

"You are to blame for their deaths." The Soultrapper gazed over the fallen women, shaking his head. He motioned to his two followers. "Bring me my sons."

"Yes, Your Divinity."

While the followers drew knives and approached a woman, I could only stare at the glyph etched by corrosive magic into Deepmand's face. I could not believe his fate was to die, not so soon before retiring with the family he loved, in the city of his birth. I glared up at the Soultrapper, the person who deserved death more than any, yet the one man who could not be threatened, let alone killed. Too many life threads wove around his own.

The Soultrapper waved his hand to the nearest onlookers. Many had run away, yet a few remained to gawk. These now stiffened, walking forward as the Soultrapper spoke.

"Remove the enchantress's golden humpback. I'd wager it's the source of her power."

Five men—three of them guardsmen—gripped me, tugging at my back. I could not believe they would listen to the Soultrapper after what he had done; by the surprise on their faces, neither could they believe it. The Soultrapper had possessed their minds.

The men struggled with the bindings that tied my hump to my gowns. Eventually, they would have them unknotted, and then I could be killed by anyone with so much as a knife.

I could only think how Tethiel had betrayed me, how I had lost Deepmand and even Janny. My worthless magic could not save me. I was alone and helpless.

UNRESTRAINED
-39-

The Soultrapper buckled my golden hump onto his back; it made him glitter like a jeweled scarab, one with a fleshy underbelly and missing three legs. He palmed his shoulder stump with his remaining hand as he walked between rows of Bone Orbs. His followers had brought them one by one, and the rain washed them free of blood.

I could scarcely focus my eyes. A boiling sickness filled me.

"Twenty-six of your sons died, Your Divinity." The followers carried a crushed Bone Orb and knelt as they rested it beside others that had broken, fractured into white pieces and leaking strong-smelling venom.

"Born before their time, at a great loss to Morimound," the Soultrapper said. "Enchantress, you murdered my sons and fifty-one women today. You do not deserve free will."

He waved his hand, and something gripped my mind, pawing at it and digging fingers into my consciousness. I felt as wronged as I had as a girl when Uncle Gobind had touched me. Then, I had struggled against shame, drowsiness, and stronger hands. Now, I felt worse, yet this time I embraced my lethargy, fleeing down the marble steps to sleep.

I had a sense of the Soultrapper reaching after me, not with his true hand but with a ghostly arm, one extending from his amputated stump. A bone hand like a five-legged white tarantula gripped my face even as I leapt upward into the laboratory.

I Repulsed the skeletal hand and Burdened it to the basalt floor, crushing it to powder. The white dust vanished.

Waking myself, I saw the Soultrapper stagger back and grip his shoulder. His tearing eyes locked on me.

"You jackal bitch! You won't refuse me once I'm fully divine." He panted, his face working in fury. "But, no, you are not worthy to even worship me. Throw her into her carriage."

Men gripped my sleeves. I caught hold of my cane and tried to beat them back, yet they dragged me across the bazaar. Before they could force me into my carriage, I spotted the followers packing the Bone Orbs with straw into barrels.

The carriage began to move; I guessed the possessed men were driving, yet I did not know where they would bring me. I gazed out the window but recognized nothing. I could not even decide if it still rained: A fog of nausea had settled over me, blurring everything.

I retreated into my laboratory, only to find it tilting, listing to one side. The floating island on which the laboratory perched was falling and would crash into the replica of Morimound. A thought from me could stop it, yet I did not see why I should bother.

I did not deserve a laboratory, or anything else, not with Deepmand incapacitated and fifty others lying dead in the bazaar, not with a Soultrapper and the Lord of the Feast free in my city.

Glowing baubles slid off shelves while I frantically asked myself if I could do anything, any one thing to help Morimound. If I slipped the Soultrapper the red diamond then it would begin dismembering the Bone Orbs over one month, and he would likely sense the spell in only seconds. I could enchant another jewel to give the Soultrapper a tumor in the frontal lobe of his brain; if he accepted it and wore it then he would have to bargain with me to cure him. Or his personality might change, and he could forget how to access his magic.

He would still hold the greater power, with the lives of thousands in his hand. He could threaten those lives if I refused to reverse the enchantment. Or he might kill all the women out of insanity.

I could think of no better option; therefore, I ripped a gem of jet from one of my gowns, crafting the enchantment even as my laboratory plummeted and I drifted upward out of the skylight.

The eclipse glared red above me, while below, the stone island hit ground, the laboratory dome crumbling and spraying black dust and colored gems over thirty city blocks. The plume rose around me, blotting out the bloody moon and multicolored stars.

Coughing, I left the dream to find the dark and round jet in my hand. I glanced out of the carriage and was shocked to see my manor.

A wagon loaded with barrels and the immobile Deepmand rattled up to the entrance beside the carriage. Twenty guardsmen escorted the wagon, and one knelt to let the Soultrapper use his back for a step down.

The Soultrapper slapped his oiled belly, which jiggled, and he gazed up at my manor. "Sunchase Hall. A suitable gift to honor the birth of my first sons. I hope, Enchantress, your master bed is soft, my back pains me so."

The Soultrapper planned to sleep in my marriage bed, and I found myself unable to object with anything more intelligent than a wet, sniffling sound. My fingers clenched the jet, and I wanted to throw it at him.

Guards seized my sleeves, leading me up to the doors. The Soultrapper walked ahead of me, two servants opening the doors for us. One of the servants was a pregnant woman, and the Soultrapper grunted in disgust at the sight of her.

"Get that fat sow away from me! I never want to see another full-bellied woman again, even if she's carrying my son."

Mister Obenji strode toward us, lifting a hand to his turban upon seeing all the guards. "Mistress Elder Enchantress, are these all guests?"

Unable to answer him, I bowed my head to hide my face.

One of the followers said, "The Divinity of Morimound has claimed this manor."

"And I will have a banquet!" The Soultrapper bellowed. "The first fruits of my long labor."

I heard Alyla's voice. "Why is that man wearing your...your gold—"

"Mister Obenji," I said, "take Alyla and Sri off the premises. Immediately."

"No, no," the Soultrapper said, "if the enchantress cares for sows, then they will stay. Guards, lock them up, so I don't have to see them."

Two of the possessed men grabbed Alyla, and as they escorted her away I heard her sob.

He spat on the marble floor. "Better that they walk about on all fours, their bellies and teats wagging like a goat stuffed with kids."

One of his followers nodded after Alyla. "Ain't nothing more ugly."

The jet dug into my palm; I knew I must be subtle in presenting it to the Soultrapper, although I had trouble formulating the words with which to do it.

"Each one shrivels my cock," the Soultrapper said, "and it's shrunk far enough. At least there's one woman left in Morimound. Senbhat, take the guards and bring me Priest Salkant's daughter."

"Bet she's a polished one," a follower said.

The other said, "Always knew you'd get her, Your Divinity, one way or another."

"Oh!" The Soultrapper lifted a pudgy finger, and the men paused, rapt and waiting. "And kill the priest. He must be punished for claiming his wine is better."

One follower left with guards, chuckling as he went. I stared after them and wondered if he could really murder a priest. Salkant of the Fate Weaver traveled with no fewer than five guards, yet the Soultrapper had twenty, almost one for each of his Bone Orbs. Once the full fifty thousand had been born, I had no doubt he would dominate the city. I could not permit that.

I lifted the jet to him. "This will regenerate your missing arm. I will give it to you, if you free Alyla and the others."

"Only a fool would accept gifts from a crocodile in a dress." The Soultrapper nodded to his follower. "Hit her."

"Er, you think I can?" The follower frowned at my gowns. "Won't she enchant me?"

"I'd like to see her try," the Soultrapper said.

The follower drew his scimitar, and with the flat of the blade, he slapped the jet from my hand then slammed my face. I fell over into my gowns from the weight of the blade.

The Soultrapper stood above me, his ample gut shadowing my head. "For breaking one measly diamond, you said I deserved to lose more than my arm. The gods thought different, and now it's my fate to protect Morimound from its enemies."

I said, "You are the city's enemy."

"What would you know of it? You've done nothing better than force me to kill women and let an elephant of a priest break down the Flood Wall with his trumpeting farts."

I touched my throbbing face. "I built the Flood Wall!"

"Yes, and you will rebuild it. I want a plan drawn up within a week. Can't have my city washed away."

I clicked my mouth shut, sick with horror and confusion—not knowing how I could refuse this request or how I could live with myself after doing anything for the Soultrapper. My face pulsed with heat and pain, and my mind refused to work.

Uncertain if I was choosing correctly, I said, "I will design a plan to reconstruct the wall, if you release my guests. And extract your foul magic from my spellsword."

The Soultrapper nodded to his follower. "Hit her again."

The follower smacked me with the blunt side of his scimitar. I heard the crack of my cheekbone breaking, and a searing pain washed over my face.

I found myself underneath an eclipsed moon, amid the rubble of my laboratory. I had fainted; my face hurt distantly even in my dream. A replica of me appeared and began to shiver as she lay on the basalt rocks.

The replica asked, "What can we do now?"

Not knowing how to answer, I knelt beside her and examined the damage done to her face. Glowing baubles floated up from the rubble as I needed them for spells, and I set the bone, creating an enchantment to accelerate the healing process.

Returning to the world of the waking, I found the follower leering over me.

"See! She ain't dead, Your Divinity."

The Soultrapper had a bottle of wine between his legs and was uncorking it one-handed. "Enchantress, you'll do whatever I want. Or I'll take your guard's soul for good, and my lads will treat your lady guests like the whores they are."

Hurt and disbelief knotted through me. I clutched my temples and groaned.

Wine tinkled as it poured into a glass, and I heard the Soultrapper sniff it. "Ah! The last bottle of Liquid Diamond with any of me in it."

A clatter of armored boots announced the return of his men; the priest's daughter was slung over one's shoulder. Her pale legs dangled from her silk shift, and when the guard set her down, her puffy eyes gaped at everything around her.

I suspected she must never have seen other men before today.

The redness of her face told of recent tears, although I saw none now. When her eyes wandered to me, she lifted her chin and said, "Flawless, these men have killed my father."

"And he was a mongrel, too." The follower handed Priest Salkant's paragon diamond to the Soultrapper. "Shat all over the place."

"This is her?" The Soultrapper grimaced at the daughter. "A diseased rat would have more meat on its bones. She won't do at all. And the enchantress is too old and too dangerous, and no muddy from Stilt Town will soil my new bed."

"Flawless," the daughter said, "these men have defied the gods by harming a priest, and I insist you arrest them."

I could not believe her courage in front of the men who had murdered her father. I was as proud of her as I was ashamed of myself.

"The enchantress isn't the Flawless. She has more flaws than a muddy leper. Now, what to do?" The Soultrapper lifted the paragon diamond to his lips as if to take a bite from a sparkling fruit. It threw prismatic sparks over his face while he grinned at the daughter. "You, what was your name?"

"Kishala," she said.

"You will be the next Flawless."

She swept one arm downward in anger. "That is for the gods and their priests to decide!"

"That is for me to decide!" Veins pulsed down his brow like thick purple worms. "I, Morimound's king and protector." He set down the diamond to lift the wineglass. "Now you must celebrate. I've saved this for you."

"Don't drink it!" I propped myself up with my cane and reached for her.

"You should stay silent, Enchantress, unless you're agreeing to rebuild the Flood Wall. If you do, Kishala here won't have to drink my wine."

"I—I will build it," I said. "First I must survey the wall, to determine priorities."

"Acolytes will inform you of the damages. You'll not be let loose in the city, and I have a place in mind to keep you." The Soultrapper gazed from the wine to Kishala. "This is hardly satisfying. You'll drink this, and the enchantress will build the wall anyway."

I screamed in denial, and Kishala shoved the wineglass away, spilling it on the Soultrapper. He cursed, and three guards pinned her down; her bare feet kicked in the air as the Soultrapper upended the wine bottle into her mouth. She spluttered and choked, and I worried they would drown her.

By the time the last drops fell from the bottle, Kishala's shift was soaked and clung to her. The girl retched. The Soultrapper spat on her, and then he turned to me.

"How refreshing to no longer have to take orders. Now, Enchantress, do you remember the boys you invited to the ball? You dressed them as women, and the one I saw turned me as a stiff as a bottle's neck. They'll have to do."

I protested that I did not remember how to find them, yet the Soultrapper threatened to bring out Alyla. Not wishing to see her tormented, I told him that Mister Obenji would know where the boys lived.

"Good, good! One last thing, Enchantress. I want your earrings—you won't be needing them where you're going."

I touched the blue diamonds at my ears. "They would not shine for you."

"Either way, you don't deserve them."

Two unspeaking guards gripped my face and tugged at my earrings. Their clasps would not loosen; even I did not have control over their potent enchantment, something I regretted when it grew obvious that the guards would rip off my ears to get them.

The Soultrapper peered at me. Perhaps he wanted to see me defend myself with magic; he might think I had powers in this world against which he must guard. I only wished he were right.

They ended up slicing my ears with their scimitars, and I began to feel this was happening to someone else. This woman could not be me on the floor, unable to do anything as she was being attacked.

The bloodied earrings fell into the Soultrapper's hands, and he dropped them. "God's fart, they weigh as much as barrels! Senbhat, lock the enchantress away where you found this rat." He kicked Kishala.

I wept and bled as they shoved me into the carriage. On the ride across the Island District, I slept and repaired my ears, even Attracting some of the blood back into the wound.

We arrived at the manor that had belonged to Salkant of the Fate Weaver. The follower forced me into Kishala's windowless room. Darkness filled the chamber now, and they threw an unlit candle after me then slammed the door shut. I winced at the "snick" of the lock.

The follower might have assumed I could light the candle with my magic; as I could not, I would have to wait in darkness. Sightless, I felt as if I hung suspended in a night without stars, and the thought of such darkness reminded me of the Lord of the Feast.

I had found the Soultrapper for him, given him the key to slaying all the city's women in one moment. I feared he would do so tonight, and I would hear the shrieking laughter of his children slaughtering in the streets.

"Great Weaver," I whispered to the darkness, "please tell me this is not our fate. Please!"

RESTRAINED
-40-

Night Forty-One, Third Trimester

I wondered if I would know when the death began. My general education course on magic had claimed that proximity to Feasting produced a sense of foreboding, yet I felt so distressed and disconsolate now that I was unsure I would be able to distinguish a difference.

Enclosed on all sides by blackness, I began to wonder if the downpour continued outside; the savanna rivers might overflow; a flood might even now sweep up the streets. Half the city could be submerged, and I would never know it.

I felt I was the last person alive, that I would be left here and forgotten, my skeleton found years later in a pile of twenty-seven gowns.

Worst of all, I imagined that this was what it would be like to have my soul imprisoned. Blackness all around, the nothing smothering me and choking me and my every effort to escape would only strengthen the Soultrapper.

Deepmand would be experiencing worse, if he died. The Soultrapper had drawn a glyph on him, and his death would mean struggling to free himself from his withered corpse, for as long as the Soultrapper lived. He had been paralyzed because of my uncertainty and inadequacy.

A.E. MARLING

"If I live," I said to the emptiness, "if I survive and Morimound does, too, Deepmand, I swear I will bring you back to health and provide for your family. I will take them into my home and honor your children as my own. Even the illegitimate one."

I saw scant possibility of that. If the city survived the night and Priest Abwar gathered the city guards to kill the Soultrapper, then every last Bone Orb inside a woman would explode.

My hands beat against the wall, and I wept. Mucus dribbled over my lips. I had no ability to save my city, and I saw now that I never had, not when confronted with men whose magic gave them the power of gods. I had spent my life studying a magic that did nothing of use, leaving me without means to defend myself or anyone else.

The squeak of sliding metal surprised me, and a rectangle of light expanded across the floor; the aperture at the base of the door had opened, and a bowl of water and rice slid through.

"Has the night passed?" I tripped over my dresses to bend down to the opening. "Is it day?"

The aperture closed, throwing me back into darkness. I had no stomach for eating, yet I felt the mounting pressure to relieve my bladder. I stumbled around searching for a chamber pot for what seemed an hour. I could have retreated into my dream to recall where it was, yet too great a lethargy bowed me down for me to wish to utilize the memory mirror, or anything else.

I forced myself to eat the rice, then I used the bowl as a chamber pot. As I rose from squatting, my gowns proved too cumbersome, causing me to tip the full bowl over and spill its noisome contents. The room stank with my shame.

"These horrid gowns!"

I tore at them, wishing to be rid of their swelter. Their silk mired my every step, forcing me to use a cane, and I wanted to be rid of it all.

"I won't die in these wretched gowns!"

Try as I might, I could not tear the enchanted fabric, nor could I untie their labyrinth of laces. I lay sweating and defeated, in drifts of velvet.

Of course, I reminded myself I could not afford to remove the gowns, especially not now. They protected me as much as mail armor protected a soldier. Underneath them, I was simply a sleepy girl who could die to any scimitar blade. With them on, everyone saw me as an enchantress: Men feared me, and even the Soultrapper knew he needed my skills. No, I could never be without my gowns.

Light flooded the room, and through blinking eyes, I saw that an acolyte had entered. He winced at the smell and at my disheveled state. Then he provided documentation on clay tablets of the condition of the Flood Wall.

The acolyte's candle illuminated the room: planters capsized, ferns and moss browning. Books were strewn from shelves. Dead fish floated in one of several bowls, their water clouded. The Soultrapper's follower must have vandalized Kishala's sanctuary during the kidnapping.

I reviewed the acolyte's notations, asked him a few questions then bid him to leave. He set parchment, ink, and quill on the table. Then he spoke.

"Enchantress, they say the Ever Always killed the women in the bazaar. All across the city, families are making sacrifices. Some women are arranging their death rites."

"Anlash Niklia killed those women."

He grimaced but nodded. "I suspected that. The acolytes of the Fate Weaver refuse to take any action, but the rest of us are fortifying the Island."

"Priest Abwar leads you?"

"He is fevered, from a cut on his hand."

"Unfortunate," I said.

"Should we attack Sunchase Hall? The traitor Anlash has the priest's daughter hostage."

"Killing him would not benefit Morimound."

"Flawless, what should we do? If you escape, could we count on you to lead us?"

"You cannot count on me for anything."

The acolyte left with the candle, returning the room to darkness.

It mattered not. By feel, I spread the parchment then wrote the plan in my dream. The Flood Wall could hardly be rebuilt with the waters already high, yet temporary barriers had a chance of preventing the flood from spreading if one diverted some of the water through the sewer system.

I outlined a plan to reconstruct the wall during the following dry season.

Awaking, I waited for the acolyte to retrieve my work. The door stayed shut, the room black. My gowns prevented me from pacing, and when I resorted to banging a fist against the door, I still garnered no response.

My thirst convinced me that the majority of the day had passed. Dipping my hand into a fishbowl to lap up water would be decidedly unladylike and unsanitary, yet I did it anyway. I wondered if night had fallen again and if the Lord of the Feast had struck; I imagined myself locked in this room, the last person alive in Morimound. The weeks of my starvation would be agonizing.

I hoped Maid Janny fared better than I, wherever the lepers had taken her. Doubtless, they only held her to stop her from blathering about Tethiel.

"Please," I said, "let her inconsequence and unappealing figure save her from harm."

The door opened in a burst of light. A man spoke, and the voice flashed a bolt of recognition through me.

"Leave the candle on the table, my heart."

A guard left the light, and the door shut behind Lord of the Feast. We were alone.

STARVING
-41-

Day Forty-Two, Third Trimester

The Lord of the Feast wore the robes of an acolyte, and for the first time, I saw him without his face powdered. I still recognized him instantly by his slumped shoulders, impassive expression, and crooked fingers. The brand of the black triangle did not show on his brow; he must have hid the stigma under a flesh-colored paste.

I wanted to scream, to throw a book at him, to weep, and to cower. My body refused to perform any of those actions, and I did no more than stare into his metallic-blue eyes.

He returned my gaze but did not speak.

I wrested back control of my breathing and managed to wet my tongue enough to form words.

"What have you done with Maid Janny?"

"She is safe."

"Is she? Is Spellsword Deepmand? He fell while you loitered. While you did nothing. Why? Why drag this out beyond mercy?"

"Soultrappers favor decoys. Now that I have seen him cast magic, I am convinced."

"Yet still you wait."

"The waters have delayed my Feasters."

I felt insignificant, no more than a colorful caterpillar. The Lord of the Feast could crush me with a thought, and now I believed he would feel no qualm in doing so.

"Did you always know," I whispered, "that killing the Soultrapper would kill the women?"

"I knew that once I began Feasting, I could not stop myself," he said, toneless as ever. "Understand, your city is delicious."

His fingers clenched as far as they could and he swallowed, his tongue running over his upper lip. Closing his eyes, he took two long breaths before speaking.

"So many worried for their unborn children. Their every breath tasted like strawberries and cream. Their uncertainty for the future was salted pork, frying on the pan. Now that the deaths in the bazaar have seasoned their fear—Ahh!"

Saliva strung between his teeth as his mouth stretched into the first full expression I had seen on his face: hunger.

"Fear is a banquet, tables set on every street, boards burdened with steak broiled in wine and dribbling with juices, with mutton roasted with truffles, with buttered carrots and enough baked pies to feed a thousand of my children."

I began to shiver and my own stomach clenched in horror.

"The Soultrapper is a snake on the table," he said, "and only with his death may the banquet begin in safety. When the women die I'll devour their terror and flood the city with nightmare. I will be the Seventh Flood."

My heart beat twice before the gravity of his words hit me: He planned to kill not only the women but their husbands as well, and their sons, fathers, uncles, nephews, and grandfathers. This was the doom predicted by Salkant of the Fate Weaver, the prophesy of "within his lifetime" off by mere days. And Sri had dreamed of a flood without water.

Tears burned my face as I stomped toward him, not realizing what I intended but with my fists raised. Before I reached him, I tripped over my gowns and collapsed weeping.

"Not tonight," he said, "but perhaps the night after. No matter what you see, no matter what you hear and feel, do not believe it. These walls will keep you from fleeing into greater danger, and you should live to see daybreak. I will ensure the survivors find you."

"There—there will be survivors?"

"Past floods drowned all but the wealthiest in the Island District. I find it poetic that the Seventh Flood will start on high and sweep downward, killing all but the poorest of Stilt Town. The survivors will need leadership in the time ahead, and you will govern them. That is my gift to you."

"Your gift?"

My hand snapped to the ruffles at my neck, and I scrounged between the folds of fabric to pull out the red diamond, wishing to throw it at him. Its gold chain prevented me from doing so, cutting into my fingers as I strained to break it.

"You kill most everyone in Morimound and call it a gift? You lied to me!"

His open-mouthed hunger contracted, his expression changing into something subtler. "I never lied."

I realized he stared at the red diamond on the necklace, and I grew embarrassed and angry with myself for allowing him to see it. "You did worse than lie. You deceived."

"You deceived yourself," he said, "if you thought I'd attempt to do good. I'm far too conscientious for that."

"I will warn the Soultrapper," I said, aware I was raving but unable to care enough to contain myself. "I'll tell him your plan, and he'll wither you like he did Deepmand."

"You will do nothing of the kind."

"I see nothing to lose by it."

"Morimound has recovered from six floods," he said, "but one Soultrapper will change it beyond recognition. You think all these Bone Orbs will satisfy him? This is only the first crop. His power will spread outward from this city, until his dominion rivals the Oasis Empire. And he won't die. His magic will extend his life even as it distorts his body, and once he at last shrivels into dust, he'll lock his own soul in his bones and still control legions of slaves."

I felt I tumbled down a cliff into despair, and I clutched the red diamond as if its gold chain were a safety rope. However, the enchanted jewel could save neither Morimound nor me, no matter how much I wished it would.

"After the Seventh Flood," he said, "I'll be gone with the dawn. This time I will not return. Enchantress Hiresha...I think you deserve better, but so do all born to this world."

With that, he left.

The candle remained on the table, yet I curled my arm around my face, hiding from the light. This candle stank of burning ox fat. As I sobbed, I wondered if the Lord of the Feast had been right: I would accept the Seventh Flood, allowing all but a few of my people to die in order to save them from enslavement.

Anlash Niklia was ill mannered and brutal, which were common traits among kings. He had professed his wish to protect the city, and I had no doubt that with his strength in magic, Morimound could become a world power. I envisioned myself at his side, advising him, petitioning him for better treatment of his subjects, for Alyla and Sri. He had some mercy in him; his magic had selectively spared girls younger than twelve from pregnancy.

My stomach rolled, and I blotted out the thought. Expecting kindness from the man who had violated women with Bone Orbs would be madness. He had no mercy, only practicality. The girls would have made insufficient vessels for the unchildren, or they would have died and thus denied his nascent empire its future generation.

The door opened again, and I was angry that the Lord of the Feast would dare to return to torment me yet again.

Lifting my eyes from the crook of my elbow, I realized it was not he. One of the Soultrapper's followers stood beside the guard, both with scimitars drawn.

MORTAL
-42-

"The candle's lit! So she *can* command fire." The follower's scimitar trembled as it pointed to me. "Don't you try your enchantery on me, you hear? Or I'll carve you into a jackal's dinner!"

His ignorance astounded me, yet not half so much as those rudely sharp blades.

The guard stayed silent beside him, yet his sword also wobbled in the air, his knuckles white on the hilt. I began to think they both feared me, and the revelation was not unpleasant, as it meant I might yet live.

"Did ya finish the plan? Water's rising, and we'll be swimming soon, if the clouds don't let up."

I waved to the parchment on the table and noticed the blood on my hand, which I had cut when yanking at my necklace. My fingers shoved the red diamond out of sight in my gowns.

The follower half-tripped over a fallen book on his way to the table. Keeping his scimitar angled at me, he attempted to scrutinize the construction procedures and diagrams while glancing my way every other second.

I thought I should warn them about the Lord of the Feast. Better for people to live, even if they suffered. Yet, the follower and guard had arrived so soon after Tethiel that I worried he might still be in the building, and he might intercept any message I gave them. I was too drowsy to decide if that was probable or not.

"The pictures seem right enough." The follower scooped up the parchment and rolled it into his belt. He backed away from me and nodded to the guard. "Well, go on. We'll be safer once it's done."

The guard stalked toward me with his scimitar.

I needed two seconds to realize the purpose to which he intended to put that blade and another to remember that I had lost both my golden hump and Deepmand. Neither of them would save me now. The blade swung toward my head.

I tried to back away, tripping instead into my billowing gowns. The scimitar sliced the air above my nose.

"Hurry, you fool!" The follower shouted from behind a bookcase. "Before she enchants us to death!"

I thrashed to my feet and tried to escape, wallowing in my silks, yet the guard had trodden on several of my hems, pinning me. He grabbed at the swaths of cloth spreading from my shoulder and yanked me toward his blade. My gowns, I realized, had just killed me.

An agony spread through me, even though the scimitar had yet to cut. I would be thrust from this world; the majority of Morimound would soon follow, and I could do nothing to stop it.

The guard's face tensed as if he struggled against something within him.

"She killed His Divinity's sons." The follower peeked around the bookcase. "They broke because of her, and the enchantress must die!"

I glowered up at the guard, angry that I would have to admit to the other spirits that a possessed nobody had killed me. Not about to waste breath on pleading, I torqued the arm holding my shoulder.

A line of pressure crossed over my neck, followed by sensations of heat and wetness. I glanced below my chin to see blood dribbling over the bronze of the scimitar.

He had severed my throat.

A calmness washed through me, along with feelings of lifting and weightlessness, as if I entered my dream.

"Good man." The follower strode from behind the shelf with scimitar raised. "Now lay her out, and I'll cut off her head for His Divinity."

The guard was holding me on my feet, and I had pressed my hands against my throat. While blood leaked between my fingers, I gazed at the men with a sense of perfect clarity. My own struggle seemed a trifling thing now, only one fraying thread in the Loom of Life. In addition, I realized that even if I could still speak to warn them of the Lord of the Feast, I would not.

Alyla and Sri would die birthing Bone Orbs; the Soultrapper would sacrifice them because he cared little for his people and much for himself, and under his rule, Morimound would rise to power but not to greatness. Better for some of my people to lay down their lives now than doom their descendents to tyranny.

The follower stopped his approach, and the guard stiffened, their eyes widening. I wondered what in my face had given them pause.

Hands lifted from my throat, and I realized they must be my hands as my blood covered them and they reached from

A.E. MARLING

my sleeves. Yet I could not recall releasing my grip on my neck, or of lifting my arms, although I could not be certain: I felt nothing now but a coldness.

My dripping fingers etched runes of blood in the air. Red energy crackled down my arms. My hands began to smoke with heat. From this, I could only conclude that blood loss was causing a hallucination.

The guard backed away from me, the follower dropping his scimitar. Both their mouths stretched in horror, and this pleased me until I realized that real men would not be able to see my hallucination. Their reactions also had to be the result of miscalculations in my dying brain.

Flame spewed from my hands; blinding waves of red blasted over both men. Books sprayed into ash, and the marble behind crumbling shelves brightened into molten dribbles.

The fire scoured away the men, vaporizing their flesh and carbonizing their bones, which shattered against the wall. Ash drizzled through the air.

When the room cleared of smoke, I found myself on my knees with cold hands still held against my throat. The bookshelves returned into being from their recent incineration, and the walls were no longer melting; my hallucination had ended. Quite peculiar, I thought, that the men lay unmoving on the floor, their skin white and faces wracked with terror. Neither man breathed.

Tethiel stood in the doorway, a black triangle on his brow. His hands were raised.

Then I understood: I had not hallucinated but seen an illusion, which had frightened my attackers to death. Tethiel had begun Feasting for my sake, counter to all his plans, and as I spluttered blood, I dreaded that I would be but the first Morimound woman of thousands to die.

Tethiel began to bloat, his head and body expanding and stretching upward while his arms thickened into trunks. More fingers sprouted beside his thumbs on his palm, and all his digits sharpened into black fangs; his hands were enlarging into the jaws of monsters.

Now I knew why they said the Lord of the Feast had three heads. The sight froze me and obstructed my breath, although that might have been the blood in my chest.

With a yell, he slammed his hands to the ground and pinned them under his knees. The teeth at the end of his arms gnashed while he bent forward to vomit a dark fluid. The tar-colored ooze rippled over the floor then melded into shadows.

As he retched out more darkness, Tethiel shrank back to normal size. Fangs diminished to bent fingers, and the black triangle receded into his skull.

"Hiresha!"

He scrambled to me. I had fallen to my side, gagging, and he rolled me forward, holding my head and shoulders steady as I coughed blood. While I gasped, he cradled me and wiped my mouth.

"Can you heal yourself, in your dream?"

I had never heard of someone falling asleep with her throat cut, yet if anyone could, she would be me. When I nodded, my neck stung.

"Then you must sleep. You will sleep and heal yourself."

A.E. MARLING

Hearing him say it made it almost sound plausible. I relaxed my grip on my neck and forced my eyes closed. Aware of blood sliding down my esophagus, I saw the stair leading to my dream dripping with red. The steps multiplied, the stair twisting and knotting itself into a maze that I could never hope to traverse before I drowned in my own blood.

I waved my hand and willed the stair back to straightness, the one hundred steps leading down to safety. As I began to descend them, blood trickled after me, slicking the steps and forcing me to worry what would happen if I fell from the stair into the darkness on either side.

By step thirty-five, blood sheeted down the stairs, and I was wading downhill. My foot slipped, and I tumbled five steps and began to slide off the edge. I threw my arms over the wet side, hauling myself back up and wobbling to my feet.

Stooping for a lower center of gravity, I flattened each foot on the step ahead of me before trusting any weight to it. This grew impossible by step seventy-one, as the blood flow had increased into a red waterfall. I did not so much walk as was swept down the last steps, relying on flailing and willpower to stay on the stair.

The hundredth step approached, and I feared that if I went past it then I would hurl downward into nothingness. Jumping too soon would result in waking to death, and with blood preventing proper footing, I was unsure if even leaping at the right moment would grant me sufficient clearance to reach the dream.

Above the ninety-ninth step, I heaved my legs downward into the blood.

My feet connected with the hundredth step and sent me soaring.

A moon shaded of amber and spessartine gems shone in the jeweled sky above me, and I stood amid broken basalt. From the rubble lifted my operations table; I replicated myself onto it, and with golden clamp in hand, I sealed her throat shut.

I Attracted the blood out of the replica's lungs, throat, and gowns, forming it into a weightless, gelatinous globe. The blood siphoned in and out of my sapphire jar, purifying, and two streamlets returned to the replica's veins through incisions in her wrists, where I had Repulsed her skin open.

Meanwhile, rocks levitated below me, reforming into the island of stone. Blocks of basalt swirled around the operations table, fitting together into a round foundation. While I repaired the veins in her neck, we rose higher into the night, and the walls of the laboratory rebuilt. My spell baubles arranged themselves on their shelves around me, jewels whirling down through a newly formed skylight.

As I angled pins around her throat and wrists to stimulate healing, elation filled me. I felt that I, similar to my jewels and baubles, glowed with a golden warmth.

The replica laughed with a high, tinkling sound. I scowled down at her.

"So sorry," she said, "but we are marvelously happy."

"I have no right to be," I snapped.

"The laboratory is rebuilt, and we are whole."

"I will thank you to stop moving." I set another six pins in place in the air, and my mind raced. "Tethiel may no longer be able to kill the Soultrapper, as he revealed himself by saving me."

"Goodness! Then what can we do?"

I checked over my work then embedded all my spellcraft into the red diamond. The jewel had the capacity to hold this enchantment as well as the one that dissembled Bone Orbs, and wearing it would keep my throat from opening until the tissue units had a chance to mend.

Hovering over the diamond dais, I considered what I could do upon waking, if anything. The realization that I would prefer the coming of the Seventh Flood troubled me no little amount, and I was shocked I could willingly sacrifice so many.

I wanted my people to live, yet as soon as the Soultrapper died, the Bone Orbs would kill all the women who carried them. To prevent that, I would have to draw him into my dream alive, an impossibility that he would never allow; I needed a hundred seconds to fall asleep, and his touch could putrefy me to death in a tenth the time.

No, the only hope for Morimound lay in Tethiel and the Seventh Flood, a catastrophe I was no longer certain lay within his ability.

I awoke in Tethiel's arms.

BARE

-43-

Night Forty-Two, Third Trimester

"I have witnessed a marvel." Tethiel gazed down at my throat and wrists. "Hiresha, yours is the most wonderful of magics."

He lifted his arms halfway up to help hoist me to my feet. I peered at his hands, yet they showed no signs of transmogrifying.

My throat was dry and tender as I spoke. "You said you could not stop Feasting once you began."

"It seems I can." He lifted one hand to waist-level and flexed its fingers. "So long as I focus on you."

My face heated, and I felt lightheaded as if after hyperventilating. "You are stronger than you thought."

"No, weaker." He picked up my cane and handed it to me. "If I had been stronger, I would've let you die."

"That is an impolite thing to say." His rudeness recalled me to my senses, and my dizziness dissipated. I walked over the dead follower, out of my prison, and into the hall.

Tethiel made way for my parade of gowns. "Now the Soultrapper may kill me as I approach, or as I kill him. Upon my death, my children will cast illusion into homes and slaughter many, perhaps even you. No, you first of all, Hiresha. They can be jealous."

"Then I must hope you live."

Although I had Attracted all the blood from my gowns, they still felt unclean, dangerously unwieldy, and entrapping. Even in the hall, I felt stifled by the close walls; I needed fresh air and openness. After days spent worrying that Morimound had been destroyed by flood or Bone Orbs, I had to reassure myself that civilization yet remained. I had to know that deluges had not yet washed away our homes, and women yet lived.

Remembering Kishala had mentioned a roof garden, I ventured upstairs for a commanding view. Tethiel hesitated then climbed the steps after me, although the train of my gowns prevented his following with any closeness. With him clothed in simple acolyte garb, I felt foolish wearing a conglomeration of colored silks. My cane tapped its way ahead of me; we reached the third flight, and I realized the rain would drench us. Yet, when I opened a door onto the roof, a full moon beamed through a break in the clouds.

Bright and enormous from its light refracting off water vapor, the moon turned the night into a silvery day. The White Ziggurat sparkled above us, a mountain of diamond dust. Past the shadows of groves and gardens, I spotted the roof steeples of Sunchase Hall.

I asked, "The Soultrapper will have sensed your magic, from my manor?"

"As a distant feeling of doom." Tethiel walked along a stone path to where I stood at the edge of the building. "He would also have felt the loss of the dominated guard, perhaps of his follower, too. He might be inexperienced enough to confuse the sensations and believe you enchanted them to death."

"Then you may yet surprise him."

"Or he'll recognize my magic and disbelieve my attack long enough to turn me into a sack of meat pudding."

His perfectly symmetrical face was calm, and I noticed that without the powder, he appeared far less deathly. Now only his slouch flawed his figure; the weight of his magic had ruined him as my somnolence had ruined me.

"You do not appear in the least afraid," I said.

He snorted. "Dying will be a relief. It's the mess that comes after that troubles me."

Thoughts of death and the Soultrapper tensed me to the point that my abdomen ached, and my heart sped to two hundred beats per minute. To relax myself, I breathed in air cleaned by rain and sweetened by jasmine.

I asked, "Will you attack tonight? I worry he may harvest more Bone Orbs for power."

"I will, but before I place my life on the betting table, I have one last request." He lifted a hand to me, and shadows around us fluttered as if a wind buffeted our clothes. "To dance with the greatest enchantress on Loam."

The night must have been a sweltering one because at that moment my gowns heated to an insufferable degree.

I found myself short of breath. "This is not, well, it's hardly a proper time."

"True, but it may be our last."

"There is no music."

"With you, I could do without."

Our shadows ebbed and flowed as if we already danced.

"I could never dance in these gowns," I said quietly.

As heat morphed into nausea, I questioned my unwillingness to dance. I needed Tethiel's cooperation to remove the Soultrapper; if in return he wished to indulge in an admittedly absurd waste of time then I might consider agreeing to the exchange, before I fainted from the heat in these terrible gowns. Dancing, I reasoned, although imprudent, would likely not result in any lasting harm.

"No, I could never dance in these gowns. Therefore, they must be removed. I insist that they be excised, using my enchanted sword."

When he grasped my hand, a prickling sensation rose up my arm, along with a soothing coldness. I attributed the feeling to his magic.

For the first time, he smiled without restraint. He straightened his shoulders, and his whole aspect changed, becoming a man emblazoned with unguarded courage and naïve lightheartedness.

"Hold steady," he said.

A blade flashed to my right, from a dandy swordsman who had stepped from the shadow of a fruit tree. He substantiated himself out of nothing, or so his illusions would have me believe.

I said, "Slice away all but the innermost gown, the sixth layer."

The enchanted sword split through silk and gold thread with a sound like wind whistling through the reeds of rice plants. My gowns peeled apart, and I shrugged my shoulders out of the plethora of sleeves and stepped into the open.

Twenty-six gowns deflated behind me, sinking to the ground in a glittering heap. Now I wore next to nothing, only one single gown.

I dropped my cane. I had no more need of it.

When I pulled off my headdress, my scalp tingled, reminding me of gliding headfirst into gusts in my dream. On impulse, I removed the pins from my hair bun, and my locks fell to my shoulders. Tethiel guided me to a wider stretch of garden path; jasmine flowers on the rooftop shone white. A fountain shimmered with water. Fresh air trespassed through my sleeves and up my skirt to breeze between my dress and skin.

"By casting elegance aside, Hiresha, you wear more than ever." He touched the red diamond hanging on its necklace amid polished amethysts at the center of my chest.

Since I could not seem to meet his eyes, I stared instead at the collar of his robes. "I admit, I constructed this gown myself, using equations for ideal aesthetics."

"And you hid it until now? A tragedy."

I drew in a breath as his fingers slid around my waist to clasp me by the small of my back. When I lifted my hands to lay them on his shoulders, amethysts on my sleeves sparkled darkly in the pale light.

Bats dove overhead; crickets chorused, and moths fluttered. We moved around in a slow circular manner, and because we went nowhere, the dancing was pointless. Yet his closeness increased my self-awareness, how silk flowed over my skin like water, the delightful prickling of the gems through my dress; the synchronicity of our movements even granted a certain manner of pleasure.

Our closeness caused an even greater amount of fright. I felt vulnerable. Touching him felt wrong, when Tethiel would soon begin to Feast, to harm the Soultrapper, yes, but also perhaps many of my people. I worried I would remember this night with him forever, even when awake.

Of course, if anyone saw me dancing with the Lord of the Feast, my reputation would be null. I took reassurance in knowing that the Feaster swordsman would cleave any witness in half with my enchanted blade.

"You might now guess," he said, his breath lifting strands of my hair across my brow, "the reason I began Feasting."

"Given the timing of that statement, I deduce you used it to save someone's life."

"As I said, it reflects most negatively on me. I thought I could use the magic to do good."

I asked, "Your magic failed you?"

"Once I had a home, as you do. A land, and a people who I called family."

He had meant "*whom* I called family," yet I decided I would not correct him.

"We were attacked, and I thought I could protect them by reaching into darkness." The shadows trembled around us, and whether conscious of it or not, he tightened his grasp, drawing me closer. "I defeated the invaders but horrified my people. They exiled me, leaving me with nothing but my magic's hunger. Bright Palms led the next invasion, to draw me out. I survived. My homeland did not."

I remembered the ulcerating pain I had felt when my people hated me for building the Flood Wall. How much greater that suffering would be, I thought, if I lost Morimound forever to the Soultrapper, as Tethiel had lost his people to the sword.

A tear rolled down his expressionless face. It landed on my hand, surprising me with its heat.

"My magic failed me as well," I said. "It has never cured my somnolence."

"But you never need be ashamed of it." His chin now brushed the hair draping over my ear. "Your magic has never goaded you, never punished you for every good deed. Your magic is pure."

I thought of my wish to have never encountered my magic, to have never experienced lucidity and known the full poverty of my waking hours. A sadness filled me, an ache I knew Tethiel shared. As he had once lost everything, so would I, tonight; either Tethiel would succeed in bringing about the Seventh Flood and slay most of the city, or Morimound would become enslaved by the Soultrapper.

"My magic failed me," I said. "And failed my people."

I had no power to save them and would be forced to accept the terrible cleansing of the Seventh Flood. I wanted to believe I could do something to protect Alyla, Sri, and the rest, yet to do that I would need to fall asleep with the Soultrapper; the unattainable desire crushed me, heavier than all my gowns had been.

My tears astonished me, flowing in rivulets down my face. I slid my arms off Tethiel's shoulders, meaning to step away from him. He did not release me, although I was unsure if he clung to me for my sake or his own.

His fingers at my back felt more like claws, each a pinprick that set hair on end all over my body. I was

A.E. MARLING

beginning to feel overbalanced by the sensations transmitted through the single gown; his arms held me, and his chest brushed against mine. Why, without even any gloves on, I could run a finger down his neck and feel the warmth of his skin.

I felt naked. I felt powerful.

The second emotion I found inexplicable but also undeniable. I thought of the opportunities that would open to me by wearing barely anything. In one gown I had the chance of ascending ladders, and I would not require the support of a cane. By extension, I allowed myself to analyze if any further benefits could be gained by removing the twenty-seventh gown.

An idea jolted me with such force that I gasped in his arms.

He leaned back to look into my eyes. "What is it, Hiresha?"

"Tethiel," I said, "I can save everyone."

FEARFUL

-44-

"I thought it was impossible," I said, "yet I only have to fall asleep with sufficient surface area of my skin touching the Soultrapper. In my laboratory, I will have control."

"Your laboratory? What is this?" He took a step back, his fingers sliding off the small of my back but still holding me. "You mean your dream? You think you can trick him into bedding you?"

"He wears an open vest. I need only lean against his chest..." I grimaced at the thought of touching his oiled breasts. "...and fall asleep, and he would not know what I was doing until he found himself in my dream."

"I think the Soultrapper would very well know if an enchantress was falling asleep on his lap."

"He would never recognize me, not with short hair. Not if I wore no clothes." I gulped. "He will believe I am one of the boys he forces to wear women's clothing."

"If you were nude, he could hardly mistake you for a boy."

"Do you think me a slattern? I will be wearing my undergarments!"

"You'd be a model of propriety in them, I'm sure, but remember, sometimes men's eyes stray and accidentally look at faces."

"I will paint my face. Hide it like you hid yours."

"That can only go so far." His gaze roamed up my body. "And I still cannot believe anyone could mistake you for a boy."

"A boy dressed as a woman."

"But without a dress on!"

He gripped my sides more strongly, and I noticed his fingers now appeared as black fangs, which pierced my dress to prick my skin. I ignored the needling, knowing it illusion.

"The Soultrapper will recognize you," he said. "With him touching you, you could be ruined in an instant. Remember your spellsword!"

"I remember what was done to him very well, no thanks to you."

"How could you sleep, knowing that any second your insides might begin to rot, your skin decay to slime, your brain shrivel to dust?"

"I fell asleep with my throat cut. I am a professional."

"This death will be faster and far less enjoyable. And to what purpose? He will spot you."

"He will not. He must not." I winced as Tethiel's fingers bit into me, and another idea sparked in my mind. "You will distract him, with your magic. Craft an illusion of me in my gowns, and the Soultrapper will never notice the true me lying against him."

Tethiel pushed himself away from me, his arms shaking and shadows crawling up his sleeves. "Don't ask me to do this. I must Feast on him. The Seventh Flood is the only way."

"You would be saving thousands of lives. Tethiel, you will be a hero."

"That is the problem! I'd be doing good, and my magic will make me regret it." His shoulders contracted into a slouch. "Far better to satisfy it now."

"By killing nearly everyone in a city? What could be worse?"

"I don't know, but it will be."

"You said you could resist your magic by focusing on me." I reached toward his trembling shoulders but hesitated, unsure of where one was supposed to touch another for reassurance. I wondered if other people knew these things instinctively or only through careful observation. My fingers brushed his neck, where I had touched him before. "I know you can be a hero. You saved me."

"I have saved no one." He pinched his eyes closed. "Now you'll get yourself withered by the Soultrapper, and I'll have to Feast on the city a day earlier."

"The Fate Weaver decides the future, not your magic. And she would never allow the Soultrapper to rule Morimound."

"What if I die? Your plan puts me at greater risk." He backed away, his boot dipping to splash in a lily pool. "Don't you understand? My magic wants me to die, I keep it too well leashed."

"Then rein it in now. Do not Feast on the whole city, merely create one contained illusion of me."

"I mustn't cast you in shadow. My magic will remember you."

I said, "I care more of Morimound's women than the hypothetical memories of your magic."

"No! My magic must be influencing you. It worms its way into people's minds and deceives them."

"My thoughts are my own, even if yours are biased." I offered him my hand. "Will you trust me? Your magic could not both inspire my plan and entertain designs of Feasting on the city, as the two goals are exclusive."

"Are they? Nightmares always find a way."

As he frowned down at me, the fangs at the end of his arms clicked together. He clasped my hand between both of his, nerves thrumming up my arm. The teeth attached to his palms transformed back into fingers: scarred and misshapen ones, although decidedly human.

"I think you are stronger than I, my heart." When his gaze lifted, his eyes no longer reminded me of common aquamarine. Reflecting the moonlight, they stunned me with the adamantine luster of silver diamonds. "But you must promise not to look at your illusion."

"I promise, Tethiel."

"Then we must hurry, before wisdom catches up to me."

He strode down the garden path and downstairs. As I followed, I glanced once more at the glittering wreckage of my gowns; spotting a shawl embroidered with a purple iris, I snatched it before hurrying downstairs.

I covered my hair with the shawl on my way outside the manor, where a brown horse kneeled before us. Tethiel mounted first, and as I situated myself to sit sidesaddle behind him, the horse vaulted forward.

I clung to Tethiel, having a legitimate suspicion that the horse meant to kill me. We raced down streets glowing with moonlight, leaping over garden plots and walls, plunging through the darkness of groves. I felt like a bat, flying blind.

At every turn in our path, silent figures waited for us. Some Feasters gleamed in their flamboyant clothes, and the horse snapped its teeth at them. One beautiful maiden glowed like starlight, bobbing down the street with her feet skimming the ground; she spoke in a curiously deep voice as we passed.

"Enchantress, if you've spoiled the banquet...."

She had mouthed the words, I realized, which had come from behind her. A black stalk connected the maiden to the forehead of a monstrosity comprised of spear-sized fangs and a gaping mouth large enough to swallow an ox and wagon.

The horse's hooves left the toothy maw and maiden lure behind us, and the next Feaster bled in a frightful manner from a gash on her chest, lifting the blood in her palms in homage. She seemed unconcerned with her own mortal wound. Hanging roots of banyans hid an even more sinister presence, and I heard an oozing and glimpsed something pale and human-sized slithering around the trunk.

I clutched Tethiel tighter, with the sole goal of positioning my jostling chin closer to his ear. "The acolyte said city guards surround my manor."

"They won't dare leave their tents," he said.

The horse leaped from the road into a park. Two Feasters with jeweled swords pointed us through the strangler fig trees, and the horse slowed, stalking between pavilion tents situated in my gardens.

My manor rose before us, lamps brightening the east wing. The horse stopped in a shadow of a mango tree, and Tethiel lowered me to the sod.

"Hiresha, I will enter by the front door with the illusion. Whatever you do, don't look at it. And in case this is the last night for either of us...."

He lifted my hand and kissed it. I was proud that his fingers did not even blacken with magic.

I padded into the garden, squinting up at the manor windows. The moon shadowed this side, yet two lamps shone in the crystal panes. Guards peered out into the night, and I felt obligated to subject myself to the incivilities of ducking behind colonnades and crouching behind topiary.

Tethiel's voice whispered through my mind. *They will see you.*

Instead of crossing between two hedges, I froze in mid-step, out of surprise more than acknowledgement of his warning. A light from a raised lamp flickered over the ground ahead of me, and I exhaled at the near miss.

A glance behind showed no sign of Tethiel, only moonlit branches and shadows. I shook my head and bent over, clutching my skirt, and hustled the last distance to the manor wall.

I had no choice but to exhibit my calves while scrambling up to a window. It was locked, and I could not reach anything higher on the wall. I pressed my hand against a crystal pane, wondering if I would have to break it after so recently replacing my windows.

A skull with blond hair grinned through the glass. I bit on my knuckles to keep from screaming, and in that instant I noticed the bone head also possessed sunken eyes and was supported by an emaciated body. Skeletal arms pried open the window to let me inside.

I asked, "Physis?"

Her ratty dress lacked a single jewel. "Father said no casting. Not this close to the soul collector."

"Do not presume yourself welcome in my home, merely because I am relieved to see you."

Her arms trembled as she closed the window behind me.

DESCENDING
-45-

A casual observer might have mistaken me for an enchantress of modest ability with her underfed servant, striding down the hall. The onlooker could not know I had attained the rank of elder, nor that Physis could—at a thought—become a statuesque beauty or a hideous monster.

Notwithstanding, no casual observer would have spotted us, as Physis closeted us out of sight whenever guard or servant approached. In one such delay, I spoke to her in a whisper.

"We must find the boys' dressing room."

"You told me that already, fluff head."

I had grown weary and begun to forget details. "If you had located it, I would not be forced to repeat myself."

The Feaster had a disturbing tendency to sniff at doorways, licking her lips. We found Deepmand in a storeroom lying like a fallen statue. He looked dead. My shaking fingers reached above his face, trying to feel if he still breathed.

Physis smacked her lips. "He lives. I can smell it. Can you get him up?"

I pointed to the glyph on his brow. "The Soultrapper might know it if I touch him. I have a better plan."

While leaving I hoped the Fate Weaver would not cut his thread before I could depose the Soultrapper. I needed only a little more time.

We soon discovered the dressing room. One boy sat sobbing. He clutched the blouse he wore and twisted the fabric, while another youth was attended by a servant painting spirals on his face.

Physis extended her fingers like claws. "Anyone scream, and I'll eat your tongue out of your mouth."

She appeared hungry enough to follow up such a threat. A boy muffled his yelp with his hands, and the servant dropped her paintbrush.

"Such incivilities are hardly necessary. Now, Physis, assist me with these buttons. And, you, I want something elaborate on my face."

The Feaster fumbled with my gown buttons, fingers shaking. When she at last had done, she whistled at the sight of my red undergarments. "I would have poisoned my sister for those."

By the time I thought of a retort, the moment had passed.

Physis flashed scissors toward my eyes, grinning at my fear, then lifted them higher to begin clipping my hair short. The servant painted a bird of paradise design on my face, with a yellow dot above each eye and red frills swooping down from my brows to my cheeks. While her brush tickled my skin, I regarded myself in a hand mirror and decided that Tethiel had been correct: No one could confuse my proportions as masculine, although my belly would match a boy's tautness. I would need to rely on the expectation that all the women in Morimound were pregnant, as well as the distraction of the illusion.

A guard opened the door, and as it swung inward, Physis scurried behind it to hide. "One of you monkeys," he said, "get in here."

I followed the guard barefoot, wearing nothing but my undergarments, a shawl, and the red diamond. My vision constricted from sleepiness; I bumped into a doorframe and once lost the guard altogether.

"You shouldn't be drinking so much at your age." He kicked me in the right direction. "'Course, might as well drink. No woman will marry you after this."

I stumbled into a dining room, and the first thing I noticed was that my furniture had been moved. With the tables shoved to the sides, a wide walkway led down the room to an ostentatious chair, on which a follower sat. He wore silk and the dead priest's paragon diamond. The Soultrapper crouched on a stool beside him, in his poorer clothes.

"Your Lustrous, er, Your Divinity," a guard said, jogging down the room and kneeling to the follower, "she...she killed them at the doors. She's inside."

The Soultrapper rose and kicked away his stool. "By the goddess's tits! The enchantress will be here soon. If she casts any spells, cut off her head."

Thoughts of my vulnerability and mortality spread through me like a poison, and I trembled uncontrollably. Many guards—I could not manage a firm count—stood in the room, and the moment one gave me a second glance, he would realize I was a woman. The sense of my doom burned inside me. I would die—I would die—I would die.

It occurred to me that I was feeling the approach of Tethiel's illusion. Nobody had noticed me yet, and I told myself that the men were distracted and as fearful as I.

The Soultrapper shoved the follower off the chair, taking the diamond from him. "Might as well wear this. *She* knows who I am."

I padded my way past two guards to the Soultrapper's side, my arms trembling so much that I could not hold the shawl, and it slid off my shoulders. Only my undergarments covered me, in front of all these men; my throat constricted, and I felt one of them would have to notice my gasping, my shivering, or my hips.

All the men stared at the door, waiting. The feeling of death approached.

The Soultrapper presented a problem, in that he had not yet sat down in the ostentatious chair. If he planned to face the illusion standing then I could do nothing. I wondered if I might act in some way to lure him into the chair, without drawing much attention to myself; if any answer to my quandary existed, it lost itself in the chaos of my thoughts.

A whimper drew my eyes to a table, where two abdomens protruded upward. After blinking, I realized that men held down Sri and Alyla, their legs forced to a spread position as if in preparation to give birth.

The Soultrapper could kill them in a moment with a twist of his unchildren. The thought left me swaying against the chair, gripping my brow.

The guards sucked in their breaths at a rising sibilance from the doorway. The sound reminded me of hundreds of snakes slithering closer.

The Soultrapper grabbed me with his disturbingly long arm, and he pulled me down as he sat. His fingers left trails of oil on my belly, and the paragon diamond dug into my back.

"You'll protect me, won't you, girlie?" He crushed me closer against his slimy chest. "The enchantress would have to burn you first, but you won't mind dying for Your Divinity, would you?"

Elation filled me because now I would have the chance to draw him into my dream. The Fate Weaver must have her hands on my thread. Unfortunately, the excitement and disgust of lying against the Soultrapper had woken me fully.

Forcing my eyes closed, I set my bare foot on the first step on the stairwell. When I reached the fifth step, the Soultrapper's words filtered down from behind me.

"You're a good girlie, aren't you? Not a squirmer at all."

I felt the Soultrapper tilt in the chair and release gas. The stench chafed my nostrils and yanked me back to wakefulness.

Gowns swarming with jewels seethed into view in the doorway, and I glimpsed a black glove before squeezing my eyes shut. On the stairwell again, I scrambled downward; I had to concentrate and sleep, as I had when dying. I reminded myself that my peril was as great now: I lay against a man who could rot my insides in a moment and trap my soul for an eternity of torment within my corpse.

My feet slapped the steps on the way down while the Soultrapper spoke behind me. "Enchantress, displease me and your spellsword will die along with these sows. Now kneel."

I reached the twentieth step when a chillingly familiar voice answered him. "It is you who should fear to displease."

The words were my own, and I paused on the twenty-ninth step, to reassure myself that I had not in fact spoken while falling asleep.

"My imprisonment was an indignation that I will not suffer again." The voice matched my pitch, yet it was more forceful and laced with malice. "Abuse one more woman of Morimound and I will incinerate you, regardless of the consequences."

I wished to turn around, to see the illusion speaking with my voice, yet I remembered Tethiel's warning and proceeded to the fortieth step.

"Good thing this girlie isn't a woman," the Soultrapper said in the distance.

I lifted my hand to the right side of my head, feeling as if an earthworm coated with mucus rolled about in my ear. Glancing halfway back to the stair, I realized that the Soultrapper was licking my ear, and the embarrassment caused me to blush and slide up three steps.

Tethiel might have followed the illusion into the room, and I realized he could be seeing me in my undergarments, with a tongue greasing the side of my face. I feared he had, and to determine the truth, I peered up at the top of the stairway.

I saw myself.

In each black glove, I clutched the scalp of a man's charred head. Blood dribbled from severed necks onto the carpet. My gowns writhed around me, scarves and folds of silk reaching to strangle anyone who strayed close. I sneered at the guards who flinched from my stare, and I relished how even the Soultrapper quavered. I had power over them. They had to obey my every command. At last, I had found another way besides raising children to earn true respect.

No, I told myself, I was seeing only an illusion. While the real me had gawked, steps had slid under my feet, dragging me toward the waking world and the shadow of myself. I gripped my head and dug in my toes, forcing myself to focus. The stairs now stung my bare feet as if coated by frost.

I had done the one thing Tethiel had warned me against, and worry slowed my progress, my muscles turning cold and my limbs thick with ice.

On step forty-five, I heard the illusion speak behind me. My words—no, her words—sounded closer, and I was uncertain if she spoke to the Soultrapper or to me.

"After deliberation, I have concluded that we will either ally, or you will die."

A shadow passed over me on the fifty-third step, and I glanced up to see a multicolored torrent of gowns swooping above the stair. The illusion landed ahead of me, on the lowest steps.

Fabric sawed outward as my look-alike spun to face me. She grinned and lifted her arms, shadows crawling out from the folds of silk to flicker on her palms as black flame.

"Hiresha." Her voice echoed up the stairwell. "You have no need to rely on your dreams, ever again. We can reduce the Soultrapper to a sniveling wretch and force him to capitulate."

Reaching step seventy, I pressed on without speaking. Any words here might cause me to mumble in the waking world, and I would not dignify this dark replica with a reply in any event. I noted her eyes lacked irises or any whites and appeared as enormous black pupils.

"You are touching him, and he could not resist us. It would be ever so easy."

I wondered if the presence of the illusion on my stair meant she had vanished from the waking world, or if a separate entity now blocked my way. If the former then I had to hurry, and I crossed the eightieth step. If the latter then I doubted this illusion, which had pierced my consciousness, was in any way under Tethiel's control.

"I will not allow you to choose unwisely." Black flame and red smoke erupted from her hands, bursting up the stairway. "You must accept my power."

The shadow inferno roared, and I felt myself pulled forward as it consumed the air in the stairway. I remembered seeing the two men being cremated in Kishala's room. That had been illusion, yet this looked real and would feel like unending torment. I could never surmount that kind of pain. I would awake screaming in the Soultrapper's arms and ruin everything.

I would have to accept the dark replica and begin Feasting.

I placed a hand over each of my ears, my head trembling from side to side. My eyes were so dry from the heat that my eyelids chafed. I remembered Tethiel had said he once saved his nation with Feasting, only to later lose it. I reminded myself of the ramifications of using that magic, the disgrace and banishment as well as the anguish and distrust that governed Tethiel.

I could not take the easy way. It would be too difficult.

Running toward the fire, I told myself that figments of my mind could not harm me: I was master of all the insubstantial. I plowed into the flame, pressing on even when I felt the agony of my scorched skin peeling from my arms, onward into the red smoke that scarred my lungs and spread toxins into my veins.

The pain faded in the next instant, the flame disappearing. I reached the ninetieth step unharmed.

"Someday, you will need me." The illusion smiled up at me with my own face, except her teeth bristled like needles. "I am willing to wait."

She Lightened herself and leapt, reaching for my face, and her black-gloved fingers gouged my eyes.

I flinched but continued into what felt as cold as a blizzard gust. A darkness blanketed my vision, and I had to descend the last steps by the feel of my numb toes.

Believing I had at last gained the hundredth step, I jumped upward and reached behind my back. My frigid hands closed on the oily warmth of the Soultrapper, yet I felt him slipping in my grasp. Sitting on his lap in the waking world, I did not have as complete a contact with him as I normally had with people when bringing them into my laboratory.

I flexed my arms behind me and caught him by his shoulder. He threaded his arm between mine and wriggled away as I continued my ascent. My hands snapped down on the last available place to grab him: his neck.

I had to hold on. He must sense something was happening to him; he was struggling. If I entered the dream without him then I would be safe from his magic attacks, yet he could still shove my real body away. Then Tethiel would see my plan had failed and begin Feasting, to the death of the city.

The Soultrapper's hand ran down my spine, pushing me. It was more a mental shove than a physical one; I continued moving upward in the same trajectory, yet he flickered in and out of existence. My grip failed, my hands clamping together with nothing between them.

I felt as if the city itself had fallen from my grasp, as if Morimound were a glass miniature that would smash onto the floor and spray back up in a gale of shards to cut me in a thousand places.

Something touched my thigh—his elbow, perhaps—and without thinking I reached my legs around and caught his head between my calves. I crushed my legs together, locking my feet in place under his flabby chin.

Not the most decorous way to catch a Soultrapper, I thought, while towing him upward into my dream. Yet, it would suffice.

A.E. MARLING

UNDONE
-46-

Only a loincloth and a blindfold covered the Soultrapper as he lay shackled to the basalt operations table. He snapped his head from side to side, trying to see; his lack of a foot allowed him to slip his stump out of a manacle. Missing an arm freed him further, and he thrashed and twisted.

All twenty-seven of my gowns flowed around me. Wearing clothes after my nakedness surged me with self-assurance, especially with the Soultrapper shivering before me in the thin, laboratory air. My dream had adorned me automatically, yet my amethyst gown seemed most appropriate for this moment of triumph. As I drifted toward the Soultrapper, layers of fabric shed from me and sublimed into glittering vapor.

He cried out. "What have you done to me?"

I smiled at my success; now, I was as impervious as a woman carved of enchanted diamond. The illusion on the stair had offered power, yet I needed none.

One last velvet dress unraveled from me to reveal my innermost gown: The purple silk glistened in waves over my body. Amethysts spiraled down my sleeves and radiated over my chest, their geometric sides flashing with my delight.

"Welcome to my world, Anlash Niklia." Burdening my hand, I pinned him to the table. "My, but you are one to squirm."

The red diamond drifted out from my embroidered collar, and when my other hand closed on it, the gold chain unclasped from behind my neck. I Attracted the blindfold off his face in order for him to see me holding the jewel over his chest.

The air rippled as the Soultrapper tried to attack me with his magic, his spell affecting me no more than fouling my mouth with a rotten aftertaste. "Release me, you jeweled vulture," he shouted, "Morimound deserves a strong ruler!"

"Death will release you soon enough. You should take the opportunity to appreciate this gem."

I felt him activate a different type of spell, one that linked to something outside the dream. He had to be scrounging for more power, thinking to harvest additional Bone Orbs in births of blood and lacerated flesh. With him inside my dream, the spell had to pass through me to reach the women, and I willed his magic into my red diamond, which channeled its own enchantment along his connection to two hundred and fifty women; they would not die but be saved.

One of the jewel's facets now shone, throwing a rose-colored beam of light onto the laboratory wall.

"I predict," I said, "that over fifteen seconds, the enchantment in this diamond will commandeer your link to fifty-three thousand Bone Orbs."

"Let me go!" His limbs thickened with muscle, his skin stretched and reddened as he strained against my arm and the gold shackles. "Or all my sons will be born today!"

"Incorrect." I smashed the sharp, pavilion end of the red diamond into his chest.

He howled as the gem began to appropriate his bond to the women, starting a process that would break apart their unchildren. More facets lit on the diamond, triangular rays lancing outward.

"Your armored man will die." The Soultrapper redirected his magic.

I snipped his bond with Deepmand. "He will die, after many more happy years of life."

"I deserve to rule Morimound!" Veins stood out in a tattered web on his oily brows, and in a bout of inhuman vigor, he bent one of his shackles. "I spent ten years of my life learning my magic."

"Only ten?"

Half the diamond's facets burst with light; in seven more seconds, Morimound would be free. He alarmed me by heaving upward, breaking one shackle and lifting my Burdened arm an inch off his chest. I felt as if a metal wall had shoved me back, and I reminded myself that the Soultrapper had possessed the resolve to cut off his own limbs. He could not harm me in my dream, yet his willpower gave him the strength to resist me.

I Burdened the diamond to the weight of a boulder, and it cracked through his ribcage and into his heart. His chest cavity blazed with red light; his ribs became black silhouettes. The enchantment needed only three more seconds to free the last of the women.

His scream turned into a roar, and he bucked me off him, gold shackles snapping into slivers. I allowed myself to be thrown into the air, flipping over his head in a sweep of purple silk.

Sitting up, he gripped the golden chain leaking out of his chest and pulled. My slippers touched the laboratory wall, and I bent backward at the waist to keep him in my sight.

He yanked and ripped out the red diamond; the gold chain trailed after it. All but two of its facets beamed, the gem now blindingly bright. One more moment of contact would save the last of the women.

Calculations of vectors of flight spun through my head, and I aligned my hand with the jewel and the Soultrapper's skull. Clamping onto the red diamond with all my mental strength, I thought of Faliti and the other women he had killed. Then I Attracted.

The gold chain whipped around as the gem sped faster than a dragonfly with a backwind of a hurricane. The jewel streaked toward my hand like a bolt of red lightning.

The Soultrapper may not have even realized the diamond had changed course in the air before it drilled through his forehead, jerking his body forward as it tore through his brain and out the back of his neck.

I released my spell and Lightened the diamond; it held scintillating in place while beads of blood were Burdened to the floor. As the dying Soultrapper slumped onto the black table, I willed the jewel to float forward. It last facets blossomed with light; the women were safe.

I closed my hands over the red diamond, which glowed between my fingers as if I held the sun. Within me, the warmth of my happiness burned just as bright.

I awoke.

Gasping, I untangled myself from the Soultrapper's corpse.

Hands of servants lifted me and wiped off the gore. I blinked, focusing on Tethiel as he covered me with a tablecloth.

"It is over," I said, grinning. "The pregnancies will reverse, and Morimound is saved."

Tethiel shook his head, his face awash in wonderment. "Hiresha, you are truly flawless."

I found myself unable to stop smiling, and I did not even care how many in the crowd had seen my undergarments.

The shadows in the room swelled, and Tethiel stepped back into them. A chill seeped into me, and my smile evaporated.

A black mist rose from the remains of the Soultrapper, and the tendrils of smoke formed into a spectral monster with three heads: one of an ogre, one of a dragon, and the last of a worm, with a maw of serrated teeth. The guards and servants recoiled, and I heard Alyla scream.

Tethiel's voice boomed through my mind. *This wine merchant was possessed, and the Lord of the Feast was behind all the horror in this city.*

He was lying, I realized. Men gripped their heads and screamed as if they could also hear his unspoken words.

"The Lord of the Feast!" All around me, people cowered, ran, or fainted.

I stood slack-mouthed as the Lord of the Feast gulped their fear from the air, and the three-headed monstrosity grew. He could not intend to continue Feasting, to cause the Seventh Flood anyway and kill the citizens I had just saved. I did not want to believe it, yet as despair gripped me, I knew it to be true.

Tethiel was betraying me in the worst possible way, and I felt as crushed as an opal between two hard blocks of granite. My defeat of the Soultrapper had been for nothing.

When the dragon and worm heads opened their mouths to devour two guards, a woman in red undergarments ran in front of me and leapt toward the Lord of the Feast. She had short hair, and a lance of fire swelled from her raised hand.

I realized the woman was me—an illusion with my face he had woven from shadows. A glance down at my own body showed only darkness.

My doppelganger speared the Lord of the Feast through his chest. He roared and shrank into a man, his face a stranger's but with a black triangle on his brow. Clutching his chest, he flew out of the room like a ghost that left a trail of black blood.

I stumbled after him, confused but hopeful. Exiting the manor doors, I saw an eight-legged beast with scales and a spined tail, its eyes frothing with a grey light; a stooped figure sat on the basilisk's back, and men covered their eyes in fear of its gaze as the creature and its rider loped away between the strangler fig trees.

Men who had thrown themselves behind hedges and flowerbeds now picked themselves off the ground. Physis approached in her enchantress's gown, and she shouted.

"Hiresha the Flawless has driven off the Lord of the Feast and saved Morimound!"

"I saw her," a man shouted, "with a spear of light!"

"She saved us! She's a paragon!"

Guards and acolytes flocked out of the tents they had constructed on my property to join a chant. Many prostrated themselves to touch my feet.

"Paragon Hiresha! Paragon Hiresha!"

I noticed a Bright Palm gazing down the street where Tethiel had fled, hand on his sword hilt. The veins in his eyes shone with white light as his expressionless face turned toward the crowd. Physis could no longer be seen among the ecstatic masses. I walked through them, and they parted around me. Alyla stood gawking and teetering between the front doors.

She asked, "What has happened, Mistress Enchantress?"

Fighting off deluges of disbelief and relief, I managed to speak. "The Lord of the Feast will at last be gone with the dawn. All is well."

Feeling weightless, I hugged her to keep myself from floating upward. The red diamond sparkled between us.

EPILOGUE

Two Months Later

The measuring tape wrapped around Sri's belly, her abdomen scarred with stretch marks but currently no more than plump. Her cheeks crinkled in a smile, her skin a healthy hue of bronze. "I have never felt so slender."

Sri stood on a stool while tailors fitted her in a pink wedding dress. Her knobby hands fondled her diamond engagement necklace.

"Nor," she said, her eyes soft with delight, "so happy."

"My utmost congratulations," I said. "May you have multiple years of blissful marriage."

Beside me, Maid Janny smacked her lips. "May you have good wine at the wedding."

"Maid Janny! I am astounded you could think of drinking wine, after it was the cause of so many pregnancies."

"Hardly the first time drink has done up a lass." She winked at me from under her bonnet. "This woman takes her chances."

"You are a paragon of impertinence."

Although my chin maintained a dignified elevation, my words lacked any disciplinary tone. I was too happy to seriously scold Janny.

Sri lifted her arms to try on another wedding dress, this one tulip yellow. "Now, Hiresha, you must be the one to give me to the groom. My father would, had he not passed to the Weaver's side thirty-six years ago."

"Indubitably, I will."

Flawless Kishala strode into the room with the bearing of a woman whom nothing could surprise. Her poise was remarkable, given that she had been brought up in a locked cell. I had passed the position of city arbiter to her because I felt she deserved it, and I planned to be far too preoccupied to govern.

"Lady Sri," Flawless Kishala said, "I would appreciate your guidance on a multifaceted case."

"Very well, my lovely girl, in return for your guidance as to which flowers I must wear with this dress."

I left the room, and between yawns, I touched the purple silk at my chest, which concealed my own jeweled necklace. I simply had to find a more suitable way to carry the red diamond. Tethiel had not returned, which was well because otherwise I would have choice words for him. Reports had come of two villages ransacked in the night, one in Morimound's protection, the other in a neighboring state.

Nonetheless, I seemed to recollect with unexplainable frequency how he had referred to me as "flawless." I could not help but think that if he were not a Feaster, I would wish for his company.

In a parlor, I found Alyla sitting beside her brother, who had returned for the funerals of his parents. Harend Chandur had fallen from the top of the Flood Wall and died, likely from a slip during the frenzy of deconstruction. The news had sickened me and driven me to heal Priest Abwar of the infected cut on his hand, as there had been entirely too much death in Morimound.

The brother bowed and left the room when I asked Alyla after her health. Despite the warmth of summer, she wore a full blouse to cover the stretch marks. Red lines had remained on her petite frame as a sobering reminder of the disintegrated unchild.

She gazed after her brother. "I worry about my Fosapam. We haven't the money for him to return to the military university."

"I will offer to sponsor his training as a spellsword," I said, "an honorable profession practiced only by the best of men. And, Alyla, when I eventually return to the Mindvault Academy, I hope you will accompany me as a novice."

She bowed her head, hands folded across her lap. "Might I stay close to my brother?"

"The spellsword dormitories are below the Academy, and you would find enchantment a wondrous and empowering magic."

Leaving Alyla alone to consider, I suffered a poke in the ribs from Maid Janny. "Making plans to keep her brother close, are you? He's an eyeful, isn't he? A bundle of shivers, a real painting, a sing-song, a lamp lighter."

"I certainly do not know what you mean. He merely exemplifies physical aptitude."

Janny's chortling only quieted when we met a tall man in the hall wearing a golden turban. His beard had thinned, and the scruff closest to his chin had turned white. He appeared gaunt, and not only because he wore no armor, yet his face had color to it, his eyes bright with life.

"Elder Enchantress, I have had long to think abed." Deepmand lowered himself before me. "I was wrong to have ever questioned you."

"Nonsense." I caught his shoulder, stopping him before he could reach down to touch my feet. "Your warnings of a certain someone came dangerously close to being correct."

"Had you listened to me, Morimound would have been lost."

"And had you died because of my not listening, I should never have forgiven myself." I stooped and collapsed to a knee, as if I had lost my balance.

Deepmand rose to offer a hand up.

Instead I reached and touched his feet, before he could think to step away from the act of deference.

"You have served the empire and the Academy well," I said. "And you retire with honor, Elder Spellsword."

Pinkness rose from the white of his beard. For the first time ever, I saw Deepmand blush.

Mister Obenji strode into the hall, his gait livelier than that of many men one-third his age. He informed us that Mistress Deepmand and her family had arrived.

Deepmand lumbered ahead of me down the entrance stair and caught up his children in his arms. His sons wore small turbans, and one of his daughters had the most precious gap-toothed smile. I hugged them all in turn, a gesture I had discovered most gratifying and expedient when wearing a single gown.

After lavishing the children with presents, I escorted the family to the manor's east wing. "You will live in my finest rooms, my bright stars."

The mother protested when she saw the master bedroom.

I insisted, saying how I had grown attached to my own guest room. Maid Janny muttered something about "slave to habit."

The children squealed with delight as they explored four sunlit rooms, all exquisitely furnished with small chairs and beds. Hopping up and down, one girl tried to reach a carnelian embedded into one of the four jeweled doors. I held her up so she could touch it.

"So red!" She covered her chubby smile with one hand. "What it doing here?"

"My little luminary," I said, hugging the child closer, "this is Carnelian's Room."

"Why?"

"Never mind the name. If the jewel pleases you, that is enough for now."

The laughter of children rang down the halls of my manor, yet even amid the excitement of their play, I began to droop with fatigue. Despite my attempts to stay conscious, I found myself sitting on a miniature bed, leaning against the wall.

The gap-toothed girl climbed up to count the amethysts on my gown. I followed her finger amid the sparkling designs, trying to help her with the numbers past seven, yet my voice faded. At the same time, her lashes slid downward, her eyes closing. My purple-gloved thumb brushed a lock of brown hair from her peaceful face, and then I saw no more.

I could not be certain if she fell asleep in my arms first, or I in hers. I only knew that I slept with a smile.

THE END

A.E. MARLING

Thank you for reading Brood of Bones,
a tale told of the Lands of Loam.

Discover Hiresha's next adventure:

Fox's Bride

at http://aemarling.com/

As an independent storyteller, A.E. Marling
lacks a corporate advertising budget,
but your recommendation is more powerful
than any ad.
Become a patron of fantasy storytelling
by recommending this book to a friend
and reviewing it online.

Meet the humble scribe:
@AEMarling

www.ingramcontent.com/pod-product-compliance
Lightning Source LLC
Chambersburg PA
CBHW071506260626
47170CB00002B/284